WARRIORS OF IRELAND

Fighting for honour and for love

In this powerful new duet
by **Michelle Willingham** step back in time
to medieval Ireland, where proud men were
willing to die for honour and for the ones they
loved—although not without a fight!

Fans of *The MacEgan Brothers* mini-series
will meet some familiar faces along the way,
but prepare to have your hearts captured
by two new fierce warriors!

Meet Killian MacDubh in

Warrior of Ice
available now

and look for

Warrior of Fire
coming soon

AUTHOR NOTE

Beauty and the Beast has always been one of my favourite fairytales. In *Warrior of Ice* I wanted to twist the tale by having a hero with a handsome face but the tormented soul of a beast and the heroine a scarred face but the heart of a beauty.

I was also very inspired by the character of Jon Snow from *Game of Thrones* in this story, and I wanted to write a tale where the bastard hero becomes the king he was meant to be. I hope you'll enjoy the love story of Killian and Taryn as they learn to look beyond appearances. Also look for the sequel to this book, *Warrior of Fire*, which tells the story of Carice Faoilin, Killian's 'adopted' sister.

If you'd like me to email you when I have a new book out, please visit my website at michellewillingham.com to sign up for my newsletter. You can also learn more about my other historical romances and see photos of my trips to Ireland.

WARRIOR OF ICE

Michelle Willingham

Published in Great Britain 2015
by Mills & Boon, an imprint of Harlequin (UK) Limited,
Eton House, 18-24 Paradise Road, Richmond, Surrey, TW9 1SR

© 2015 Michelle Willingham

ISBN: 978-0-263-24792-3

Harlequin (UK) Limited's policy is to use papers that are natural,
renewa͏
sustaina
to the l

Printed
by CPI,

RITA® Award finalist **Michelle Willingham** has written over twenty historical romances, novellas and short stories. Currently she lives in south-eastern Virginia with her husband and children. When she's not writing Michelle enjoys reading, baking and avoiding exercise at all costs.

Visit her website at: michellewillingham.com

Visit the author profile page
at millsandboon.co.uk for more titles

To Fitch, the best cat in the world.
You've kept me company through each of my books and,
although it's difficult to write when you plant your furry
behind on my keyboard, you always make me smile.

Chapter One

Ireland—1172

His sister was going to die.

Killian MacDubh could see it, even if everyone around him was in denial. Though Carice was still the most beautiful woman in Éireann, her body was fragile. She left her bed rarely, and when she did, she often had to be carried back. Her illness had struck hard, several years ago, and she'd wasted away ever since. This evening, she had sent word that she needed to speak with him, but he did not know why.

Outside, the rain pounded against the mud, but another storm brewed inside Killian. There was a restless anticipation within him, as if an invisible threat hung over all of them. He couldn't place it, but all day, he'd been pacing.

His tunic and leggings were soaked through,

and he stood at the back of the Great Chamber. The moment he stepped inside, Brian Faoilin's face was grim with distaste, as if a stray dog had wandered into his house. The chieftain loathed the very air Killian breathed. Though he'd allowed Iona to keep the bastard son she'd brought with her, Brian had forced both of them to live among the *fuidir*. All his life, Killian had slept among the dogs and dined upon scraps from the table. He was forbidden to possess any rights of the tribe or own any land. It should have taught him his place. Instead, it had fed his resentment, making him vow that one day, no man would call him slave. He hungered for a life where others would look upon him with respect instead of disdain.

He'd spent time training among the finest warriors in Éireann, intending to leave the tribe and become a mercenary. Better to lead a nomadic life on his own terms than to live like this. But then Carice had fallen ill. He'd delayed his plans to leave, for her sake, after she'd begged him not to go. Were it not for her, he'd have disappeared long ago. She was the only family he had left, and he knew her life was slipping away. For that reason, he had sworn to remain with her until the end.

The chieftain leaned over to one of the guards, undoubtedly giving the order to throw Killian out. Within moments, his friend Seorse crossed the Great Chamber, regret upon his face. 'You know you cannot come inside without orders, Killian.'

'Of course not.' He was supposed to remain outside in the pouring rain, amid the mud and the animal dung. Brian refused to let him be a part of their tribe—not in any way. He was expected to work in the stables, obeying all commands given to him.

This time, Killian crossed his arms and stood his ground. 'Will you be the one to throw me out?' His voice held the edge of ice, for he was weary of being treated like the bastard he was. Frustration clenched in his gut, and he didn't move.

'Don't start a fight,' Seorse warned. 'Take shelter in the tower if you must, but don't cause more trouble. I'll bring you food later.'

Killian gave a thin smile. 'Do you think I care about causing trouble?' He enjoyed fighting, and he'd earned his place among the men as one of the best warriors. Beneath his fur-lined tunic, he wore chain-mail armour that he'd taken from a dead Norse invader during a raid. He had no sword of his own, but he knew how to use his fists and had broken a few bones over the years. Every time he won a match or bested a clansman, it was a thorn in Brian's side.

Seorse dropped his voice low. 'Why are you here, Killian?'

'Carice sent for me.'

His friend shook his head. 'She's worse today. I don't think she can leave her chamber. She was sick most of the night, and she can hardly eat anything.'

A tightness filled up Killian's chest. It bothered him to see her starving to death before his eyes, unable to tolerate any food at all. The healer had ordered Carice to eat only bread and the plainest of foods, to keep her stomach calm. But nothing seemed to work. 'Take me to her.'

'I cannot, and you know this. Brian ordered me to escort you outside.'

He wasn't about to leave—not yet. But as he moved towards the entrance, he glanced behind him and saw a hint of motion near the stairs. Brian's attention was elsewhere, so Killian hastened up the spiral steps. Seorse sent him a warning look, but his silent message was clear. He would not let Brian know that Killian was still here.

Carice was struggling to walk down the stairs. Her skin was the colour of snow, and she held on to her maid's shoulder, touching the opposite wall for support. Instantly, Killian went to the stairs and offered his arm. 'Do you need help, my lady?'

'Call me that again, and I shall bloody your nose, Killian.' Her dark brown hair was bound back from her face, and her blue eyes held warmth. She was far too thin, and he could see the bones in her wrists. But her spirit was as fiery as ever.

'You should not have left your room, Carice.' He moved up the spiral stairs, and she gestured for her maid to go.

'I'll sit here a moment and talk with you,' she said. 'Then you can carry me back to bed afterwards.'

'You're too ill,' he argued. 'You need to go back now.'

She shook her head and raised a hand. 'Let me speak. This is important.'

He climbed a few more of the stairs to reach her side. Carice sat down, steadying herself. 'Father shouldn't treat you this way. You *are* my brother, and always have been, even if we do not share the same parents.' She reached out her hand and squeezed his palm. In so many ways, she reminded him of his mother. Gentle and strong-willed, she'd made it her task to take care of him. 'You deserve a better life than this, Killian. It was wrong of me to ask you to stay.'

He didn't deny it, but he knew that once he left, he would never return to Carrickmeath. 'One day I'll go. Perhaps when you are married and are no longer fighting my battles for me.'

She drew back, her face serious. 'I'm not going to marry anyone, Killian. This winter is my last. I may not live until the summer.'

Uneasiness passed over him, for her proclamation wasn't a jest. Each season grew harder on her, and it was only a matter of time before she lost her fragile grasp on life. Though her body was weak, her inner strength rivalled a warrior queen's.

'Father doesn't believe me. He thinks I'm going to get well and wed the High King, becoming Queen of Éireann. But he is wrong. And so I have taken matters into my own hands.'

'What do you mean?' She wasn't planning to take her own life, was she?

'I will not marry Rory Ó Connor,' she said. 'I have made arrangements to leave this place.' Her face softened, and she admitted, 'Father has been delaying my journey to Tara for my marriage. He's told the High King of my illness, but soon enough, the King's men will come for me. And I will not have my last moments be shadowed by marriage to such a man.' She reached out and smoothed his hair. 'I know Rory is your father, but I am glad you are nothing like him.'

'I will never be like him.' The stories of the High King's ruthless actions were well known. Rory had plundered and burned the lands of Strabane and Derry, even ordering his own brother to be blinded, in order to seize possession of the throne. It was one of many reasons why no one dared to stand against him.

'In one way, you will.' Carice's hand rested upon his cheek. 'You have the blood of the High King within your veins. You are destined to rule over your own lands.'

While he wanted to believe that, he didn't know if he would ever overcome his low birth. Men respected his fighting skills and his strategies, but he needed far more than that to win a place for himself.

'I am a bastard,' he pointed out, 'and the *Ard-Righ* will never acknowledge me as his son.' It was well known that the High King had sired dozens of bastard children, and he had little interest in them. Brian had travelled to visit Rory, hoping to receive compensation for Killian's fostering, but the King had been away, and his retainers had refused to grant anything. During those years, Rory had been King of Connacht, before he became High King of Éireann.

'That could change,' she argued. 'And I know you will fight for the life you want. Just as I will fight for the death I want.'

The words were chilling, for Carice was the one good part of his life. Her quiet spirit and kindness had helped him to push back his hatred of Brian. Without her, there was no one to fight for.

'Carice, don't,' he said, not wanting to speak of it. 'You cannot give up.'

She ignored him and continued. 'I have asked the MacEgan tribe for help. Someone will come and take me to our holdings in the west. I ask that you help me to leave. Do not let Father's men stop me.' Though her face remained strong, he caught the rise of tears in her eyes. 'If I stay, I will have to marry the High King. And I do not wish to endure that wedding night.'

She took a slow breath, her hands trembling. 'Help me escape, Killian. You're strong enough to fight this battle.'

He bowed his head, knowing that it was

peace she wanted. And so he gave a vow he knew he could keep. 'I swear, on my life, that I will never let you wed King Rory.'

Her shoulders lowered with relief, and she touched his hair, resting her forehead against his. 'Thank you. I cannot say when I will leave, but one day soon, I will be gone. I know Father's men will search for me, but keep them searching to the north instead. Tell them I went to visit friends, if you wish. The MacEgans will protect me with other false stories, if needed.'

'So be it.'

She leaned against the wall, and he suspected she had not the strength to return to her bed. 'You are the brother of my heart, Killian, no matter what my father says. I pray that one day you realise how worthy you are.'

He reached out to lift her into his arms. 'I'm taking you back to your chamber. Rest, and trust that I will keep you safe.'

Taryn Connelly had never rescued a captive before.

She knew nothing at all about how to infiltrate the High King's fortress at Tara and steal a prisoner away, but her father's time was running out. If she didn't organise soldiers to save him, his life would be forfeit. But finding warriors was proving to be a problem.

Her father, King Devlin, had been a good man and a strong ruler. But the last group of men who had gone to rescue her father had all been returned to Ossoria—without their heads. She shuddered at the memory. King Rory had made it clear that he was not going to release his prisoner.

Her mother, Queen Maeve, had insisted that the remaining soldiers stay behind to guard their province, and they were all too glad to obey.

Taryn refused to leave Devlin there to die. It wasn't fair and it wasn't right. Someone had to save him. And though she wasn't strong enough to lead men into battle, she could find a warrior who was.

A sudden rise of nerves caught in her stomach, for she had never left Ossoria before. For so many years, she had remained hidden away, so that no one would look upon her scarred face. Her father had warned that others would scorn her for the physical imperfections if she dared to leave. But now, she had no alternative. Given the choice between facing a jeering crowd and saving his life, she would set aside her fear and risk everything.

Her mother opened the door to Taryn's chamber, staring at the open trunk of Taryn's belongings. Inside lay not only fine gowns, but a box filled with gold pieces, silver chalices, and a small bag of pearls.

'You cannot save him, Taryn,' Maeve said. 'You saw what happened to the last group of soldiers who went to the High King.'

'If you were in his place, would you want us to go about our lives, not even trying to bring you home?' she countered. 'He's my father, not a traitor.'

She was certain of that. Devlin had answered a summons, only to be taken by the King's men and bound in chains. And whatever the reason, Taryn intended to bring him home. 'I will not turn my back on him.'

Her mother was silent, her expression tight. Around her throat she wore a gold torque set with rubies, while her long red hair fell to her waist. 'I know you believe Devlin was a good father. He tried very hard to make you think well of him.' Her voice was calm, but it held the unmistakable edge of loathing.

Taryn tensed, for she'd known that her parents' marriage had never been a happy one. Her mother had miscarried many children over the

years, and it shadowed her moods at all times.
She controlled every moment of each day and
kept the servants at her beck and call. Those
who disobeyed were punished for any infrac-
tion.

Maeve sighed and paced across the room. 'I
am sorry, but you cannot go to Tara. And you
may not send more of my soldiers on Devlin's
behalf.'

My soldiers? Taryn bristled at that. As if she'd
already given up on her husband?

'They are still Father's men, too,' Taryn corrected.

But Maeve's face turned cool. She walked
to stand at the window and said, 'I have not,
nor will I, give permission for you to take soldiers against King Rory. Every last man of them
would be killed, including yourself. And I am
not a woman who sends others to die need-
lessly.'

Not even for your husband? Taryn wanted
to ask, but didn't.

'I do not intend to take an army,' she told
Maeve quietly. 'I go only to plead for Father's
life. Surely there is no harm in appealing to
King Rory. I am no threat to the High King.'

'You will not leave,' Maeve said. 'And that

is final.' Her gaze swept over Taryn. 'The *Ard-Righ* will not listen to anything you have to say.' She reached out to touch Taryn's scarred cheek. 'And unlike other women, you cannot use your looks to win his attention, I fear.' Her mother's touch burned into her skin like a brand.

Taryn knew she would never be beautiful, and she would bear the disfigurement of her face and hands forever. But to hear it from her mother was a blow she hadn't expected. She stepped backwards, lowering her gaze to the floor. 'I do not want King Rory's attention.'

Far from it. She knew she had a face that made men shudder, and she was too tall. Her hair was black instead of her mother's fiery colour. They shared the same eyes, however. More than once, Taryn had wished that she did not have to see those icy blue eyes staring back at her in a reflection.

Sometimes she wished that her mother had been taken captive, instead of her father. Maeve never seemed to care about anyone but herself. And it hurt to imagine Devlin in chains, suffering torture.

Taryn closed the trunk and stood. 'I do not understand why I may not take a small escort when I speak with the High King. Two or three men are harmless.' More than that, she could see no reason why her mother would care what risks she took. 'If I fail, there is nothing lost.'

'Nothing, save your life,' Maeve countered. She continued staring out the window, and at last she said, 'A messenger came this morn. Devlin is to be executed on the eve of Imbolc.' With that, she turned back. 'I do not think you want to witness your father's death. And if you go, the *Ard-Righ will* force you to watch.'

Horror wrenched her stomach at the thought. Taryn gripped her hands together tightly, wishing she could control the trembling. 'And you'll do nothing to stop it.'

'I will not interfere with the High King's justice, for I value my own life.' Maeve moved closer, cupping Taryn's chin. 'Just as I value yours. Devlin is gone, and there is nothing more to be done.'

The Queen's face held traces of regret. 'I can read your thoughts, my daughter. You plan to slip away and try to save Devlin. But I will not let you endanger yourself or others. Your father is not the man you think he is.' She paused a moment, as if she wanted to say something more, but then held her silence.

Taryn said nothing, not at all believing her

mother. Devlin was a quiet, wise leader whom the people respected. Her blood ran cold at the thought of her father's death. Their small province would fall into chaos, for Maeve would rule with an iron hand. Devlin had brought peace and prosperity among them, but it would not last beneath her mother's commands.

She swallowed hard, her stomach churning at the prospect of facing the High King. But face him she must, if it meant saving Devlin's life. Imbolc was only a few weeks away.

'May I go now?' she asked her mother. There was little time left, and she wanted to leave Ossoria at dawn. She dared not travel with more than a single guard, and it would be difficult to find anyone who would go with her, if she asked it of him.

'To your chamber, yes,' Maeve answered. 'But nowhere else. And, Taryn, if you *do* attempt to leave against my orders, my soldiers will bring you back. Be assured of it.'

Taryn said nothing, but curtsied to her mother before leaving. An uneasy fear gathered in her stomach, for she suspected her mother would punish any servants who dared to accompany her.

Once she reached the hallway, she leaned

back against the stone wall, terrified of the next few weeks. It would take at least a sennight to reach Tara, and even then, she needed men to defend her. Not an army—but enough fighters to help her rescue Devlin, if King Rory would not listen.

Who would agree to such a task? She didn't know how to hire mercenaries, and if she asked a neighbouring chieftain or king, they would never consider allying against the High King.

She needed leverage, something King Rory wanted.

You cannot use your looks to win his attention, her mother had said. And Taryn knew that all too well. The very idea of offering herself was impossible, for men did not want a scarred bride—they only wanted her kingdom. Most behaved as if they didn't see her, or they turned their backs to avoid her presence. Her stomach twisted at the unwanted memories. Although no one dared to mock her openly, it was easier to hide herself away from others, pretending as if she was unaware of their revulsion.

She forced back her thoughts, still wondering how to save her father's life. She'd heard Devlin speak of the betrothal between King Rory and Carice Faoilin. The young woman was rumoured to be the most beautiful woman in Éire-ann—a perfect bride for the High King. But Taryn doubted if any woman alive would want to be wedded to such a cruel man.

Then, again, it was unlikely that Carice had a choice.

A union between the High King and the Faoilin tribe would be a powerful one, giving the King more influence in the southern ter-ritories. Rory Ó Connor needed strong armies and alliances that would protect Éireann, since the Norman invaders were gaining a stronger foothold. War was brewing, and they knew not who would win.

Would the King listen to a plea from his bride? Taryn wondered if she could convince Carice to let her travel with her as a companion. Though she had never met the young woman, perhaps she could visit Carrickmeath and seek help on her father's behalf.

Inwardly, Taryn worried whether pearls or gold would be enough to gain their assistance. She had little else to offer in exchange for Dev-lin's rescue. And now that her mother had for-bidden her to take soldiers as escorts, she could not travel in a wagon. It meant she could only

bring wealth she could carry. Even then, she
might not gain the help she needed.

An idea began to form as she thought about
Carice Faoilin. Perhaps a distraction was what
was needed. Carice had not yet married the
High King…but what if Taryn accompanied
her to the wedding? A celebration would offer
the strongest diversion yet, where hundreds of
wedding guests would attend, offering the perfect chance to rescue her father in secret.

She didn't need an army—only a small group
of well-trained men to slip past the guards.

And she knew exactly where she would find
them.

The overcast sky darkened as the afternoon
stretched into evening. Taryn huddled within
her fur-lined cloak while the damp conditions
turned into frost. Her guard, Pól, accompanied
her, carrying the small bundle containing a bag
of jewels and silver, as well as a second gown.
She'd had to leave almost everything behind,
since they hadn't taken a horse. Pól had protested, saying that it would take far too long to
travel on foot.

Taryn had argued back that she wanted to
disappear quietly. The truth was, horses terrified her. Her heart sickened at the memory of

her older brother's death, and never would she forget that terrible day when he had died after being thrown from his horse. She had tried to avoid riding ever since.

No, if she could not travel in a wagon, she would walk. It wasn't that far to Carrickmeath—less than a day's journey on foot. And without a horse, it was more difficult for her mother's soldiers to track them.

She was so tired, her feet were numb. She'd been walking since the middle of last night, in order to get past her mother's guards. Her hair was sodden from the earlier rain, hanging across her shoulders against her blue woollen gown. Weariness cloaked her, but she could not stop this journey. Her mother would send men to bring her back, and she had to put as much distance as possible between them. Once she reached the safety of Brian Faoilin's ring fort, she could stop.

After another hour of walking, she spied a fortress in the distance. It was a wooden structure atop a hillside with a deep trench surrounding it. Sharpened stakes were set at even intervals all around it, with a wicker fence to keep out invaders.

Thank goodness. She would beg hospitality

with the Faoilin tribe for this night, and gain their protection, if possible. But when she drew nearer, she spied two dozen soldiers approaching the fortress, their commanders on horseback. They were riding towards the gates with spears clenched in their fists, and it was clear that they had not come for an amicable visit. One carried the High King's banner, and they looked as if they were waiting for the right moment to attack.

Why would the High King's men wage a battle here? Were they here to lay siege upon the fortress? Or had the Faoilin chieftain betrayed the High King? Whatever the reason, Taryn was not about to intrude. At least, not until she knew why they were here.

She slowed her pace and exchanged a look with her escort. 'I think we should wait before approaching the ring fort.'

'I agree, my lady.'

Taryn motioned for Pól to follow her into a grove of trees. The wind whipped at her cloak, freezing her skin. Even worse, the rain started up once more, mixed with ice. Taryn hurried towards the oaks, taking shelter beneath a large tree. She had no idea what to do now or how long she should wait. The last thing she wanted was to sleep out in the open. At night, it would begin snowing, and the ground would harden into ice. It was dangerous to sleep in the midst of such treacherous weather.

'What should we do?' she asked Pól.

The older man rested his hand upon his sword, shrugging. 'We'll have to wait until they've left. Or at least until they've gone inside.'

Taryn despised waiting. She much preferred to take action and hope for a good outcome. Yet she knew better than to act on impulse and endanger their lives. The wooden gates remained closed, and four men stood within a guard tower, overlooking the entrance. For a time, the High King's soldiers remained in front of the gates, and she could not tell what was happening. Eyeing the men, she wondered how they would respond if she approached.

'We cannot wait all night,' she mused aloud. 'We have to find out why they're here.'

Her guard shrugged. 'Whatever the reason, I would not be asking them, my lady. I can build a fire and a shelter for you in the meantime.'

The older man had insisted upon accompanying her to Tara, and she was grateful for his loyalty. But he wasn't the strongest escort, and she questioned his ability to defend her. He could wield a sword, but his hands suffered aches and pains during damp weather. Pól was nothing like Brian Faoilin's men, who were among the strongest fighters in Éireann, second only to the MacEgans.

Taryn exhaled, her breath forming clouds in the air. Somehow, she needed to ally herself with Carice Faoilin. The High King's bride was her safest means of getting close to Tara.

She started pacing, worried about why these soldiers were here. Would they allow her to approach the fortress? Likely if the Faoilin tribe kept their gates closed, then there was a reason for it.

'Do you want me to move in closer to learn more about why they've come?' Pól asked. 'So long as I leave my weapons with you, no one would suspect me.'

It was a dangerous risk, but one they needed to take. They had to get inside the fortress and seek shelter for the night.

'Yes, you should go,' she ordered the guard. 'Return when you know what's happening.'

Pól bowed in agreement before he walked towards the main road. Then he adjusted his gait to add a slight limp, making it seem that he was a harmless old man.

With every moment she was alone, Taryn's apprehensions increased. What if Pól didn't return? She couldn't remain here alone. Yet, if she approached the High King's men, they might harm her. She knew she wasn't beautiful, but as a woman, there was still a strong risk. Then, too, if she appealed to Lady Carice, there was still the chance that the young woman would refuse to let her join her ladies—even if Taryn confessed her reasons. The more she dwelled upon her rash decision, the more unlikely it seemed that she would succeed.

You cannot give up, she told herself. No one else would save her father.

And so, she continued to wait. Pól had given her a dagger, which she had secured at her waist. She had no idea what to do with his sword, for she could hardly lift the heavy weapon. In the end, it seemed best to prop it up against a tree.

After nearly an hour, the men still had not entered the fortress. Something was very, very wrong. Minutes crept onward, and when Pól did not return, Taryn couldn't stand the waiting any longer. She simply *had* to know what was happening.

This is dangerous and foolish, she told herself. But what choice did she have? She was alone, with no shelter for the approaching night. She could die at the hands of these men, or she could freeze to death.

They might not kill her, she supposed, as she began walking towards the fortress. They had no true reason to take her life. It was a small consolation.

The rain had slowed to a soft drizzle, and she kept her head and scarred face covered with a woollen *brat*. No matter how she tried to square her shoulders and walk with confidence, like the lady she was, she couldn't stop her teeth from chattering or her hands from trembling.

Within moments, one of the soldiers spied her. Word began to spread, and it wasn't long before all two dozen men were staring at her. Taryn adjusted her head covering, searching for a glimpse of Pól. But he was nowhere to be found, and she realised that he had likely hidden himself.

'Were you going somewhere?' one of the commanders asked. He wore an iron helm, and a sword rested at his left side. Trying not to show her alarm, she averted her gaze. She never had time to answer before another man emerged from the fortress.

He strode forward, his gaze narrowed upon the soldiers. And the moment she glimpsed his face, her pulse quickened.

Never in her life had she seen a warrior so handsome. He was like the son of Lugh, a god walking among them. He was tall with dark hair that hung below his shoulders. Every perfect feature looked as if it were carved from ice, with steel-grey eyes, an aquiline nose, and a mouth that tightened as he stared at the armed men. He seemed to be assessing their strength and ability to fight. Though he was dressed in ragged, worn clothing, she spied the glint of chain mail beneath it.

He carried no weapons, but she suspected he was not a man who needed them. There was not a trace of fear in his demeanour, and he didn't seem to care if he lived or died. But when his gaze swept over her, she caught a warning in his eyes, as if he'd ordered her to say nothing. Her cheeks warmed beneath his gaze, and she tried to suppress the embarrassment of such a man watching her.

She lifted her chin, still keeping her face covered by the woollen *brat* so that only her eyes were revealed. Though it was vain, she didn't want him to see her scars. For a moment, she wanted to look upon this warrior as if she were his equal.

The man turned to the soldiers and said, 'Our chieftain would like to know why you've come with armed men to Carrickmeath.'

The commander moved forward, two riders on either side of him, armed with spears. His eyes narrowed for a moment as he confronted the man. 'You have the look of the *Ard-Righ* about you.'

The man did not seem pleased by the observation. 'I am the High King's bastard son. And you still have not answered my question of why you are here.' His words were iron, revealing his impatience.

'Brian Faoilin betrothed his daughter to the *Ard-Righ*,' the commander answered. 'And yet, he has not brought the bride to King Rory, despite messengers that we sent over the past few months. The King wishes to know his reasons for delaying the marriage.'

'Lady Carice has been ill,' the dark-haired man said. He crossed his arms over his chest and met the man's accusations openly. 'The High King already knows this.'

'I have my doubts,' the commander said. 'It looks as if she was about to flee.' He stared hard at Taryn, and she ignored his gaze, feeling a sudden rush of fear.

He hadn't seen her face. He thought *she* was the Lady Carice because her scars were hidden. Her heart beat faster, and she had no idea what to say. Taryn stole another look at the dark-haired god, but he did not deny the soldier's mistake. Instead, his eyes fixed upon her, and in them, she caught another warning. Whatever was happening, he wanted her to follow his lead.

It was clear that she had to maintain a pretence. A frozen chill washed over her at the thought of such an illusion. It would never work—not in a thousand years. The moment anyone saw her face, they would know the truth.

But whatever it was that the man wanted from her, he would owe her a favour if she did as he asked. She *needed his* help, more than he needed hers. And for that reason, she met his gaze evenly and gave a slight nod.

'Lady Carice was not trying to flee,' he said smoothly, reaching out his hand to her. It was an offer of sanctuary, so long as she obeyed him. Taryn hesitated a moment, for this man was a stranger to her. She had no idea whether or not she should trust him.

His grey eyes were as cold as frost upon stone. There was no trace of emotion or any reaction upon his face. It was as if he cared not what she did.

Taryn took a slight step forward, feeling uneasy about the deception. But she kept her face shielded by the wool, lowering her gaze to the ground. Each step brought her closer to this man, and she had no idea why he wanted to perpetuate such a lie.

But perhaps her acquiescence would lead to the help she needed. One wrong move, and the High King's men would attack this fortress and bring violence with them—she had no doubt of it.

When she reached the dark-haired god's side, Taryn could feel the tension stretched tightly between them. She risked a glance at him and sent a pleading look, praying that he would help her.

Despite his ragged appearance, his hard body strained at the wool and hidden armour, revealing a warrior's build. He crossed his upper arms, and the bulge of muscle made it clear that he had the strength to fight any of these men. But more than that, he held an unshakable confidence.

She took his hand, and he squeezed it lightly in a veiled command to remain silent. She decided that this was her best chance to save her father's life. All she needed was to maintain the deception long enough to gain their cooperation. Just a little longer.

But the wind tore at her woollen *brat*, whipping free the dark locks of her hair. She seized the edges of the wool, trying to hide her scarred face.

For a moment, she held her breath, afraid that they had seen her. But instead, the commander gave a nod, as if her identity had been confirmed. 'What have you to say, Lady Carice?' He eyed her and remarked, 'I presume you were trying to flee and realised your mistake.'

She sent another questioning look towards the dark-haired warrior. But this time, he gave no indication of what he wanted her to say. Instead, he seemed to be waiting for her response.

Taryn needed help from the Faoilin clan. Her best means of gaining an army was to offer them assistance in her own way.

'You are right,' she told the commander, trying to sound sheepish. 'I *was* trying to flee. But then I realised how foolish it would be to do so.'

She lifted her chin, keeping the wool firmly in place to reveal nothing but her eyes. 'I am Lady Carice. And I suppose you've come to escort me to Tara for my wedding.'

Chapter Two

W ho in the name of the gods was this woman? And why was she here?

Killian had never seen her before, but her presence had been the answer to a dilemma. He had left the fortress, intending to speak with the armed men, and the woman had appeared out of nowhere. The pleading look in her blue eyes was a silent cry for help, and he'd acted on impulse, letting the commander believe what he wanted to.

Because Carice's freedom depended on the decisions he made now.

These men had come to seize his sister, and it would have ended her chance of escaping. But now, there was a fragment of hope.

The woman had kept her face hidden, and the effect had magnified those beautiful eyes.

Her hair was wet from the rain and snow, like a length of black silk. Every man there had been unable to take his eyes from her, and that was why the High King's men had believed she was Carice.

Fate had delivered a way of saving his sister into Killian's hands, and he had acted on that instinct. The woman clearly wanted help, and he would give it—at his own price.

Carice wanted to leave, to have her freedom, and this young woman was offering herself as part of the deception. He didn't know how he would use her—perhaps they could switch places. But for now, he would take her inside, and find out what she wanted later.

His breath became mist in the frigid air, and he kept his gaze fixed upon her. She was terrified and with good reason. Everything rested upon the decision he made now.

'My men have travelled far,' the commander said. 'They need food, wine, and a place to sleep before we depart on the morrow.' His gaze narrowed upon the young woman. 'Open the gates, and we will give her this night to ready her possessions.'

Killian had no wish to bring the soldiers inside the castle, but neither could he raise their suspicions. To deny them hospitality might make them question their motives. He inclined his head once. To the woman, he said, 'You should return to your chamber. I will escort you there.'

And then he would have the answers to his questions. Though he doubted if she posed any threat, he would find out before he allowed her to dwell among the women. He kept her gloved hand in his, noting the slight tremor in her palm. But even so, she carried herself with a quiet grace that was different from the other women he'd known. And he knew, without her revealing her true identity, that this woman had noble blood.

Before they could walk further than a few paces, the commander stepped forward to intercede. 'We go with her, lad.'

'I am Killian MacDubh. Not your lad,' he said. But he motioned the commander to follow. When they reached the entrance, he ordered the men to open the gates.

'They are here at the High King's command,' Killian told the guards. 'They have come to escort Carice to her wedding.' Which was the truth, and none here would deny it. He deliberately said nothing about the strange woman, for once the gates were open, he intended to have words with her and learn her reasons for the deception.

While the soldiers rode inside, Killian moved back to wait for them. The young woman drew away from the horses, gripping his palm as if she was trying to gain strength from him. Her fear had not diminished at all, and he wondered if she had been fleeing from someone in pursuit of her.

Not once had she let go of the woollen *brat*, and he now was beginning to think she was trying to hide her true identity. For what purpose?

Against her ear, he murmured, 'Do exactly as I command and say nothing.'

She nodded, and Killian brought her forward while the men gave over their horses to the stable boys. His friend Seorse was watching, and Killian kept his voice low, saying, 'Take the High King's men to dine with our chieftain while I escort the Lady to the solar.'

Seorse looked as if he wanted to ask more, but Killian shook his head slightly, denying him that. There would be time for answers later.

Thankfully, the High King's men followed Seorse into the Great Chamber. His friend welcomed the men, and Killian kept the young woman back so that she was hidden from Brian Faoilin's view. Once the men were speaking to the chieftain, he seized the opportunity to escape. He took the young woman towards the spiral stairs leading towards Carice's chamber. For a moment, he paused, waiting to see if any of the High King's men would follow. When no one did, he pulled her into the shadows and covered her mouth with his hand.

In a low voice, he murmured, 'I'm going to take my hand from your mouth, and we're going to talk. You're going to tell me who you are and why you're here.'

Although she had offered herself in Carice's place, that didn't make her worthy of trust. If anything, her lie made him more suspicious. She was here for reasons of her own, and he knew not what threat she posed.

Killian removed his hand from her mouth, but the young woman kept the *brat* over her face, hiding her features. She met his gaze evenly. 'I am Taryn Connelly of Ossoria. My father, King Devlin, is a prisoner of the High King and will be executed on the eve of Imbolc. I came here to seek help from your chieftain.'

For a moment, Killian studied her. Of royal blood, was she? He could almost believe it, given her demeanour and the way she held her posture. But no king's daughter would travel alone.

'Where are your escorts?' he demanded.

She glanced behind her and shrugged. 'I... brought only a single guard. I sent him here before me, but I have not seen him. I do not know where he is now.'

The worry in her voice did nothing to dispel his distrust. She was hiding the truth from him, as well as her face. Though he knew why she had veiled herself among the soldiers, he wondered why she would not uncover her features.

'Lower the *brat*,' he ordered. 'I want to see your face.'

Her blue eyes held wariness, and she shook her head. 'No. Not now.' She gripped the wool as if it could make her invisible from his gaze.

The stricken expression in her eyes warned that she did not want him to see her.

He couldn't imagine why. With her midnight-black hair and spellbinding eyes, she captivated his attention.

Killian ignored her refusal and took the edges of the wool, forcing her to remain still. He lowered the *brat* from her head, revealing her face. It was then that he saw the jagged red scars upon her right cheek. It looked as if someone had tried to tear her face open, and he could only imagine the pain she'd endured. There was a matching scar upon the left side, though it was whiter in colour.

This was why she had wanted to shield herself. If the men had seen the scars, they would have known she was not Carice.

He was at a loss for words. Not because the scars and reddened skin made her unattractive—it was because they revealed a suffering that no one should endure. And this beautiful woman would bear the marks of this attack forever.

Her hair hung down in waving locks against her shoulders, and it was still soaked from the rain. When she pulled the wet strands against her cheeks, the scars were barely visible. Like Carice, Taryn had blue eyes, but they held a stronger resemblance to the sea. Worry creased her expression, as if she did not want him to see her true appearance.

'And now you see why I hide myself,' she admitted. 'I am ugly. No one would ever want to look upon me.'

Killian supposed that men did avoid her— and yet, the scars revealed a woman who had been through the worst and survived it. It didn't bother him at all; instead, it intrigued him.

'Do not hide yourself from me,' he told her. 'You have nothing to fear.'

She gave him a half-hearted smile, as if she didn't believe him. And still she held the silken strands to her face, like a shield. 'I don't know why the men possibly believed I was Lady Carice,' she said. 'I look nothing like her.'

'No,' he agreed. 'But the men have never seen her before.' Carice had brown hair with hints of red and gold. Her blue eyes were lighter than Taryn's, similar to a bright summer sky. His sister had lacked no shortage of suitors, but Brian had no intention of letting any man have his only daughter, save the High King.

'Why was your father taken prisoner by the High King?' he asked Taryn.

She shook her head, admitting, 'I don't know. Whenever I ask why, my mother will not give me an answer.' At last, she released the strands of hair, letting him glimpse the reddened scars. 'I want to plead for his life, but she refused to allow it. It is why I travelled alone. I thought I could ask your chieftain for help, and I would offer compensation to the warriors in return.'

He said nothing, for he doubted if Brian

would want to be involved. The chieftain would do nothing to threaten his close alliance with the High King.

Taryn paused a moment and added, 'Or if Lady Carice is travelling to her wedding, I could accompany her and speak with King Rory while I am there.'

'You may ask Carice,' he offered at last, 'but Brian would never bring soldiers against the High King. Not when he hopes his daughter will be Queen.'

She thought for a moment. 'I know you are right. I did not mean to suggest that his men would fight against the King. Only that...perhaps someone could help my father escape in secret.' She raised hopeful eyes in his direction, and he knew she was referring to him.

'No.' Killian wasn't about to go anywhere near the High King. This wasn't his fight.

But she wasn't so easily deterred. 'Your men are stronger and better-trained than ours were. They could easily—'

'Were?' he interrupted. At the guilty flush on her face, he suspected the worst. 'Are they dead, then?'

Her hesitation only confirmed his belief. Her men had failed, and it had cost them their lives.

'I was not there to know exactly what happened. But yes, they died.' She rubbed her shoulders as if to fight off a chill. 'Perhaps it would be different with stronger men, like you. And you already have a reason to travel to Tara.'

'You want me to risk my life for your father?' he prompted. 'My loyalty does not lie with Ossoria.' Only with Carice, whom he would protect with his life. But he had no desire to lay eyes upon the father who had refused to acknowledge him.

'Would you intercede with the chieftain for me?' she asked at last. 'I presume you are his son or…one of his commanders?'

Killian folded his arms across his chest. 'I am little more than a slave here, Lady Taryn. But Carice is like a sister to me.'

Confusion crossed over her face. 'Then why did you—' She stopped speaking and chose different words. 'That is, if you are only a slave, why did you speak to the High King's men on Brian Faoilin's behalf?'

'Because if the soldiers killed me, my life would be no loss to the chieftain.' He spoke the words matter-of-factly, though the real answer was because he'd recognised the High King's banner. There was no question that the King's men posed a threat to Carice, and he'd gone to protect her.

The Lady straightened and regarded him. 'I don't believe a man like you would ever willingly go to die.'

'You don't know what sort of man I am.' He lived each day with the knowledge that he was nothing to Brian Faoilin, beyond his fighting skills. And Taryn was wrong—he *would* die to save Carice's life. She was the only person who cared anything for him. The only woman who had given him kindness after his mother had died. He traced the outline of the silver ring upon his smallest finger that Iona had given him before her death.

'No,' she agreed. 'I don't know you at all. But I suspect you might be someone who could help me. For a price,' she added.

Though it was true that he did need gold or silver to raise his status, he was wary of trusting a stranger. He knew nothing of this woman, aside from her claims.

'My only concern is in protecting Lady Carice,' he told her. 'She does not wish to wed the High King.' *And she is dying,* he thought, but didn't say it. The journey to Tara might weaken her even faster. He would do whatever was necessary to prolong whatever life she had remaining.

The Lady gave a nod. 'I understand.'

Killian didn't miss the slight shiver when she spoke, as if she feared the High King. And likely she had reason to, for few women wanted to wed a man so ruthless. His own mother had fled from Rory Ó Connor, remaining in hiding for the rest of her life.

'I don't think you do,' he countered. 'Carice wants to slip away and escape the marriage altogether. She was planning to flee before the soldiers came.'

'Perhaps I could help her,' she offered. 'That is, if she will let me travel with her.' Taryn gripped her *brat*, drawing it closer.

'You will have to ask.' Killian stared at her, wondering exactly what she intended to do, once she reached Tara. Travelling alone was a disastrous idea, one more dangerous than she could imagine.

And yet…she *could* help his sister slip away at nightfall. Or Taryn could help to deceive the King's men by disguising herself at night, letting them believe she was Carice and thereby granting his sister more time.

He wasn't a man to make a decision lightly,

especially when there was so much at stake. If he refused to let Taryn get involved, Carice would be taken against her will in the morning. It would be far too difficult to help his sister escape.

But a deception at night could work, especially if Taryn remained behind in Carice's place. The soldiers might believe it for a few hours, if she kept her face shielded.

He couldn't fathom why he was even considering this. It would never work.

'May I warm myself by your fire?' Taryn asked quietly.

He decided it was best to consult Carice in this, for it was her decision to make. 'I will take you to my sister's chamber, and you may warm yourself there,' he told her, 'but she has been ill and is resting. If she awakens, you may ask her what she wants to do.'

'I would think she'd be relieved and eager to help me.' Taryn's mouth twisted. 'Especially if she can somehow avoid the marriage.' There was a faint trace of unrest in her eyes. For all her bravado, this woman was afraid of Rory Ó Connor.

He led her up the stone staircase and when they reached the top, he blocked her way. 'I will let you meet my sister. But if Carice refuses to let you travel with us, you're going to leave.' He would find another way of helping his sister escape the marriage—even if it meant carrying her out of the fortress in the middle of the night.

Taryn nodded slowly in agreement, though he suspected she would not give up that easily. Killian knocked upon his sister's chamber and heard her weak reply, 'Come in.'

He pushed the door open and found Carice curled up on her side, her strained expression revealing her pain. The room smelled of sickness, and it was clear that she hadn't managed to eat the bread that her maid had brought.

'Leave us,' Killian told the serving girl. She obeyed, glancing at Taryn as she did. After the girl was gone, he went to Carice's bedside. 'I've brought someone to meet you. There has been a change in our plans since we last spoke.'

Taryn remained on the far side of the room, but he beckoned for her to draw nearer. When she did, she held her hair against her cheeks, hiding the scars. Though he understood why she did it, it bothered him. His sister was not the sort of person who would judge someone by her appearance.

Upon the foot of the bed, a smoke-grey cat

arched his back and stretched, clawing at the coverlet. Harold began purring and jumped down, rubbing against Killian's legs. He scratched the cat's ears and lifted Harold up, giving the animal affection before he sat beside his sister. By the Rood, she looked weary and frail.

Carice opened her eyes and looked first at Killian and then at Taryn. 'I have seen you before,' she said to Taryn, her voice barely above a whisper. Her fingers dug into the sheets as if another stomach cramp plagued her. 'You are Lady Taryn of Ossoria.'

Taryn nodded. 'I am, yes.' Even with her hair shielding her face, she held herself back, keeping a goodly distance from both of them. Killian sensed that she was nervous.

'Why have you come?' His sister struggled to sit up, and Killian assisted her, propping up a pillow behind her shoulders.

Taryn glanced back at him, as if questioning whether or not she should tell Carice everything. He nodded for her to continue. 'Tell her.'

'I know you are betrothed to the High King,' Taryn said. 'My father is the High King's captive, and I cannot let him die as a prisoner. I

must get close in order to save him, and I... I
wanted to accompany you to Tara.'

Carice stared at the young woman as if uncertain what to say. The cat jumped down from
the bed again, padding towards Taryn. The moment he approached, she tensed and moved
aside to avoid him. Harold responded by purring and nudging her legs, but Taryn wouldn't
even look at the animal.

'King Rory's men arrived less than an hour
ago,' Killian told his sister. 'They want you to
journey to Tara in the morning.'

'They what?' Horror came over his sister's
face. She glanced towards the door as if trying
to think of an escape. 'So soon?'

He squeezed her hand in quiet reassurance.
'I haven't forgotten my promise, Carice. Trust
in me.'

Taryn came closer. 'I will help you to avoid
the marriage,' she told the other woman. 'I could
disguise myself in your clothing until you've
managed to leave. And then Killian will bring
me to Tara in your place before anyone knows
you have gone.'

Killian studied his sister, who had laid her
head back down. God above, he wished he could
take this suffering from her. She should have

had a life before her, marriage and the children she wanted. Instead, every moment was filled with pain.

'What do you want to do, Carice?' he asked, gently touching her cheek.

His sister let out a weak smile. 'It seems that Fate has changed our plans, doesn't it, Killian?' She closed her eyes for a moment. 'While I understand your offer, Lady Taryn, I fear it cannot work. My father would never allow us to carry out such a deception, much less an escape.' She reached out a hand to the cat, who came closer and rubbed his head against her fingers. 'If the King's men are here, my father will insist upon accompanying me.'

The desolate weariness on her face was like a blade in Killian's chest. If she had to leave with the High King's men, it would end her life even faster.

He wanted to plead with Brian to end the betrothal, but the chieftain was blind to his daughter's illness, believing that she would overcome it. He wanted Carice to be Queen of all Éireann, no matter what the cost. If these men wanted her to leave with them, Brian would send his daughter.

'Your father doesn't have to know,' Taryn

said. 'Let him believe that I am merely accompanying you to your wedding. No one will suspect anything if you begin the journey at my side. We could travel in a litter, and then you can slip away at night. If I remain hidden, it would give you time enough to flee. Perhaps my guard could take you wherever you want to go.'

His sister took a shaky breath. To Taryn, she admitted, 'What you are suggesting is dangerous. If I do escape, when you arrive at Tara, the High King's men will tell him what happened. You would be punished for deceiving his men.'

'It is a risk,' Taryn agreed. 'But I am willing to try, for my father's sake.'

'And what if the High King demands that you take my place?' Carice asked. 'You are Lady of Ossoria, after all. What if he forces *you* to marry him?'

Taryn's face reddened, and she shook her head. 'He would never wed someone like me.' She fingered the ends of her hair, and Killian knew why. She didn't want anyone to see her features. And though he could demand that she show his sister the scars, he was holding back her secret. There was no need to voice what both of them knew. The High King of Éireann would never accept a scarred woman as his bride.

Even so, Taryn was not as unattractive as she seemed to believe. No, she did not have the strong beauty of Carice, but her long black hair framed a face with bold blue eyes. The freezing rain had dampened her face, and her wet hair rested over her shoulders. Her gown clung to a slender body with a slight swell of hips and generous breasts.

A sudden vision flared, of peeling back her gown to reveal that creamy skin. He imagined tasting the water droplets as they rolled over erect nipples and between the valleys. Would she sigh with pleasure, arching and grasping his hair?

Gods, where had that thought come from? It had been a while since he'd been with a woman, and certainly he'd never had a noblewoman in his bed. This one seemed timorous somehow, though she had braved her journey here alone.

Her appearance might be marred, but Taryn of Ossoria had something that others lacked—courage. He knew of no woman who would offer to deceive the High King at a risk to herself.

'King Rory will seek vengeance if you do this,' Carice insisted. 'He is old and cruel. And he acts swiftly before considering the consequences.' She paused a moment and looked at him. 'He is also Killian's father.'

Taryn didn't flinch, but she admitted, 'I heard him say that when he spoke with the soldiers.' She glanced over at him as if she expected to see traces of his father there. And perhaps there were. Killian prided himself on never allowing emotions to cloud his judgement.

'I am the High King's bastard,' he reminded her. 'Not a true-born son.'

He expected the young woman to regard him with derision. Instead, she seemed more curious, her gaze discerning.

'Killian and I are not brother and sister by blood,' Carice said. 'But I've always thought of him in that way. His mother sought sanctuary with my father, and we grew up together, though we had different parents.' She ventured a smile, but he sensed that she was growing even more tired.

Taryn moved closer to them, and upon her face, there was sympathy. 'Why does your father want you to marry the High King, if you find him to be cruel? Especially if you've been so unwell?'

'Because Brian wants me to be High Queen,' Carice admitted. 'And because he does not believe how ill I am. He cannot accept weakness in anyone, and he keeps sending for healers who bleed me and give me potions I despise.' Her voice dropped to a whisper. 'I suppose, in his own way, he wants a better life for me. You know what a father will do for his daughter, do you not?'

Killian caught the sudden flash of pain over the young woman's face when she nodded. 'I do, yes. And I know what a daughter would do for her father.'

A silent understanding passed between them. Then Carice added, 'I know you are trying to help him. But you should not endanger yourself. There are other ways you might send men to Tara.'

Killian wasn't so certain. If the Queen had refused to intervene on her husband's behalf, then there were reasons for it. In the meantime, he wasn't going to lose the opportunity to get Carice to safety—not when Taryn had offered to help.

'I will speak with Brian and see what can be done,' Killian offered. He placed the cat beside Carice and pulled the coverlet over her, brushing her hair aside. 'Rest now.' Harold curled up beside his sister, and she stroked his ears.

Her eyes held sadness, as if she'd resigned herself to an unwelcome fate. But Killian wasn't
about to give up hope. There had to be a means
of saving her—and he wouldn't stop until he'd
found a way.

Taryn followed Killian into the hall, but he
did not return towards the stairs. Instead, he
beckoned for her to follow him towards another
chamber.

'Aren't we going to speak with your chieftain?' She wasn't certain quite where he was
taking her.

Killian seized a torch from an iron sconce on
the wall and opened another door. 'Not yet.' He
stood before the entrance, waiting.

Though she knew he was expecting her obedience, she took a moment to study him closer.
She could see the chain mail beneath his dark
woollen clothing. His forearms were scarred,
and his face held the dark bristle of unshaved
cheeks. His grey eyes were the colour of the sky
on a winter's morning.

Taryn took a single step inside the chamber,
then froze. The room was small, hardly large
enough for a chair, and it had no window at all.

'I'm not going in there.' She didn't know this man at all and certainly didn't trust him.

He placed the torch upon one wall, and it illuminated the space, casting shadows on the wall. 'We need to talk about Carice. Close the door and stand beside it if it makes you feel safer.'

While she thought about it, the grey cat wandered into the room, weaving against her legs before it went back to Killian. He picked it up, and the animal began purring.

She took another hesitant step inside the chamber and closed the door. Killian remained on the far side of the room, the torchlight flickering across his face. 'You don't like animals, do you?'

It surprised her that he'd noticed. 'Oh, I don't mind animals. It's just that they don't seem to like me.'

Killian set down the cat. 'You're afraid of them.'

'Sometimes.' She saw no reason to be dishonest, but when the cat approached, she couldn't help but retreat.

'Don't show your fear,' he advised. 'They sense it.'

She knew that, but she'd never been able to suppress the way she felt. Not only because of her brother Christopher's death, but also from her own scars. She didn't remember how she had been attacked, but she had nightmares about wild teeth tearing into her flesh. Every time she was near animals, the hairs on her arms stood on end, and fear enveloped her. The reaction was instinctive, though she knew most animals meant her no harm.

'What should we do about your sister?' she asked, needing to change the subject.

Killian paused a moment. 'I've been thinking, and there may be a way to solve both of our problems.'

He was watching her, and Taryn pulled her hair forward again, not wanting this man's discerning gaze upon her face. 'What do you want me to do?'

He crossed his arms. 'Accompany Carice to Tara, and do not leave her side. Not at all.'

Curious, she leaned against the wall, wondering what sort of deception he intended.

'We won't be explaining ourselves to anyone,' he continued. 'When anyone addresses Carice, you will be beside her. If all goes well, the High King's men won't know which one of you is the bride. Let them believe what they want.'

The idea was a bold one, but it would indeed

create an illusion. 'And what will we do about her illness?'

'Hide it as best we can.' He spoke of her standing at his sister's side, granting her physical support so she could walk to the litter. 'Brian will want that as well.'

'And what will we do about him?' The chieftain would undoubtedly give away Carice's identity if he accompanied them.

'If he escorts Carice, I will ensure that he does not stop her from leaving,' Killian answered.

The ice in his voice frightened her, for she knew not what he intended to do. Whatever it was, Killian was not a man she would ever want as her enemy.

And yet, she could not fault him for wanting to protect the woman he called sister. Would he hold the same loyalty towards his own woman, if he were married? Perhaps. And yet, she believed he was a man who walked his path alone. He wore an air of isolation, as if he wanted to remain apart from others.

'What will happen to Carice?' she asked him. 'How will she escape?'

'Within a day or two, one of the MacEgan men will "kidnap" her,' he answered. 'Carice will disappear, and you will take her place for a few hours that night, before anyone notices she's gone.'

'And if I do this, will you help me to free my father?' she ventured.

He studied her for a moment but shook his head. 'I will take you the rest of the way to Tara, but that is all.'

It wasn't what she had hoped for, but it was a start. 'What of the other men? Is there someone else who might help me?'

His silence was not reassuring. There was so little time left, and she had to find someone quickly. It would take days yet to reach Tara, and if she did not find someone here, she would have to seek help from mercenaries. Such warriors would sooner steal her gold than do her bidding.

'Brian's men will not stand against Rory,' he said at last. 'And even if you did find someone to free King Devlin, your father could never return to his kingdom. Not if the High King wants him dead.'

Her spirit dissolved in fear, for that was true. She might save Devlin's life—but she could not save his reign. The only way to truly bring him back was to mend the breach between the two kings. Someone had to intercede on her father's behalf…someone with the ear of the High King.

Like his son.

Killian MacDubh might be a bastard, but surely the *Ard-Righ* would listen to him.

Yet Killian wanted no part of his father. He was trying to keep Lady Carice from wedding the man. It was unlikely that he would even consider her request.

'I could pay you in silver or pearls,' she said. 'If you found men willing to help me.' She eyed him, adding, 'Certainly, the task would be too difficult for only one man.'

His expression tightened at her challenge, as if he wanted to rise to the bait.

Just how proud are you, Killian? she wondered. Was he willing to help her, in return for the riches he lacked?

'Too difficult, is it?' he countered. In one swift motion, he extinguished the torch. Darkness enveloped the room, and Taryn huddled against the door. Only the faintest embers glowed against the wood, and she could hear nothing at all.

Silence permeated the space, and a moment later, his hands were upon her shoulders, his breath against her ear. 'When I want to be unseen, this I can do, *a chara*. Like a shadow.'

Shivers erupted over her skin, and she tried to calm the rapid beating of her heart. Never before had any man come so close to her, and she could feel the hard planes of his body behind her.

'It will be dangerous at Tara.'

She told herself to step forward, out of his hold. And yet, her feet stubbornly refused to move. A reckless side to her imagined what it would be like if he pressed her back against the wall and claimed a kiss.

He turned her in the darkness, keeping her hand in his. Against her palm, she felt the calloused skin of a swordsman. 'It is, aye.'

'And you've said that you will not help me,' she reminded him. 'Unless there is something else you want that I can grant.'

The moment she spoke the words, she regretted them. It sounded as if she were offering herself as the prize.

His hand moved through her hair, his thumb skimming the ridged scars upon her cheek. The touch only reminded her that she was a woman no man would ever want. He didn't have to speak a single word for her to know the answer.

Abruptly he opened the door, and light speared her eyes from the hall. 'Stay with my sister for the rest of the night. I will tell Brian that you are here.'

He made no promises, and she could not imagine what he was thinking right now. A strange ache caught within her, knowing that she was utterly alone in wanting to save her father.

Taryn closed her eyes against the light in the hall, pushing back the hurt feelings before she emerged. She knew she should do as Killian had ordered, returning to share the chamber with his sister. And yet, she did not want to be brushed aside so soon.

She tiptoed down the stairs, hiding herself against the curve of the wall so that she had a view of the Great Chamber. From here, no one would see her. The chieftain was seated at a long table, upon a dais, surrounded by other men. The High King's soldiers were dining at the lower tables, tossing bones to the dogs, and drinking ale.

Killian walked towards the chieftain, striding past the men as if he ruled over all of them. But Brian Faoilin looked displeased to see him.

The chieftain motioned for one of his guards to come forward, and he spoke quietly to the man.

Killian stared at Brian, waiting for his chance to speak. But instead of agreeing to an audience, the soldier approached and ordered him to leave. It was clear that the chieftain had no intention of acknowledging a *fuidir*.

Taryn was startled to realise it. Why? What harm was there in speaking to the chieftain? Though it was true that Killian lacked full membership in the tribe, due to his low status, surely Brian would allow him a voice.

Killian didn't move at all, but folded his arms and held his ground in his own defiance. Fury darkened the chieftain's face, and he stood. The first soldier seized Killian, shoving him against one of the benches. But instead of losing his balance, Killian moved with swift reflexes and flipped the man over, tossing him across the table. Food and drink went flying on to the floor, and a moment later, he stood before the chieftain, a faint smile upon his face.

You cannot force me to go, he seemed to be saying.

The violent hatred in the chieftain's eyes stunned her. He looked as if he wanted Killian to be beaten bloody and left to die. Within seconds, other soldiers joined in on the fighting, trying to force him out. Even the High King's men stood from their benches, surrounding Killian. All, save two men, whose expressions held anger and displeasure at the disturbance.

Instead of surrendering, Killian remained in place. A moment later, he was no longer standing there. Never in her life had she seen any man move so fast. A fist swung towards his jaw, but he dodged the blow and it collided with another man's face.

He was indeed like a shadow, here for a fleeting second, and gone the next.

The drunken men continued to fight, but Killian somehow managed to move away from them. When anyone tried to hit him, he spun and shoved them off balance. It soon became clear that he was defending himself, not provoking more fighting. But when one soldier's fist connected with Killian's jaw, it turned violent. Killian struck back, beating the man bloody, until his opponent backed off. It was an unmistakable silent message sent to the others. At last, he threw a dark glower at Brian and strode towards the back of the hall, as if he didn't want to waste words on the chieftain.

Taryn hurried from her hiding place and

followed him outside. The rain had stopped, but the air was moist and smelled of damp earth. Within the inner bailey, she glimpsed her guard, Pól, and she sent him a nod, thankful that he'd made it safely inside. She raised her hand in recognition, intending to speak with him later.

Killian continued towards the stables, and she hurried to keep up with him. Her footing slipped a time or two, but eventually she reached the outer door.

For a moment, Taryn rested her hand upon the outbuilding, taking the time to push back the unreasonable fears. The horses would be enclosed within the stalls, she told herself. If she kept her distance, no harm would come to her. Though it was foolish to be afraid of horses, a darker memory lingered on the edges of awareness.

It was your fault that Christopher died, came the voice of her conscience. She closed her eyes, wanting so badly to push back the grief. But against her will, she saw her brother's lifeless body in her vision, her heart still hurting for the loss.

She'd been a young girl, only four years old. Christopher was twelve and was home from his fostering, visiting for Yuletide. She'd idolised him and had followed him around everywhere, wanting so badly to be near him. Her brother had an easy smile and he'd never seemed to mind her attention. Sometimes he would swing her up on his shoulders, letting her feel as tall as a grown woman.

Sweet Jesu, she had loved him.

But one morning, she had run through the courtyard, eager to bid him farewell before he went off hunting with their father. She hadn't paid any heed to where she was going, and Christopher's horse had reared up without warning, throwing him off. Her brother's head had struck a stone, and he had never awakened again.

The bitter guilt had remained with her all these years, for it *had* been her fault.

Taryn took a tentative step inside the stable and was relieved to see that all of the animals remained still and quiet with only an occasional nicker. Killian stood on the far end, resting both palms against a stall. Tension lined his shoulders, and she suddenly questioned her decision to follow him.

'You were supposed to stay with Carice,' he told her.

In his voice, she sensed the caged frustration.

But even so, she wanted to understand what had happened in the Great Chamber. 'Why did the chieftain refuse to let you speak?'

He didn't turn around, and his knuckles tightened against the wood. 'Brian wishes that I had never been born. He's hated me since I took my first breath.'

'Why? What threat could you possibly pose to him?'

He faced her, and in his grey eyes, she saw a man of ice. There was no pain, no emotion at all. Only a frozen mask of indifference.

'I'm a bastard, Lady Taryn. I was not born a member of the tribe, and I'm not worth even the dirt beneath his feet. Why *would* he speak to me?' Killian studied her with a mocking smile. 'Brian wants naught to do with me. He wanted me hidden from everyone, like a secret meant to be forgotten.' He spread out his hands, gesturing towards the stable. 'Look around you, Lady Taryn. This is my home. I sleep here, among the horses and dogs.'

She didn't like that at all. A man's worth had nothing to do with his birthright.

'You are not to blame for your mother's choices.'

'A choice?' He looked incredulous at her

words. 'My mother had no choice at all. She was with child when she fled the High King. Brian took her in, but we were both treated as *fuidir*.' He shrugged as if it meant nothing. Still, it bothered Taryn to see a man so mistreated, merely from circumstances of birth.

'Why did she leave the High King?'

He sent her a disbelieving glance. 'It's more likely that she never wanted to be with a man like him. She wouldn't speak of Rory, though everyone knows I am his son.'

'Does he know about you? That is, did you ever go to see him?' Though it was quite a distance to Tara, she couldn't imagine that he'd remained here.

'No. Brian told him about me, but Rory cared nothing about my existence. I had no desire to meet him, based on my mother's experience.'

She suspected there was more that he hadn't revealed. In his eyes, she saw the hard resentment of a man who hated his life. Most of the *fuidir* she'd encountered were not as proud as this man. But Killian seemed unwilling to accept a fate such as this, and she could not blame him.

'If this is not the life you want, you could leave,' she suggested.

He said nothing, and she realised that she *did* have something to offer this man. A home where he would not be treated as a slave. 'If you free my father, you could come and live among our people at Ossoria. You would have a place with us.'

The doubt upon his face made it clear that he did not believe her. 'I intend to see my sister to safety. That is the only reason I am escorting you to Tara—to help her escape. After that, I will go my own way.'

She wasn't ready to give up so soon. Not when there was a chance he could save her father's life.

Yet, there was so much bitterness locked away in Killian, it was festering deep inside. Despite the High King's reputation, there was a blood bond between them, of father and son. There might be a way for him to gain Rory's favour.

'And after Carice is safe? What then?' she pressed. 'Will you return here and live among men who treat you like the dirt they walk upon?'

Rage flashed in his eyes and she knew she had struck upon his weakness—pride. This was a man who had the demeanour of a king, though he was trapped in the life of a slave.

'My decisions are my own.' He took a step towards her, letting his height intimidate her. But she refused to back down—not when she believed he had the power to save her father. This man had single-handedly fought back against the chieftain's strongest men, proving that he could overcome the odds. When she looked upon his face, she saw a man of determination, a man of courage.

He reached down and caught her wrist. 'Don't think I'm unaware of what you're doing, *a chara*. You want me to speak on your father's behalf to King Rory and ask my father to free Devlin.' He sent her a sidelong look. 'As if a bastard son has any influence at all.' She tried to pull her hand back, but he gripped it tight. 'I'll not be risking my life for his.'

He wouldn't want that, no. But there was something else that might sway him.

Taryn reached beneath her skirt to a pouch she'd tied beneath it. From the pouch, she withdrew a silver coin. She held it up and said, 'If you do go your own path, you will need to build your own wealth. You could start with this.'

She pressed the silver into his palm, but he caught her hand and held it. The small piece of metal warmed beneath their joined hands, but there was more than a simple touch. 'This is what my word is worth,' she continued. 'If you rescue my father, I can give you a chest of silver so heavy, you cannot lift it. You could buy anything you want.'

Killian's steel eyes smouldered with fury, and he looked as if her offer had wounded his pride. Taryn's skin tightened, her body flushing at his intense stare. She tried to look away, but every part of her was strangely attuned to him. Her body had grown sensitive, and the coldness of his face caught her breath.

Like a fallen angel, his features were darkly handsome. Though he didn't bruise her skin with his grip, he was letting her know who was in command. And it wasn't her.

'I've never met anyone of noble blood whose word could be trusted.' He pressed the coin back into her hand, as if to say he wanted nothing she could give.

His words infuriated her. She had done nothing to warrant such distrust, and it was insulting. 'You don't even know me, Killian MacDubh. I am a woman who keeps her promises.'

'Are you?' he asked softly. 'The first words you spoke were lies and deceptions. Why should I believe you?'

Her face flushed at the memory of how she'd told the soldiers she was Carice. From the shielded expression on his face, she realised that Killian was a man who trusted no one, save himself. No matter what vows she made, he would not believe them.

'Then perhaps I won't help your sister after all,' she countered. 'I'll confess to the soldiers who I really am, and your father can take her to Tara to be wedded to the High King. I'll find other soldiers to save my father.'

She started to move away, but he caught her waist, trapping her against the wooden horse stall. 'Don't.'

His hard body was pressed against hers, and she was completely at his mercy. Though he was likely meaning to intimidate her, instead, it felt like an embrace. Her body softened against his hardness, and she found herself spellbound by his iron eyes. The fierceness of his expression was of a warrior bent upon gaining her surrender. He kept her wrists pinned with his hands against the wall. But instead of feeling trapped, her traitorous mind imagined what it would be like to be claimed by this man.

She suspected that Killian would only take what he wanted, never giving anything of himself. And though it should have frightened her, she wondered if there was any warmth at all behind his heart of ice.

'You will do nothing to harm Carice. Not ever.' Though his words were spoken softly, the threat was not lost upon her. 'Not in word or in deed.'

Taryn stared back at him, facing him without fear. 'I will do whatever I must to free my father. We can be allies and help one another…or we can be enemies. The choice is yours.'

Chapter Three

Killian awakened in a pile of straw with three dogs sleeping near him and Harold's furry face nudging his. It was so cold, he could see a layer of ice upon the water trough. He stretched, feeling stiff and sore from the sleepless night, while the cat rubbed against his side.

Taryn's threat, to reveal everything to the High King's men, had infuriated him. For whether or not he wanted to admit it, he did need her assistance. One of the MacEgans might help Carice to escape, but without Taryn to disguise herself and buy a few more hours of time, the soldiers would pursue his sister.

What the Lady wanted in return was far too great a price. He had no desire to get entangled with her father's fate, nor did he want to lay eyes upon Rory Ó Connor. He remembered all

too well what had happened when Brian had returned from Connacht, fifteen years ago.

*The chieftain had stared at him with loath-
ing. 'Come here, boy.'*

*Killian had obeyed, keeping his back straight.
He'd hardly slept last night, dreaming that he
would be sent to live at Connacht with the King.
He imagined a life where he had a pallet to
sleep upon instead of a pile of straw in the stables. Would he finally go to live with his true father? Would Rory be proud of him? He was six
years old, and he was growing stronger each
day. He might be one of the finest warriors in
Éireann one day, if he worked hard.*

*'He doesn't want you,' Brian said. 'He has
sired over a dozen bastards, and he doesn't want
another.' The chieftain spat at his feet. 'That's
all you're worth to him.'*

*A coldness seized up in his chest, the hope
shattering. He'd wanted so badly to live with
someone who wanted him, now that his mother
was dead. He twisted the silver ring on his
thumb, so afraid of what would happen now.*

*'Did...did you see him?' Mayhap there had
been a mistake.*

*'No,' Brian answered. 'He was organising a
raid on Munster.'*

'Then it might have been a mistake.' Killian brightened at that. If his father was waging war on Munster, he might not want a son right now. But later...

'There was no mistake.' Brian sent him a scathing look. 'His men gave him the message, but Rory offered nothing at all for you. Were I not a merciful man, I'd turn you out.' He crossed his arms and regarded Killian. 'As it is, I will let you live in the stables and tend the horses. Unless you'd rather go out on your own?'

Killian had been too frightened to understand any of what had happened, but he'd obeyed. At least at Carrickmeath, he had food and shelter. It was better than starving to death, and he'd been too young to survive alone.

But now, he would have his freedom. Once he saw Carice to safety.

The wolfhound beside him stretched and trotted over to him, resting his head upon Killian's knee. He rubbed the dog's ears, still thinking about Lady Taryn. She had silver and wealth beyond his dreams—but what he truly wanted was land and kinsmen who would look upon him with respect. And that was something that could never be bought—it had to be earned.

The voice of temptation lured him closer, reminding him that Taryn could grant him everything he wanted. All he had to do was risk his life for her father.

Likely the man was already dead. The High King resented the other provincial kings, particularly those who did not revere him. Though Killian didn't know what Devlin's crimes were, the odds of saving him were nearly impossible.

The dilemma weighed down upon him, for in a matter of hours, everything had changed. He would protect Carice, aye. But beyond that, once she was safe? What then?

Taryn's words dug into his pride. *Will you return here and live among men who treat you like the dirt they walk upon?*

That was what bothered him most. Never had he been given the chance to fight for the life he wanted. This woman held the power to change everything—all he had to do was risk his life for a stranger.

He didn't know what to think of this turn of events. Nor did he know what to think of Taryn Connelly. She was acutely conscious of her scarred face, but she was not a woman to hide herself away from the world. She'd faced him down, fighting for the life of the father she loved. Just as he was fighting for Carice.

They were more alike than he'd wanted to admit.

When he'd lost his temper and had pressed her back against the wall, he'd never expected the sudden interest that had flared up within him. He'd meant to intimidate her, to make her understand that he would allow no one to threaten his sister. Instead, he'd been fully aware of the lines of her body and the softness that had pressed back against him.

Her eyes had widened, as if she didn't know what to do. He'd expected her to pull back in revulsion, but instead, she'd studied him as if she could see past his anger. As if she saw the man he wanted to be instead of the man he was. Never had any woman looked at him in that way. Most wanted a hasty tumble in the dark, but nothing more than that.

The wolfhound placed his paw upon Killian's knee, offering despondent eyes. 'You're right,' he admitted to the dog. 'I wasn't thinking. I shouldn't have given in to my temper.' The wolfhound nuzzled his hand, and Killian stood.

All three hounds stared up at him as if he was their lord and master.

'King of the dogs, that's what I am.' He shook his head in exasperation and left the stable with a trail of animals following behind him. Even Harold joined them, for the cat seemed to believe Killian was his owner. When he drew closer to the *donjon*, there were a few smirks from his kinsmen, but he ignored them.

When he reached the entrance leading to the Great Chamber, he saw the Lady Taryn descending the stairs. She was dressed in a green silk gown, with jewelled rings upon her hands and a silver torque at her throat. A veil covered her hair and shielded most of her scars from view.

When she saw him, she stopped at the foot of the stairs and waited. Killian knew she expected him to approach, but he stopped where he was and watched her. Her eyes were a frosty blue as she regarded him.

One of the wolfhounds moved forward and began sniffing at her skirts. Taryn paled and moved backwards up the stairs, trying to get away.

He was convinced that her scars had been the result of an animal attack. With a whistle, he called back the wolfhounds and ordered them to go.

'The dogs won't harm you,' he said, standing at the foot of the stairs.

She nodded but appeared unconvinced. 'I wanted to speak to you before I meet with the chieftain.' Keeping her eye on the retreating wolfhounds, she remained in place and asked, 'What have you decided? Am I to travel with Lady Carice, or should I seek help elsewhere?'

He ought to let her go, for this wasn't his fight. There were other ways to help his sister escape, even if Taryn did reveal the truth to the High King's men.

'You are waging a battle you cannot win,' he told her. The moment she set foot within the High King's holdings, she risked her own safety. If she freed her father and was caught, King Rory would hold her responsible. If she didn't, she would watch him die. And no matter whom she hired to do her bidding, she would face the consequences from the High King.

'He is my father,' she said quietly. 'If your sister were imprisoned, you would do the same for her.'

Her blue eyes stared into his with finality.

She *did* understand the risks, then. But it didn't seem that she cared.

'Go with my sister,' he said at last. 'And we will talk later about your father.' He would make no promises beyond that.

In her expression, he saw the relief. 'Thank you. If you have need of my guard, Pól, he is loyal to me and can be trusted.'

Her offer was a welcome one, for he needed to ensure that the MacEgans were aware of the change in plans. He had intended to travel to Laochre on his own to seek help, though he hadn't wanted to leave Carice behind at the hands of these soldiers. Now there was an alternative.

If her guard alerted the MacEgans, Killian could keep a close watch over Carice. 'We will send your man to Laochre this morning,' he said. 'I will see to it that he has a horse. But when you dine with Brian, you must convince him to let me accompany you,' he said. The chieftain didn't want him anywhere near Carice, and it would be difficult to gain his permission. 'And you cannot let the King's men know who you are.'

'Leave that to me,' she agreed. 'Give Pól your message, and I will handle Brian Faoilin and the others.' There was such confidence in her voice, he could almost believe her.

She paused. 'And if you decide to help my father, know that I will grant anything you desire. His life is worth whatever price I must pay.'

The urge to accept her challenge was tempting. But he could not let the desire for land cloud his judgement.

'If I did try to free him, what makes you believe I will succeed?' he prompted. 'Both of us could die in the attempt.' He wanted her to fully understand how difficult this task was.

'I have seen you fight.' She raised her chin and added, 'And you are not a man who gives up. The only question is whether you are willing to risk your life for the reward I am offering.'

After Taryn's guard departed with detailed instructions about who to speak with at Laochre Castle, Killian slipped inside the *donjon*, heading for the spiral stairs. He wanted to see Carice this morn, to determine if she was well enough for the journey.

He crossed through the back of the Great Chamber and saw Taryn breaking her fast with the chieftain. Her eyes narrowed upon him, and she gave him a nod before she bent to Brian and spoke again. It was clear that she was talking about him, for her gaze passed over him once more. The distaste on Brian's face was evident, but he motioned for Seorse to come forward.

Killian didn't doubt that they were going to throw him out again, so he began walking up the staircase. But before he could reach the upper floor leading to his sister's chamber, Seorse called out to him, 'Killian, wait.'

Though he suspected he wouldn't like hearing this, he paused until his friend reached the top of the stairs. Seorse tossed over a scrap of bread and said, 'He wants to speak to you.'

There was no question that *'he'* meant the chieftain. Killian wondered whether Taryn had succeeded in convincing Brian to allow him to come along with them. He tore off a piece of bread and ate it. 'What does he want?'

Seorse shrugged. 'I can't be saying. But whatever the reason, you'd best go now.'

With reluctance, Killian returned down the stairway, finishing the remainder of the bread. No one paid him any heed as he approached the dais, feeling uneasy about the audience. Had Lady Taryn reached an agreement with the chieftain?

He crossed past the rows of tables, well aware

of all the eyes upon him. Several of the men glared at him, particularly those with bruises and swollen jaws from the fight last night. The High King's men were not among them, and he guessed they were preparing for the journey.

When Killian stood before Brian, the chieftain turned back to Taryn. 'You are certain he is the *fuidir* you want to accompany you?'

'I am. I have seen that he is a strong fighter, one who would serve well for my needs. I have need of a protector.'

They spoke of Killian as if he weren't there, as if he were a slave to be bought and sold. A hardness tightened in Killian's chest when Brian faced him at last. 'You will join us on this journey to Tara, to guard the Lady Taryn and obey her bidding. I have agreed to her request, and you will follow the wagons on foot.'

Not once did the man ask if Killian was willing—the assumption of obedience was unquestionable. But there was a knowing look in Brian's eyes, making Killian wonder why the man had agreed to this. Perhaps the chieftain was waiting for Killian to lose his temper, to lash out and refuse the command. And the moment he did, it would give the chieftain a strong reason to throw him out.

Instead, Killian bowed and walked away. Let Brian wonder why he'd obeyed.

He passed his friend Seorse, who followed him down the stairs and outside. 'What did the chieftain want with you?'

'I am to guard the Lady Taryn and do whatever she commands.' He kept his tone even, though he didn't like the insinuation that he was to obey her bidding.

Seorse only smirked. 'I wouldn't mind letting a lady order me around. She might want you to help her bathe or—'

'No.' Killian cut the man off and took a step forward. 'She is helping me to guard Carice while she travels to Tara.'

'Is she?' Seorse teased. 'Or does she want you to guard *her* at night? In her tent, perhaps?'

He swung his fist at Seorse, but the man ducked out of the way. 'Peace, Killian. I'll take you to the armoury, where you can get weapons.' He motioned for him to follow him. 'If you're obeying the chieftain's commands, there is no reason why you shouldn't have every means of *guarding* the Lady.'

He ignored the dig, realising that this was a benefit he hadn't thought of. Although he had spent a few summers training with the MacEgan soldiers, never before had he owned a sword. But Seorse was giving him the right to choose. Killian could hardly wait to get his hands upon these weapons.

He walked with Seorse to the far end of the fortress, towards a staircase that led up towards the battlements. After they reached the top, Seorse pulled out an iron key and unlocked the door.

Below them, within the inner bailey, Killian saw Taryn watching. He guessed that she wanted to speak to him, to tell him more about her conversation with Brian. He lifted his hand to acknowledge her before following Seorse inside.

His friend led him into the small armoury and picked up a torch from an iron sconce. Swords, maces, and daggers lined one wall while spears and *colc* swords hung upon another.

Killian studied each of the swords, ignoring the decorative hilts. Though a longer sword might be visually attractive, he preferred a sharp, light blade. In the end, he chose a *colc* sword. He also selected two daggers, neither one with jewels—only blades that were so sharp, the lightest touch drew blood upon his thumb.

'I want these,' he told Seorse.

The man gave him a belted scabbard for the sword and Killian secured one dagger at his waist and another in his boot.

The door opened, and light filtered into the room. Taryn stood at the entrance, and Seorse approached. 'How may we be of service, Lady Taryn?'

'I wish to speak to Killian alone. Leave us, if you will.' Her regal demeanour made it clear that she expected to be obeyed. Seorse did, but he sent Killian a knowing look as he departed, closing the door behind him.

'What did he say?' he asked quietly.

She leaned back and crossed her arms. 'Brian agreed to lend me your service, as my personal guard.'

'Did you tell him anything else?' He didn't know if the Lady could be trusted yet. Carice's life hung in the balance, and he knew not what she had said to Brian.

'He already knows that my father is the High King's prisoner, and that is why I am accompanying Carice. Brian told me that King Rory ordered the provincial kings to send soldiers to help defend Éireann against the Normans. He wants to build an army of men from all across our lands.' She paused, then added, 'My father did not send the soldiers. I suppose he thought to keep peace in Ossoria, protecting our people from having to shed blood in a war.'

But the man's refusal was undoubtedly seen as rebellion, Killian suspected. 'Rory will take the men, if that's what he's wanting.' He came closer, studying the young woman. In the dim torchlight, the silver torque gleamed about her throat, though most of her face was shielded by the veil. 'To deny the High King's will is treason.'

She tensed when he drew closer. 'I know it. But I can't let him die.' She wrapped her arms around her waist. Before he could speak again, she continued, 'Brian was not going to let you come to Tara. When I mentioned it, he said that he didn't want you near Carice. I didn't like the way he spoke of you.' She raised her defiant blue eyes to his, and they seemed to hold a greenish hue in the light.

'I told him that I would be grateful if you would…become my guard. He offered me a man called Seorse, but I refused.' Though she was trying to keep her tone neutral, he sensed her reluctance to tell him the truth.

'There's more, isn't there?' He faced her fully, waiting for her confession.

Taryn faltered a moment and admitted, 'I let Brian believe that my interest in you was…more than the desire for a guard.'

He didn't know what to say to that, for it was the last thing he was expecting. 'Why would you say that?'

The young woman's gaze lowered to the floor as if she were humiliated by the idea. 'It was the only thing I could think of. And he…he agreed.' She looked as if she wanted to disappear into the wall, but her daring had caught his attention in an intriguing way.

'You let him think that you wanted me?' The idea was so startling, he could hardly grasp it. 'We're hardly more than strangers.'

Taryn closed her eyes. 'I know it. But surely you know that you are…a handsome warrior. It was as good a reason as any. And he believed it.' She raised both hands to her cheeks as if to cool the flush.

That wasn't the reason. The chieftain knew that Killian would rather die than be servant to a woman. It was a means of putting him in his place, of humiliating him. If he refused, then he could not guard his sister. If he agreed, then it forced him to obey the whims of Lady Taryn.

His anger rose up again, and he warned her in an iron voice, 'I am no one's slave.'

She stiffened, and her hands moved to her sides. 'I never asked you to be.'

He took a step nearer, adding, 'I am not yours to command, either. You need me more than I need you.'

'You're wrong,' she murmured. 'And while it's not the way I wanted to travel, I've done this to help you.' She took a breath and faced him. 'I know that I am not fair of face, and it is an insult, asking you to join me in this ruse. But I thought you would want to be near your sister.'

There was no self-pity in her tone—only a woman who spoke with frankness. To hear her speak of herself in that way bothered him. Aye, she had scars that had transformed her face. But he did not find her repulsive at all.

Killian reached out to her chin, forcing her to look at him once more. When she opened her blue eyes, he saw traces of fear and anxiety. 'Were you wanting me to share your tent?' He wanted to see if her shyness was real or feigned, so he loosened the veil and drew his hand across her scarred cheek.

'No! Of course not.' She jolted at his touch, trying to pull back. And yet, he sensed that no one had ever paid attention to this woman. She was trying to make herself invisible, trying to hide behind her veil.

He caressed the line of her jaw, moving down to her throat. Beneath the linen, her silken hair fell against his fingertips. He could almost imagine the touch of those strands against his skin. When his gaze shifted to her gown, he realised that she did have generous curves. Enough to tempt anyone.

The thought interested him more than it should have. Her eyes held fear, but she bit her lower lip in a way that tempted him. This high-born woman was so far above him, and yet she did not seem to disdain his advances. Instead, she appeared startled, as if she had never been touched before. Likely she was still an innocent, her virginity meant as an offering to her future husband.

'What would your father say, if he knew you made this offer?'

'He…he would be angry with me.'

She averted her gaze, and he prompted further, 'And what of your betrothed husband? Surely King Devlin's only daughter is promised to wed a king or a king's son. Will he not be angry?'

Her face turned scarlet, and she tried to pull away. 'None of them wanted a scarred woman for a wife. My father offered a generous bridal price, but once they saw my face, they refused.'

There were years of hurt feelings bound up in her words, but he would not let her go. Not yet. 'I don't believe you. There are men who would wed a—'

'A monster like me?' she interrupted. She removed her veil and pulled back her hair, revealing her scars. 'I know that. But why would I want to wed a man who only wanted my bride price?'

'It happens all the time,' he told her. 'Men marry for a fortune and do not care who they bed.'

'My father never demanded that of me.' She squared her shoulders. 'My mother would have wed me off to the first man who offered, without hesitation. But my father was more careful about arranging a betrothal. He allowed me the right to refuse any man I didn't want, and I owe him my loyalty for that.'

No one had ever been loyal to him, save Carice. But he understood Taryn's reasons.

'So during this journey, I am to be at your bidding at all times?' Killian drew his hand down her spine, cupping the small of her back. 'Is that what you want?'

When she didn't pull away, he wondered whether she was afraid of him…or whether there was any truth to her claim that she'd wanted him as more than her guard. He leaned in closer, until his mouth was hardly more than a breath away. If he'd wanted to, he could have kissed her. But he wanted to see her response… and in her expression, he saw only uncertainty.

She drew his hand away. 'You will let Brian believe that you are obedient to me, yes.'

Her answer softened his frustration, for it now seemed that she was not trying to assert dominion over him.

'And what else do you expect from me in front of the others?'

'You don't have to touch me and pretend that you desire me,' she said. 'That isn't necessary. Obedience is enough.'

There was a brittle tone to her voice, and he realised that she truly believed no man would want her. 'Brian will be watching us.'

Taryn shrugged. 'I suppose he will. It matters not.' The resignation on her face held years of hurt, and Killian wondered if she'd been locked away from the world, believing that no man would want her.

He drew his knuckles over her cheek, and she flinched from his touch. 'No one will believe you, if you react in this way.'

'I've already said, you need not put on a ruse. I've seen my likeness. Men who have seen my face turn away from me. They loathe the sight of me, and I cannot blame them for it.'

'You were not born this way,' he guessed.

She shook her head. 'No. But it happened when I was a child. Few people remember what it was like before I was scarred. Including me.'

'How were you hurt?' he asked quietly. He framed her face again, tracing the scars that ran along her jaw. The edges were jagged, and he suspected again that an animal had attacked her. It brought out a protective instinct he hadn't anticipated.

She stilled at his touch but didn't pull away. 'I don't want to talk about it. Let me go.'

Beneath his fingers, he could feel the rapid pulse in her throat. She was afraid of him, and that wasn't what he wanted.

Immediately, he let his hands fall away. He stood a hand's distance away from her, and in the intimate space, he expected her to flee.

Instead, she said, 'I let Brian believe that I desired you, for the sake of your sister. You promised to escort me to Tara, and I made it possible for you to do so. You'll obey my orders, and I will grant you a place at my side.'

'And at night?'

Her face was pale, her breathing hushed as her shoulders rose and fell. She might be a noblewoman, but she was not immune to him. There was fear there, but also an attraction to the forbidden.

'At night I want nothing from you,' she whispered. 'You will sleep nearby to guard me, but that is all.'

Killian rested his palms against the wall, trapping her in place. For a long moment, he studied her, wondering if she understood the implications of this. She lowered her face and covered her scars with her hands, trying to shield them from his view. Slowly, he reached out to her palms and pulled them back. 'You have nothing to hide from me.'

Taryn stared back, as if she didn't believe him at all. He continued, saying, 'On this journey, we will help each other. If you help Carice to escape, I will take you to Tara—regardless of what happens afterwards.'

* * *

Taryn's heart was racing. Her cheeks flushed from the touch of Killian's hands upon her face. She fled the armoury, not looking back. With every step, she cursed herself for coming here to speak with Killian. His touch had shaken her senses, as if he could take the scars from her skin and heal them. Not once had he looked upon her as if she were a monster. Instead, he'd treated her as if she were far above his reach.

God help her, she'd found it all too easy to fall under his spell. His dark grey eyes had held resentment at the idea of being her guard. And when he'd pressed her against the wall, her wayward feelings had crumpled.

It was the first time in her life that a handsome man had looked upon her in that way. She'd been unprepared for her racing heart and the way her body had responded. Harsh and ruthless, this man would never yield to anyone. She shouldn't like that at all. And yet, she'd found it thrilling to find a man who looked upon her as if he were about to steal a kiss.

She would have allowed it. She wanted to know what other women felt when a man captured her lips. She wanted to feel the breathless moment of surrender, to feel her first kiss.

Taryn slowed her steps, pulling her veil closer to hide her face as she drew nearer to the High King's men. A man like Killian MacDubh would never kiss her of his own free will. It was only her imagination conjuring up such a vision. This man would never blindly follow her bidding—he would forge his own path.

As she made her way back to the *donjon*, she felt the eyes of strangers watching her. Taryn kept her face hidden as she climbed the staircase leading to Carice's chamber. When she reached the door, she could almost sense the weariness within. The young woman had been sick throughout the night, and Taryn had found it difficult to sleep through her suffering.

Perhaps this journey *would* help her. If Carice could leave her room with its air of sickness, the fresh air might ease her.

Taryn reached the chamber at last and found the young woman still abed. Her eyes were closed, and she looked as if she were dying. A maid was packing Carice's belongings, and Taryn ordered her out. 'I will see to your lady. Go and see to it that they prepare the litter for her.'

The girl obeyed. Taryn went to the windows and threw back the shutters, letting in the light and fresh air. Though the morning was cool, the tainted odor of sickness lingered. Better to cast it out and begin anew.

'Good morn to you,' Taryn greeted Carice, when she stirred at the sunlight. 'Are you ready for our journey?'

The woman struggled to sit up. 'I don't know if I can move. Last night was…very hard for me.'

Taryn didn't doubt that at all. 'Do you want to break your fast?'

A pained look came over Carice's face at the mention of food. 'Later, perhaps.'

'I sent your maid to prepare a litter for us. You won't have to ride.' Secretly, Taryn was thankful that it gave both of them a reason to stay away from the horses.

'I suppose I'll have to rise and get dressed.' Carice drew a deep breath and steeled herself.

In the corner Taryn spied some food that the maid had brought. There was plain dark bread and nothing else. There wasn't nearly enough to sustain Carice for the journey. She told the young woman, 'Wait here and I'll return with more food.'

She left Carice's bedchamber and went down the stairs. A servant was about to take a tray of dried apples and meat to the chieftain, but she intercepted the man. 'I'm going to bring these to the Lady Carice,' she said, as she took a handful of the apples and a capon wing. The meat and fruit might provide more nourishment.

Once she returned to the chamber, she found Carice standing in her shift, clutching the bedpost for balance.

'Let me help you dress,' Taryn said, setting down the food she'd brought. Carice was painfully thin, her bones outlined against her skin. 'Eat this,' she ordered, handing her a piece of dried apple. 'I had some, and it was good.'

'I'm only supposed to eat bread,' Carice said. But even so, she accepted the apple slice.

Taryn helped her pull a crimson gown over her head, pulling the laces tight. 'And who told you that?'

'Our healer. He said that bread was bland enough that it would not make my stomach hurt so much.'

Though she knew it was none of her affair, Taryn worried about Carice. The young woman wasn't eating nearly enough to be well. She handed her the capon wing and asked, 'How long have you been ill?'

'Only during the past two years,' she admitted. 'It's been getting worse.'

And while it was probable that this was only a wasting sickness, Taryn knew that a chieftain's daughter could easily be a target of his enemies. 'You don't think the healer was trying to harm you by having you eat so little, do you?'

Carice turned to face her, shaking her head. 'No. Food was never denied to me, but he thought it might go easier for me if I ate only bread.'

Taryn hesitated a moment, holding back her uncertainties. 'I hope you'll feel better soon.'

'I wish I could,' Carice said quietly. She broke off a piece of meat and ate it slowly, as if she did not believe it was possible to eat without feeling pain. In her eyes was the quiet resignation of a woman who had already accepted the promise of death.

While she ate, Taryn picked up a comb and began pulling it through the young woman's long brown hair. Carice had bound it back, but the curls were tangled, her hair almost brittle.

Taryn tried to form a loose plait, gently weaving the strands and trying not to pull her hair too hard. When it was done, she tied it off with a bit of ribbon. Carice turned around, and her hollowed eyes held a sudden strength that Taryn hadn't expected. Despite her thinness, her deep brown hair framed the face of an angel. There was no question which of them was the more beautiful woman.

And yet, in that moment, Taryn suspected that Carice would trade places with her in a moment. This woman's days were numbered, and she knew it all too well.

'We will walk below stairs now, and you will help me to the litter. I think I can make it that far.' She reached out to take Taryn's arm.

Taryn kept her steps slow, to make it easier for the woman. Though Carice had to lean heavily upon her, she'd lost so much weight, it was easy for Taryn to assist her. 'Tell me if you need me to stop.'

When they reached the doorway, Carice squeezed her hand. 'Wait a moment.' She steadied herself and added, 'You were the answer to a prayer, Taryn. Despite what happens to me after this, I thank you for keeping me from this marriage.'

'I have to save my father's life. No one else will fight for him.' She squeezed the woman's hand in return. 'You would do the same for Killian, wouldn't you?'

At that, Carice smiled. 'He's stubborn, proud, and hot-tempered. And though we are not of the same blood, he will always be my brother.' Her gaze turned curious a moment. 'You like him, don't you?'

Blood rushed to her cheeks. 'I don't even know him. And every time I've spoken to him, he's snapped at me.'

And touched you, her body reminded her. *Which you liked very much.*

'He's fiercely loyal, Killian is. The sort of man who would lay down his life for you.' Carice started walking again and added, 'But he's been cast off by so many people, his heart seems made of stone. He lets no one love him, except me. And that is why I am so protective of him. My parents could never have another child—my mother miscarried several times. He's the only brother I'll ever have.'

She softened her tone and added, 'I know that you will have to wed a nobleman, just as I must. But as Killian's sister, I'll warn you that I will claw the eyes out of any woman who hurts him.' Though she spoke in teasing, undoubtedly the words were true.

'You've nothing to fear from me,' Taryn answered, indicating her scars with a wry smile. She knew there was no danger of anything more than companionship between them. 'Killian is going to accompany us to Tara.' She dropped her voice into a low whisper. 'At least until you are taken away by the MacEgans. We sent my guard to them, just this morning, to deliver the message.'

Carice nodded her approval. 'I am glad to hear it. But how did you talk Brian into allowing Killian to come with us? My father rarely listens to my wishes.'

Taryn felt her face turn crimson. 'I, ah, lied to him.'

'In what way?'

She didn't want to admit the truth, so she hedged, 'I told him that you wanted Killian to travel with us.'

At that, Carice stopped short. 'You must truly believe me to be a fool. I know, full well, that Brian cannot stand Killian's presence. What was the real reason he agreed?'

Taryn held her silence, hoping she would not have to say more. But Carice added, 'We won't take another step until you tell me.' There was a hint of fire in the woman's voice, despite her fragile state. For someone so close to the hand of Death, Carice held a stubbornness that rivalled Killian's.

'I told the chieftain I wanted your brother to

serve me,' Taryn blurted out. 'In...every way I wanted him to.'

Whatever she expected, it wasn't the snort of laughter that came from Carice. The young woman appeared delighted at the confession. 'And how did Killian respond to this? That he is to be your *servant*.' She was holding her hand to her mouth, her shoulders shaking.

'He wasn't happy about it. But I knew he wanted to go with us, to watch over you.'

There was a trace of wickedness in Carice's eyes. 'Instead, he has to watch over *you*.' She was gleeful, her mood transformed as if she were plotting.

Taryn said nothing more, but opened the door and helped her towards the stairs. When they reached the spiral steps, she went first, while Carice held on to her shoulder and followed behind.

'You caught Killian's attention,' she said to Taryn, halfway down the steps. 'I saw him watching you. Whether or not he will admit it, he was interested in you.'

'I'm not beautiful the way you are,' she argued. 'Men are afraid of the way I look.'

'You're wrong,' Carice said. 'For courage holds its own beauty.'

Chapter Four

Killian trudged behind the travelling party during the late afternoon, heedless of the miles they had travelled. Taryn had taken his advice, remaining at his sister's side at all times. It was a dangerous game they played, and thus far, the chieftain had not given their identities away. But the Lady was careful to hide her scars. With the veil to shield them, her appearance was striking. Deep blue eyes stood out against a heart-shaped face that held a quiet bravery.

He could only hope that their deception would last for only a day or two. He had sent Lady Taryn's guard to the MacEgans, with the message to send help in the form of Trahern MacEgan. The bard was a giant of a man, one who would guard Carice easily. Once Trahern arrived, he could breathe easier.

Brian rode ahead of the litter, while Killian remained behind everyone else. He'd been ordered to stay out of the way, except when the Lady Taryn summoned him. He wasn't entirely certain what to think of her. She was a contradiction, both bold and fearful. When he'd touched her scarred face, she'd appeared shocked that he would dare to cross that boundary. But she didn't seem angry, only surprised.

Killian didn't know what to think of that. He had many scars of his own, from the years of training for battle. He didn't view them as a physical imperfection, only a lesson learned. Many times, he'd earned his own scars when he wasn't swift enough.

Since he'd not been allowed to train with the men when Brian could see, he'd trained with Seorse and some of the others in secret. Later, he'd spent a few summers with the MacEgan tribe when Seorse had taken him along as a servant. Those were among his favourite memories, for during those seasons, he'd never felt like a slave. A year ago, he had considered leaving the Faoilin tribe to join the MacEgans, except that he was not free to do so—at least, not yet.

One of the High King's soldiers walked to the back, approaching Killian until he strode alongside him. The man's expression was grim, and he sent him a sidelong glance. 'I think we're being followed.'

Killian glanced behind him, but could see nothing, save the forest that stretched out behind them for miles. 'What makes you believe that?'

'I saw the glint of armour when we crossed the last hill.' He added, 'I want you to scout the enemy and find out how many there are. I'll speak to our commander and take the women east, towards that round tower.' He pointed towards a high column in the distance. The tower was often used by the priests, both as a means of sighting danger and a place to hide religious treasures.

'Stay hidden,' the man ordered, 'and meet us there when you know how many soldiers they have and what banner they carry.'

Killian nodded. While it was possible that it could be the MacEgans, he doubted if Taryn's guard could travel that fast. The soldier was right—if they were being followed, he needed to know what threat they were facing.

'I'll return within the hour,' Killian promised. He wasn't certain how far back the men were, but he could run swiftly and find them.

He slipped into the trees, cloaking himself

as he began to run. Over the next few miles, he kept his pace swift, until he reached the clearing. There, he kept low to the ground, hiding himself amid the heather and gorse.

He wasn't prepared for the sight of two dozen men, heavily armed, as they rode over the next hill. Nor had he expected to see a woman riding in the centre of the men. Her red hair was vibrant, her posture rigid. As they drew nearer to his hiding place, he guessed who it was— Taryn's mother, the Queen of Ossoria. His prediction was confirmed when he spied the standard raised high by one of the men. The white banner was trimmed in red and gold, with a rampant lion upon it.

If the Queen's men intercepted the wagons now, it would unravel all of their plans. She would identify her daughter and take Taryn away. Somehow, he had to slow them down and make it impossible for the soldiers to catch up.

It didn't surprise him that the Queen would pursue her daughter. Lady Taryn should never have travelled alone with a single guard. It was clear that she'd come here without permission. Strangely, there was no sense of urgency, since the Queen already knew where her daughter was going. They would catch up to them within the hour, for carrying the women in a litter was slowing down the High King's men.

In the end, Killian decided a diversion was best. If the men of Ossoria were following the wagons, then hiding the women elsewhere and leading the wagons on a slightly different path might be enough. He only needed a day or two before Carice would flee.

He kept low to the ground, inching his way back towards the trees. Only when he was surrounded by the wood and underbrush did he break into a run. He moved as deeply into the forest as possible, the branches cutting his arms as he ran. His lungs burned with exertion, but he wouldn't stop. Time was slipping away, and he needed to get the women out.

After half an hour of running, he finally reached the clearing where the church and round tower lay. They had stopped to rest, and the moment he approached, the soldier he'd spoken to earlier came forward. Killian caught up to him and said in a low voice, 'They have about two dozen men, all armed. The Queen of Ossoria is travelling with them.' He eyed the litter and added, 'She did not want her daughter to travel to Tara.'

'Then we will leave the Lady behind with her mother,' the soldier said, appearing unconcerned about the idea. 'You may stay with her, and we'll continue on with Lady Carice.'

Killian said nothing, for he wasn't about to abandon his sister. There had to be a way around it. The Queen of Ossoria would not interfere with Carice's journey—but it was clear that she intended to stop her daughter from travelling to Tara.

'It is better this way,' the soldier continued. 'The King of Ossoria is the *Ard-Righ's* prisoner, and he intends to make an example of him. The Queen and her daughter should stay far away from Tara.'

Which was what he'd anticipated. Rory Ó Connor kept hostages, but an execution was rare. If crimes were committed, fines were set by the *brehons* who passed judgement. A death sentence meant that Taryn's father had committed a serious offence.

'The Lady wishes to plead for her father's life,' he told the soldier. 'It's why she wanted to accompany Lady Carice to her wedding.'

The soldier shook his head. 'King Devlin is guilty of treason. The High King will never let him live.'

So that was the reason. Killian doubted if he wanted to be involved with helping Taryn's father, but he wanted to know what had happened.

'What did he do?'

'He tried to raise an army against the High King,' the soldier answered. 'He wanted to take the throne for himself.'

If that was true, then the soldier was right. Rory would never allow a rival king to lay siege to what was his. Killian thanked the soldier for the information and added, 'I will speak with the Lady Taryn and tell her.'

He walked past the guards, towards the litter where his sister and Taryn were seated. The moment he came closer, Brian drew his horse in front of them, blocking his path.

'What do you want?' the chieftain demanded.

I intend to warn the women, he wanted to say but didn't. Instead, he answered, 'I came to speak with the Lady Taryn. We are being followed by her mother's guards.'

Brian glowered at him. 'I will grant you leave to speak with her, but do not bother Carice.' At that, he waved his hand in dismissal and moved his horse.

Killian walked alongside the litter and glimpsed both women through the curtained space. He spoke in a low voice. 'Lady Taryn, your mother has sent guards after you. She's wanting you to return to Ossoria.'

From a small opening in the curtains, he saw Taryn peer out at him. Her eyes held fear, and she kept her voice in a whisper. 'How many men are with her?'

'Two dozen. They will catch up to us within the hour.'

He spied her dismayed reaction. 'I cannot let her see me. I've come this far, and I don't want to give up.' She closed her eyes, as if struggling to think.

He straightened and regarded her. 'You could hide in the round tower, if we go now. Her men will continue following us while you make your escape.'

But his sister had a pointed look upon her face. 'And who will stay with her, Killian? She cannot go there alone.' He didn't answer, for he could see that she was trying to make him feel guilty.

'I'm not leaving you, Carice. Not until you're safe.' There might be another of Rory's men who could accompany Lady Taryn. But it would not be him.

His sister's face softened with acceptance.

'The soldiers know who I am, Killian. Even if Taryn leaves, it's too late for any sort of deception. Either Trahern MacEgan will save me, or he won't.'

He didn't know what to say, but the idea of leaving her was unthinkable. His sister had improved a little, but she could hardly walk at all. 'I won't abandon you.'

She struggled to sit up, and Taryn assisted her. 'You have to let me go, Killian. There's nothing more you can do.'

The finality in her expression spoke of a woman who had accepted her inevitable death. Her gaze moved from Taryn to him and then she said, 'You must go to the MacEgans. Their castle is not far from here, and you could take the Lady there by tomorrow evening. Find out if Trahern is coming for me. If he is not, you can send someone else.'

Taryn lifted the hood of her cloak over her hair. 'I agree. If you continue travelling, my mother's men will follow. I will go to the tower to hide, just as you suggested. And at dawn, Killian can lead me to the MacEgan holdings.' She turned back to Carice. 'If they have not already sent Trahern, we will gather enough men to rescue you.'

He understood what she was proposing, but it still meant leaving Carice behind. And that wasn't something he was willing to do.

Carice's face was slightly flushed, but she nodded. 'It is the simplest plan, and one that will work. And if the Queen catches up to us and makes enquiries, I can try to send her men elsewhere.'

'Why do you not wish to return to your family?' Killian asked Taryn. He could not understand why she was fleeing from them…unless her mother was responsible for the scars. At Taryn's shudder, it made him wonder.

'I cannot,' was all she said, clenching the edges of the cloak.

God help him, he didn't want to leave Carice and follow this woman. Their plans were falling apart, and he wanted to ensure that his sister escaped.

'Killian, you must do this for me,' Carice insisted. 'Take her to the tower and hide her. I will be fine, I promise you.' To Taryn, she added, 'Go with him, and follow his orders without question. He will see you safely to Laochre Castle. God willing, I will meet you there.' She reached her hand out to his and squeezed tightly. 'Now go before they catch up to us.'

He met her gaze and saw the quiet strength in his sister's eyes. 'I will be all right. I believe that.' There was a slight difference in her demeanour, almost a new intensity.

And when she met his gaze, Carice was direct in her silent orders. *Take her with you. In this, we have no choice.*

He gave a slight shake of his head. *I don't want to leave your side.*

Her mouth tightened, and she lifted her chin in defiance. *Do this for me, Killian.*

He didn't back down, and neither did she. But she released his palm in farewell. 'Trahern MacEgan will come for me,' she whispered. 'Trust in that.'

'And if he doesn't?' he demanded.

'Then you can save me before we reach Tara.' She tightened her grip and commanded, 'Let me go, Killian. And perhaps this night, I will be gone from here.'

He didn't like the way she was speaking, as if she expected to die within hours. But her resolve was unshakable.

'Stay behind with Killian, Lady Taryn,' Carice continued. 'Trust in him, and he will bring you to safety. I hope to see you within a day or two.'

* * *

Taryn walked beside Killian towards the tower, forcing herself to stand tall, while her knees were shaking. Brian Faoilin continued on with his travelling party, but only after he peered inside the litter to verify that Carice hadn't left. Taryn let the chieftain believe she intended to speak with her mother.

Killian won't stay with you, her mind warned. Why would he? He had already said that his only loyalty was towards Carice. His promise to bring her to Tara had fallen apart, now that her mother's men were in pursuit. Her only hope was to get help from the MacEgan tribe.

The wagons continued on the main road while they waited. 'Go with your sister,' she told him. 'I know that's what you're wanting to do.'

'It is,' he admitted. 'But Carice is right. I cannot leave a woman behind unprotected.' He took her hand and led her towards the stone chapel. 'You should have told me about your mother's soldiers.'

She hadn't, for he would never have agreed to help her. 'I had hoped she would not find me this quickly.' There was naught to be done for it now.

It was late afternoon, and she studied their surroundings. The stone chapel was quite small, with rectangular blocks fitted together, and a wooden roof. She detected the scent of incense, and it reminded her of the Holy Mass she'd attended at her father's side.

Sunlight filtered through the open windows of the chapel, casting shadows upon the stone floor. Behind Killian, she spied Carice's cat, Harold, who apparently had decided to stay with them.

It shouldn't have bothered her, but she remained wary. The feline nudged at her skirts, circling her slowly. Almost as if he were contemplating the best time to attack. She remained frozen in place, and Killian bent down to rub the animal's ears.

An old priest was on his knees praying, and neither of them spoke, waiting for him to finish. At last, he rose to his feet and greeted them. 'May the peace of Christ be with you both.'

Taryn murmured her own offer of peace, and Killian greeted the old man with the same. Then he said, 'Soldiers are pursuing us, Father. We would ask if you might grant us a place to hide until nightfall.'

'Of course, you may seek the sanctuary of the church,' the old man began, but Taryn could see that he didn't understand the dire nature of their circumstances.

She moved closer and said, 'They are searching for *me*, Father. I would not wish to bring danger upon you. All I ask is that you give us leave to hide ourselves, and you need not know where we are. You may let the soldiers search where they will, and they will not harm you if you allow it.'

The old priest's face grew grave. 'What have you done that would cause soldiers to be in pursuit of you, my child?'

Taryn regarded him with honesty. 'I am trying to save my father's life. And there are those who want to stop me from helping him.'

The priest studied her as if searching for a lie, but she had given none. 'Then go. If this is true, then God will hide you beneath the shadow of his wings.'

'Thank you,' she murmured, offering him a small pearl from her gown by way of thanks.

The priest took it and said, 'Go wherever you wish, and I will pray for you both.'

Killian nodded his thanks and took her hand. 'We'll leave now.' As he passed the doorway, Taryn hurried past the cat to avoid him.

''Tis only Harold,' he told her, scooping up the animal in his arms again. 'He won't harm you.'

While she knew that, she'd had her ankles and skirts attacked by felines for no reason at all. Best to keep her distance from the animal. Even so, the cat trailed after them while Killian was hurrying towards the round tower. 'We'll hide in here.'

Taryn didn't like that idea at all. 'It's too easy to find us inside.'

'It will take them a while to get in,' Killian predicted. He led her to a smaller storage building, where he located a ladder. Then he brought her towards the round tower. The high pillar stretched tall above the land, and its diameter was narrow. The doorway was high above her head, and at the moment, it was sealed.

She now understood the reason for the ladder. It would give them the means of climbing up to the door, and they could pull it up behind them.

Killian set it against the tower and held the base of the ladder. 'Climb up. When you reach the door, raise this along the door opening to lift the latch inside.' He handed her a thin blade.

Taryn tucked the blade at her waist and obeyed, feeling uneasy about how high she had to climb. It was well over the height of a tall man, and when she reached the doorway, she found that there was no knob or latch at all. As Killian had instructed, she slid the blade along the side until she felt it catch upon the inner latch. Slowly, she lifted it, and the door opened inward. Then she grasped the door frame and pulled herself inside the round tower. Killian hurried up behind her, and she moved back into the darkness, pressing her shoulders against the wall while he closed the door.

'What should we do now?' Taryn asked. It was so dark inside the round tower, she could hardly see anything at all. High above them was a tiny circle of light.

'We climb,' he said. 'Keep your hand against the stone wall so you won't fall.' He guided her to go first, and she did as he'd suggested, running her hand over the stones. Around and around she climbed the stairs, spiralling up the tower while Killian followed behind.

With each step, her stomach ached with nerves. Though she should have expected Maeve to pursue her, as she'd promised, she didn't know if it was possible to evade them.

'If they find me, you should hide yourself and go after Carice,' she said, gritting her teeth as she forced her legs to keep going up the stairs. 'You could still reach her.'

'They're not going to find us.'

'But if they do, you—'

'You don't trust in me, do you?' he said, cutting her off. His voice held an edge of anger, and she paused a moment.

'I do not know you at all,' she admitted. 'Except that you are one of the most stubborn men I've ever met.'

'Stubborn, aye. But I usually get what I want.' There was a hint of teasing in his voice, as if he acknowledged his own arrogance. But it didn't quite diminish her fear.

He paused a moment and asked, 'Are you afraid she'll punish you?'

'A little,' she confessed. 'Maeve was furious with me for wanting to go after my father. I sometimes wonder if she wanted him to die. The things she said—' She broke off her words, not wanting to reveal too much. 'I don't think any man would make her happy. And despite what she thought of my father, I couldn't stand by and do nothing.'

Her legs were burning from climbing all the stairs, and she stopped a moment to catch her breath. She didn't know why she was telling

Killian all of this. He likely wouldn't want to hear any of it.

Instead, he said, 'I learned from the soldiers that your father tried to raise an army against the High King. He tried to overthrow Rory and failed.'

She could hardly believe what he'd said. Why would Devlin have any desire to force Rory from his throne? 'I don't understand. That doesn't seem like something he would do.' Her father had a strong will, and there were certainly times he'd disagreed with the High King. But why would he go to such lengths? Now it made sense why he had been taken prisoner and sentenced to die. But she found it difficult to reconcile the man she had known all her life to one who had greater ambitions.

'Men often want to raise themselves up to a different life,' he responded.

And there was truth in that, Taryn supposed. Just like her father, Killian MacDubh undoubtedly wanted more than the destiny Fate had given to him.

The higher they climbed, the more sunlight they saw. Near the topmost floors, there were treasures set in piles. Taryn spied two silver chalices and a jewelled bishop's crozier, along with fine linens. At the top of the tower, she saw six iron bells hanging in a cluster.

Her legs ached, and when at last they reached the top, Killian helped her through the opening. The wind was harsh, blowing from all sides, and she wasn't certain she liked being this high up. It was dizzying, seeing the trees so far below.

In the distance, she could see the glint of metal armour. Her mother's army was indeed close. Taryn huddled with her knees drawn up. 'Can they see us up here?'

Killian shook his head. 'Not if you stay seated.' He pushed down the hinged wooden door that covered the opening. It sealed them off from the rest of the tower, removing all light from inside. At least now, it was more difficult for anyone to see, even if they did search the tower.

Taryn shielded her eyes against the sun and saw Carice's litter and the High King's men journeying further to the east. 'Will the Mac-Egan warrior save your sister, do you think?'

He shrugged. 'If he doesn't, then I will get her out before she reaches Tara.'

Guilt slid over her, and she knew that he resented being here with her. Especially when he'd wanted to guard Carice.

'Why didn't you leave with her?' she asked. 'Surely your sister would have trusted you to bring her to safety.'

He turned and faced her. In his dark grey eyes, she saw a bleakness. 'I don't know if it matters any more. She's grown so ill, I doubt if she'll survive the journey.'

Though Killian was naught but a stranger to her, she understood his pain. Without a word, she reached for his hand and took it in hers. His palm was warm, and his fingers curled around hers. It was only a small comfort, but she wanted to give him what sympathy she could.

He sat beside her in silence and admitted, 'Carice was the only good thing that ever happened to me. And she doesn't deserve the life she was given.'

There were no words that would ease his grief. Taryn had witnessed the depth of Carice's illness and knew he was right. It would take a miracle to save the young woman's life now. She kept her hand in Killian's, offering him solace in the only way she knew how.

For a while, he held her hand and Taryn grew self-conscious of the sudden warmth between them. She knew she ought to pull away—and yet, she felt a tightness welling up in her throat.

Killian hadn't recoiled in disgust, though her hands were as scarred as her face. He didn't seem to mind it at all, and she struggled to ignore the yearning that rose inside her.

Her cheeks flushed, and she closed her eyes to push back the wayward thoughts. Instead, she remembered the last time a man had touched her hands, on the morning of her betrothal.

She had dressed so carefully, as if it were her wedding day. Her hair was pulled back in intricate braids woven with flowers, while the rest hung against her cheeks and down her back. She had worn her best purple gown and a jewelled torque around her throat, while her hands were covered with gloves. Her heart quaked within her chest as she descended the stairs to join the man who had agreed to become her husband.

Lucas Ó Rourke was the younger son of a chieftain who lived near the western coast, and when she'd glimpsed his handsome face from her window, she'd felt both hopeful and terrified.

Aye, she knew it was the promise of her kingdom that had attracted him here. And because he lived so far away, he would not know of her

*appearance. She had taken great care to hide
her scars beneath her hair, and she hoped he
would find her acceptable.*

But as she drew closer to the Great Chamber, she heard the sound of arguing.

*'I want to see her before I agree to the betrothal,' Lucas was saying to her father. Taryn's
pulse quickened, for the tone of his voice held a
note of warning. Although it was to be expected,
her instincts went on alert. Quietly, she entered
the chamber, hoping he would be pleased by
what he saw. Her father beckoned for her to
come forward and made the introductions.*

*Lucas Ó Rourke studied her for a moment,
but he didn't smile. Instead, he strode forward
and stood before her. 'Were you hoping to deceive me?'*

*Her heart sank as he pulled back her hair,
revealing the scarred flesh. To Devlin he added,
'Did you think I would not know what you were
trying to do? All of your servants spoke of how
happy they were that their mistress would finally be married after what happened to her.
But I do not want a deformed bride.'*

*Taryn stared back at him, disbelieving what
she'd heard. Deformed? It was not as if she had
been born this way. Why would he say such a*

thing? She couldn't bring herself to speak or move when he removed her gloves, showing the scarred, reddened knuckles. He gripped her hands to stare at them before he released them with disgust.

'I am not deformed,' she heard herself say. 'I was hurt in an attack.'

But Lucas was already shaking his head. 'I will not sign this betrothal. I do not want any sons of mine to bear those markings.'

She could hardly believe what he was saying. 'You must truly be empty-headed if you believe that any of my children would be scarred.'

'Be silent, Taryn,' her mother warned. Maeve held up a hand and said, 'We could lower her bride price, if needed.' She sent a pleading look towards her husband, and Taryn was stunned that she would even consider it.

Did her mother truly believe she was so desperate for a husband that she would accept this man? She didn't want a man like Lucas as her husband. Not if he viewed her as some sort of misshapen woman.

'I am sorry your journey brought you this far,' she said to Lucas, 'but I do not wish to wed you, either.' She straightened and turned

to leave, locking her hands together to hide the trembling.

Behind her, she overheard her mother arguing for Lucas to stay, while her father sided with her.

'Surely we can come to an understanding,' Maeve was arguing.

'There is no need for Taryn to wed a man who does not want her,' Devlin countered. 'Other men may not mind her appearance, or she can always remain here, with us.'

Taryn paused on the stairs, listening to them.

'I want her gone from here,' Maeve insisted. 'Far away from this place.'

'You only say that because you know she prefers my company to yours. She knows that I have taken good care of her and will always do so.'

It had meant a great deal to her, knowing that her father wanted her to be happy. After Lucas had departed, the rift between her and her mother only widened. Maeve tried to control her even more, never leaving her alone, always following her.

Even now, she feared that Maeve would find them and force her to return.

It was less than an hour before soldiers surrounded the chapel. Killian heard the voices of the men as they gathered around the outbuildings, searching each one. And sure enough, he saw them climbing up the ladder to the round tower.

'They're going to find us,' Taryn whispered. 'You should have destroyed the ladder.'

'If I'd done that, they would have known we were hiding in here. The priest would have no reason to do such a thing.' He'd thought of lifting the ladder away but had decided that the ten sets of stairs might be a better deterrent. It was difficult to climb the stairs wearing heavy armour, and the soldiers might give up after six or seven floors. He motioned for the Lady Taryn to join him, sitting atop the hinged opening that led to the topmost floor. Their combined weight would keep it closed.

'And what if they find us here? I don't want to be taken back.'

There was fear in her voice, and he covered her mouth with his hand, needing her to be silent. Below them, he heard the soldiers searching. They were coming closer, and he saw the fear rising in Taryn's face. She closed her eyes, and it made him wonder why she was so fearful of being caught. Was it her need to save her father? Or was she trying to save herself?

He wasn't certain. But she buried her face against his chest, as if to blot out the terror. He stroked her hair back, soothing her in silence.

Without warning, a blade pierced the seam of the trap door. Taryn clamped her hands over her mouth to muffle any sound, remaining frozen in place. Killian unsheathed a dagger of his own and was poised, waiting for the inevitable attack.

But there came nothing. Only the shouts of the men as they retreated back down the stairs. He only breathed easier when he heard the sound of the horses retreating. They had eluded capture for now...but he could not say for how long.

Taryn sat with her knees drawn up, her black hair shielding her face. When she shivered against the wind, he reached for her hand.

'They're gone,' he said at last, when he was certain of their safety. 'We can go back inside.'

She moved away from the door. 'It's g-getting colder.'

And it was. The air held the biting chill that warned of snow. Killian held open the trap door and Taryn climbed down inside the round tower. It had grown dark, and it took a moment for his eyes to adjust. Taryn huddled against the wall, and her cloak was doing little to warm her.

'I wish we had a fire,' she admitted. So did he, but there was nothing here that they could burn. In silent answer, he moved beside her. His shoulder rested against hers, as a means of offering her body heat.

She startled him when she leaned her face against him, huddling closer. It was strange to think that a noblewoman would want to be closer to a man like him. She drew the edge of his *brat* over both of them, to offer more heat.

'There,' she said. 'That's better.'

With her body pressed close, he inhaled the delicate scent of her skin. Never in his life could he imagine that a lady would seek to touch him. Though he knew she was only wanting to keep warm, it bothered him for her to be so near.

Killian moved away from her and gave her the *brat* to wear over the cloak. 'You can keep that. I've no need of it.' Then he leaned against the opposite wall, pretending as if none of it mattered.

He *was* cold, but he didn't want this woman to rely on him for anything. Sleeping beside her would only bring temptation too close. The only thing he'd agreed to do was bring her to Tara. Beyond that, their lives were too different.

He drew his knees up and leaned back, closing his eyes, though he wasn't tired at all. It was a means of avoiding her. Silence filled up the space between them, but after a few moments, he heard her approaching with quiet footsteps.

Then she lowered the woollen *brat* across his torso saying, 'I understand why you don't want to be close to me. But you don't have to freeze.'

The wool held the heat from her body, enclosing him with her scent. Though she spoke in a calm tone, he suspected that he'd hurt her feelings. And that hadn't been his intent at all.

'I said you could keep it,' he told her. 'You need it more than I.'

'Why do I make you so angry?' she whispered. 'What have I done to you in all this time?'

She didn't see it, did she? He removed the *brat* and said, 'Would you treat your guard in this way? Would you sleep beside him?'

Taryn gave no answer at all, as if she'd suddenly realised what he meant.

'I am no different from Pól, a soldier assigned to protect you. I'm your hired sword, nothing more.'

'You are *nothing* like a hired sword, Killian

MacDubh,' was her reply. 'You are no one's servant. And never will be.'

Her words startled him, for he'd never expected a lady to treat him with respect. No one, save Carice, had ever viewed him in that way.

'Keep the *brat*,' he told her. 'We won't travel this night, in case we're caught in the snow. Try to sleep, and we will go to Laochre in the morning.'

He was beginning to wonder if his sister had another reason for sending him to guard Taryn. Matchmaking was not something Carice had ever done, but he wouldn't put it past her.

Chapter Five

Taryn's limbs were stiff and cold the next day. Killian called up to her, 'Come down, Lady Taryn.'

She saw that the round tower door was open, and a sharp beam of light illuminated the bottom of the tower. It took several minutes for her to follow him down all the stairs. After she reached the door, Killian went back down the ladder. He held it steady for her as she climbed the rungs.

Nearby, she saw a horse tethered to a small sapling. The animal stood taller than her head, and he did not appear in the least bit friendly. Her nerves sharpened immediately, but she tried to suppress the fear.

'Where did you get the horse?' she asked, trying to sound calmer than she felt.

'Father Martin agreed to let us borrow him. I'll bring him back when we return from Tara.' Killian took the animal by the reins and held them out. 'Hold him for a moment while I get food and water. If we ride quickly, we should arrive at the MacEgan holdings by nightfall.'

No, she was not getting on the horse. Her insides clenched at the very thought of it.

'We should not take Father Martin's only horse when we do not need it. We can walk, just as easily.'

He eyed her as if she'd lost her wits. Then he walked over to her and took her by the hand, placing the reins inside her palm. 'Hold this.'

Her mind and body froze, her knees shaking. All she could think of was the horse rearing up and the sickening sound as her brother's head struck the stone. The horse leaned closer, sniffing at her, and the moment she felt his warm breath, Taryn dropped the reins and fled towards the chapel. She didn't care how cowardly she appeared—she simply had to run away.

When she reached the chapel, she leaned against the stone wall and sat down, burying her face in her knees. Her cheeks were burning with humiliation, and it hurt to breathe. Her heart pounded so fast, she felt as if she'd been running for an hour.

She knew Killian would pursue her, but she simply could not ride a horse. Not any more.

But when she felt the shadow of his presence, he said nothing about her sudden flight. 'Come here,' he said quietly.

'I'm not getting on that horse.' It was best to be perfectly clear about this. 'I will ride in a wagon, if we must. But I will not ride on horseback.'

He said nothing but offered his hand. Her instinct warned her not to take it, but then, she knew that she could not sit here all morning. They had to leave, or risk her mother's men finding them.

With great reluctance, she took his hand, and he helped her to stand. Then he returned to the horse and spent several minutes securing food and water to the animal. It seemed that he intended to take the gelding with them, though she was adamant about not riding.

Then he mounted the animal and rode the horse towards her. A sinking feeling caught her stomach. He wasn't going to let her walk; that much was clear.

She stood her ground and faced him. 'I said we don't need the horse, MacDubh.'

'We do, *a chara*. And you've no reason to be afraid.'

He was wrong in that. She had watched her brother die in the accident. And no matter how he tried to convince her otherwise, she had no intention of going anywhere on horseback. She hurried her pace, even knowing he would likely catch up to her.

Closer he rode, and she pushed herself to run faster. But within seconds, he reached down and caught her by the waist, lifting her up with almost no effort at all. She stifled a shriek as he hauled her atop the horse.

The motion of the animal terrified her, and she fought Killian's grasp. For a moment, the fear drowned her, until she was unable to stop her response. He was trying to subdue her, but the memories were so strong, she hardly knew what was happening.

In her memories, she heard her brother's shouted warning. There was a moment of confusion when she'd watched the horse's hooves rise up. Christopher had gripped the reins, but to no avail. He fell backwards, his head striking a stone.

And then the blood. The haze of red haunted her still.

* * *

The horse reared up, and for a moment, time seemed to stand still. There was a curious moment of calm when the horse threw her off. Taryn felt herself falling and wondered if this was what her brother had known before his life had ended.

Instead, she hit the ground and rolled over. Pain reverberated through her, and for a moment, she couldn't move. She stared up at the grey sky, startled to realise she was alive. Seconds later, a furry face peered down at her.

It was the cat, Harold.

Taryn grimaced, but the animal sniffed at her face before walking on top of her with soft paws. Gingerly, she sat up, trying to move away from the feline. Then Killian came towards her, his face infuriated. 'Why did you fight me? You were perfectly safe until you frightened our horse.'

She didn't know whether to laugh or begin weeping. Of course, he didn't know why she was afraid. Even if he did understand, she guessed that Killian MacDubh was not about to let her walk all the way to Laochre.

'I told you I didn't want to go on horseback,'

Taryn said meekly. She rubbed at her back, knowing she would be bruised for days.

Killian stared at her, and she felt even more self-conscious beneath his gaze. It was as if he thought her a foolish girl who couldn't even ride a horse. And well, that was true, but she had her reasons.

Taryn rose to stand and regarded him. 'I know what you think of me. But I cannot control the way I feel when I'm around animals.' She rubbed at her lower back, trying to ease the ache. 'I don't like being afraid, but it's impossible for me to ride.'

It was so humiliating, feeling as if she became another person when the fears took hold. Killian moved in, and he stood before her. She tried to walk away from him, but he caught her hand. 'What happened to you?'

She kept her gaze fixed upon the ground, wishing she could go back and stop all of the helpless feelings. Around this man, she was more aware of her weaknesses, and right now, she wanted to disappear.

But then she realised he believed this was about her scars, when that wasn't the truth at all. 'I am afraid because I watched my brother die when he was thrown from a horse.'

Killian met her gaze, and in his cool grey eyes, she saw a trace of sympathy. He didn't apologise, nor did he dismiss what she'd said. But he gave a brusque nod.

'Walk with me,' he said. 'I won't ask you to go on horseback. At least, not yet.'

At that, she released a little of the tension within her. Her body hurt as she tried to walk, but there wasn't a choice. They could not stay here.

He led her back to the animal and said, 'Stop here, and come no closer.'

That, at least, was an order she was comfortable obeying. Killian continued walking towards the horse, speaking in a low, calm voice. He took the reins of the animal, soothing the gelding with words and the touch of his palm. The animal nosed him, but it seemed more of an affectionate gesture than a threat.

'He was afraid you were going to harm him,' Killian continued. 'But he's a calm one. His name is Francis.'

She almost smiled, for the gentle name didn't appear to fit the large plough horse. But she remained standing in place while Killian talked to the horse.

'I'm going to let you touch him and know him

better,' he continued. 'So that you may walk beside him without fear.'

She didn't particularly want to pet the horse, but she could understand Killian's reasoning. After her behaviour, it was likely that the animal would be more than a little skittish.

'I don't want him to bite me,' she admitted. 'Especially after what happened before.'

Killian gripped the reins and took slow steps forward. 'Stay where you are, and do exactly as I say.'

She did, and as they continued towards her, the smoke-grey cat brushed her legs. It was as if Harold was seeking affection, but she remained where she was.

Killian continued walking past her and stopped when she was at the horse's side. He took her hand and brought it to the animal's back. 'He's a good lad, is Francis. Touch him here.' He showed her how to run her hand over the coarse hair, and the horse's ears pricked up as she did.

Did he know how frightening this was for her? She half-expected the animal to swing around and take a bite out of her arm.

'Your hand is trembling,' Killian said.

He was right. No matter that she was trying

to do as he bade her, she could not control the shaking fingers. This time, he placed his hand over hers. His broad palm completely covered her hand, and the sudden heat of his skin startled her. For a moment, he held it there, and he moved her fingers over the horse's back. 'Like this.'

Taryn's mouth went dry as the Irishman drew her hand across the horse's back. She could almost imagine his hand touching her in the same way, stroking and soothing. His fingers were laced with hers as he murmured to the horse.

And then he moved her to the animal's neck, still patting and caressing the gelding. The horse swung his head towards her, and Taryn tried to back away. But Killian had already anticipated her move and blocked it. 'Stay where you are.'

She was trapped with his arms around her, his right hand holding the reins, while his left hand covered hers. He drew her hand over the animal's face, and she tried to push back the fear when the horse's brown eyes met hers.

'Good lad,' Killian said, his fingers still laced with hers. But he was so close, she could feel the hard planes of his body against hers.

'I haven't put you at ease yet, have I?' he

guessed, pressing her hand down the horse's neck again.

No. She was too aware of him, too conscious of his hand upon hers. Slowly, she extricated her fingers from his palm and turned to face him. His grey eyes met hers, and there was no anger in them. Instead, she caught a glimpse of another reaction, before he masked it. It was as if he'd suddenly grown aware that he was holding her.

He took his hand from the horse, still holding the reins. 'We'll walk alongside Francis for a mile or so. Then I'll let you hold his reins. Perhaps later, when you're more comfortable, we can try again.'

She wasn't ever going to be comfortable, but she wouldn't tell him so. Instead, she gave a nod and began walking beside him.

But with every step at this man's side, she realised that there was something even greater to fear than an animal—her own unspoken desires.

They walked alongside the horse for the next hour, and eventually the cat jumped down from the basket, trotting along behind them. Killian started to hand her the reins, but she declined. 'Not yet.'

He didn't force it, but his greater worry was getting her to shelter before it turned dark. Walking was not a wise move, and he had to find a way to help her ride.

But he understood the haunted fear in those blue eyes. She had lost her brother in an accident, and the grief had never left. He feared that he would know that same pain unless a miracle cured Carice.

'When was the last time you rode a horse?' he asked. 'Have you ridden at all since that day?'

'I tried to ride a few years ago.' She turned to face him, and there was a strange glint in her eyes. Almost as if she were angry. 'I know how cowardly I must seem. But I cannot stop myself from feeling this way.'

He reached out and took her hand, warming her gloved fingers in his palm. 'We have to reach Laochre before nightfall. For now, we will walk, and if there is a wagon we can borrow, you may ride in that.'

She squeezed his palm in agreement. 'Thank you.'

He didn't want her to be utterly reliant on that possibility, however. There were few structures nearby, save an abandoned abbey that they had already passed.

'King Patrick and his brothers will welcome us, for I know them well,' Killian continued. 'They also might know more about what happened with your father and the uprising.'

Taryn was nodding in agreement and appeared more relaxed now. But he wanted her to understand the necessity of using a horse. 'If we cannot find a wagon, we will have no choice but to ride. We must find a place to stay, and it will take hours to reach Laochre on horseback. If we walk, we will never reach their boundaries before night.'

And it wasn't safe to remain outside in the cold. Killian sensed snow was coming, from the clouded sky above, and daylight was growing short. Best to coax Taryn by building her trust with the animal.

He guided her hand to the reins. 'I'm not letting go of the horse,' he told her. 'All I want is for you to hold the reins with me.'

Taryn hesitated, her lips tightening. The fear was still evident in her eyes, but she nodded. Slowly, she exhaled and grasped the reins beneath his hand. He kept his grip steady, letting her walk alongside him.

After a time, he asked, 'Shall I be letting

go of the horse now? Would you like to lead Francis?'

She looked up at him, and in her blue eyes, he caught a glimpse of a woman who wanted to be braver than she was. 'I'll try. But if he pulls away from me—'

'Then I'll be taking him back from you.' He waited to release the reins until she lowered her head in agreement.

'All right.' For a short while, she led the animal, her grip so tight upon the reins, her knuckles were white.

'You don't have to hold him so firmly,' he told her. 'Trust that he won't harm you.'

She sent him a wry look. 'My backside does not believe you.'

''Twas only because you fought. A horse like this one is used to pulling a plough or a wagon. He's a gentle one, I promise.'

Killian ran his hands over the gelding's neck and then spied Harold falling further behind. 'Keep walking. I'm going to get the cat.' He left her briefly to pick up the grey animal, before he deposited the feline in the basket on the horse's back. Harold curled up inside the dark space and was content.

'Why did the cat follow us instead of staying with Carice?' she asked.

'Harold believes he's my cat. He goes where I do.' And he rather liked the animal. 'He sometimes brings me mice, in case I've nothing for dinner.'

The appalled look upon Taryn's face was almost laughable. 'You...you don't get *that* hungry, do you?'

He sent her a mischievous smile. 'Not often.' He let her make of that what she would, though he'd never dined upon mice in all his life. 'But it's good that Harold wishes to take care of me.'

Her steps were slowing, and he knew she was growing tired from all the walking. A lady was not accustomed to such a long journey, and he wanted her to attempt riding once again.

'Lady Taryn, do you want to try to ride now? If I hold on to you and lead the horse?'

She was already shaking her head. 'No, walking is fine. I'll be all right.'

He ignored her and scooped her up into his arms, continuing the walk. 'You're weary. I can see it in the way your pace has slowed.'

'Killian, put me down,' she protested. 'This isn't necessary.'

'You walked from Ossoria to Carrickmeath,'

he reminded her. 'I was wondering where your horses were, but now I know. If you made that journey, then likely your feet are raw from all the walking.'

She said nothing, which only confirmed his suspicions. 'You should not walk another great distance, my lady.'

'But you cannot carry me to Laochre. It's too much of a burden on you.' She held on to him with her arms around his neck, and he was quite conscious of her softness pressed against him. Her black hair fell across his shoulders, and the scent of her body was like a spring meadow. He wondered what it would be like to feel her hair falling upon his bare skin. She was blushing being this close to him, but he didn't mind her weight at all.

'I'm going to lift you on to Francis's back, but I won't take my hands off you,' he said. 'I'll be holding you and can take you off at any moment.'

She was about to argue again, but he met her gaze. 'Trust in me, Lady Taryn.' She held his gaze, and he saw the worry in her eyes. 'I won't let any harm come to you, and I won't be letting go.'

Again, he waited. She was studying him as if

trying to decide whether or not to believe him.
'I know I should try,' she said. 'But the very
thought makes me tremble.'

Her honesty reminded him of a wild creature
that was too afraid to come near. He needed to
build her trust, to coax her to believe in him.

'I won't let go,' he said again, lifting her up.
She had her eyes closed, and sure enough, he
saw her hands shaking. He kept his hands upon
her waist, and she gripped his wrists with both
of her palms.

'If you lift your leg over, you'll feel more balanced,' he advised.

She was biting her lower lip, but eventually,
she managed to adjust her skirts and lift her
leg over.

'I don't like this,' she whispered. 'I'm so far
from the ground. I feel like the horse knows
how afraid I am.'

In that, she was right. Francis was obediently
walking, but there was a tension in him, as if the
horse sensed Taryn's distrust. Killian needed to
ride behind the Lady, to take command of the
horse and increase their pace.

'Move forward on the saddle, and I'll ride
with you,' he said.

'I'd rather not,' she confessed. 'If you get on, he'll throw us both off again.'

He suspected nothing would talk her into it, and if they wanted to reach Laochre by nightfall, they had to ride. Killian moved her foot from the stirrup and stepped into it, swinging up behind her.

'I said—'

'I know what you said.' But he had to take charge of this situation, before they lost more time. He held Taryn around the waist and told her, 'Relax and let me control Francis. Don't fight me on this.'

Her hands dug into his knees, and when he leaned in, he saw that her eyes were tightly closed. Francis could sense her discomfort, and if she continued to hold herself in this way, the horse might fight back.

'Breathe, my lady.'

She nodded, but her knees were tense around the animal, her body rigid with fear. 'I'm trying.'

It wasn't enough. He kept both hands upon the reins, her body between his legs. 'Relax your legs. Let them go loose around Francis's back. He can feel how nervous you are.'

'I *am* nervous,' she said. 'And I can't simply stop feeling this way.'

'Open your eyes,' he ordered. 'Look at the woods surrounding us.' The morning light cast beams across the barren branches of the trees. In the distance, he heard the noise of a stream trickling across stones. It was cold, and a bitter wind swept over them as they rode.

Taryn lifted her face upward, clearly trying hard to set aside her fears. He touched her right knee. 'Stop trying to hold on with your knees. Let them be.' He kept his hand there, but when she pressed her bottom back against his groin, his reaction was swift.

By the gods, she smelled good. Her hair rested against him, and her neck was bared. He wondered what it would be like to taste that delicate skin, to touch her. Her earlobe appeared soft, and he imagined taking it into his mouth while he reached around to cup her breasts in his palms.

Her scars marred that perfect skin, but her black hair and blue eyes were striking. He kept his hands frozen in place, forcing back the attraction he didn't want to feel.

'Calm yourself,' he said quietly. 'Breathe

slowly and watch the trees. Let your arms and legs relax and trust that I will control the horse.'

Her shoulders lowered, and it did seem that she was trying. Even so, he kept his arms around her waist while he held the reins.

'How far are we from their castle?'

'We won't be there by nightfall, unless we hasten our pace.' But he hoped to reach the vast meadow surrounding the castle, where they could see their destination.

'Do you think your sister has fled by now?'

'If Trahern found her, then by tonight or early tomorrow, she will join us at Laochre.' And if she did not arrive, he would do whatever was necessary to find her.

Killian clicked his tongue and urged the horse into a trot. Francis obeyed and Taryn struggled with the new rhythm. 'I think I prefer him walking,' she said, wincing at the rocking motion.

'When we're free of the woods, I'm going to take him a little faster,' Killian warned.

'Faster? I think this is fast enough,' she insisted. Her voice held traces of panic, though she was valiantly trying to remain relaxed.

They had made it this far, and he wanted them to make up for all the lost time from earlier. 'It won't be for long,' he promised. But he suspected if he could get her to fully trust in him and in the horse, she might enjoy the feeling of riding fast.

He let go of her waist to tighten his grip upon the reins. 'Don't let go of me,' she pleaded.

Killian adjusted his seat until he could hold her with one arm, still keeping control over the horse. 'Is that better?'

'Yes.'

They rode through the forest, down the winding path, until they reached the clearing. Once they were there, he asked, 'Are you ready?'

'Not at all.'

But he urged the horse into a canter and then into a gallop. Francis was strong from years of pulling the plough, but he wouldn't have the endurance to go far, carrying the weight of both of them.

'Are your eyes open, Lady Taryn?' he asked.

'N-no,' she said.

He leaned into her body, whispering against her ear. 'Look around you. I'll wager you've never gone this fast in your life.'

Killian could tell she didn't want to, but she obeyed. He studied the profile of her face as they rode. The fear never left her eyes, but he saw a hint of wonder in them. He kept the pace swift as they crossed the flat lands in a sea of green grass. Sheep grazed in the open meadow, and in the distance, he spied the silvery river.

He kept up the gallop until they drew close to the water's edge. Then he slowed the horse down to a walk. At last, he dismounted and helped Taryn down. Her hair was windblown, and her eyes were bright.

She walked towards the water and bent down her hands to scoop up a drink from the river. Francis approached her, and Killian handed over the reins.

'Let him drink,' he told her. She accepted the reins and guided the horse to the water. Francis drank thirstily, and Taryn rubbed his neck as he did.

'It wasn't as frightening as I thought it would be,' she admitted. 'Thank you.' Upon her face, he saw a soft smile. It had been so long since a woman had smiled at him, it caught him without warning.

'You did well, *a chara*.' He stood on the other side of the horse, and used a bit of dried grass to rub down the gelding. Taryn looked away from him, and there was a sudden shyness about her.

Careful, he warned himself. *She's not for you.*

He was only travelling with this woman for

her own protection and because Carice had pleaded with him. It meant nothing at all.

After the horse had drunk its fill, Killian took back the reins and let the animal graze for a while. He offered the Lady a bit of bread and cheese, and she broke off her share, leaving him the rest.

Once again, she was treating him like an equal, and it raised his wariness once more. He told himself that it was out of thankfulness that he'd remained with her. And yet, he couldn't imagine that she shared her food with her personal guard in this way.

He decided to keep his distance, and he sat down on a stone near the river. There was a film of ice forming near the shoreline and the air was frigid.

Instead of finishing her food alone, Taryn brought it along and came to sit near him. Once again, he grew wary. 'Was there something you were wanting, Lady Taryn?'

The edge of her *brat* slipped downward, and she grasped the woollen wrap, pulling it over her shoulders. She continued eating and answered, 'No, I do not need anything just now.'

Then why had she come to sit by him? Killian started to stand, but she beckoned him to remain seated. 'Stay and talk with me awhile.' She tucked a long strand of black hair behind one ear and broke off a piece of bread while she stared at the river. It seemed that she had grown accustomed to his presence and was comfortable with her scars.

But he was wary of her. He couldn't seem to tear his gaze from this woman, and her blue eyes held him captive. She had proven that she could overcome her fears, and he was falling prey to her siren call. When she had leaned against him, burying her face in his heart, he had felt the strong urge to guard this woman. Even now, her presence warmed his frozen heart.

Taryn Connelly was dangerous in a way he hadn't anticipated.

'What will you do if Carice does not arrive at Laochre?' she asked him.

'She will. I trust the MacEgans to bring her there.' Any one of their warriors was stealthy enough to bring Carice to safety.

Taryn's expression held worry, and she bit her lower lip. He clenched his fist, for he was wondering what it would be like to taste those lips, to draw her body close to his. God, she had smelled so good. And her body had fit against his in a way that provoked him.

'But what if…what if she doesn't?' She lifted her gaze to his and reached out her hand to him.

He forced himself not to touch her. If he took her fingers in his, it would only tempt him to take the offering she didn't want to give.

'As I told you before, I will go after her myself, if needed.' He stood and started towards the horse, only to have her follow him again.

'Killian, wait.'

He stopped in place, and the tension inside him tightened even more. She moved to stand in front of him. 'You're angry with me, and I want to know why. I thought, after all this, we could be allies. Perhaps friends.'

He stared at her in disbelief. Didn't she realise how tightly strung he was? If she touched him, he didn't trust himself to leave her alone. It had been so long since he'd enjoyed the softness of a woman's body, he was rigid with frustration. The night he'd spent beside her had been torture, for she had fallen asleep with her head in his lap. It had been all he could do to leave her untouched.

And yet, she didn't seem to know that he was on the edge of his control. She was far too desirable, and he had to do something to keep her at arm's length. Anything.

'We could never be friends, Lady Taryn. I know what I am, and I know my place.' He didn't want or need her pity.

She crossed her arms over her chest and glared at him. 'For a man who wants to raise his status, you seem intent upon reminding me that you are a *fuidir*. Would you rather I gave you orders? Do you want to be treated like a slave?'

He stiffened at that, but she wasn't finished yet. 'I've been kind to you, and I've tried not to let my fears hinder you. I don't deserve your hatred, and I cannot change the way I look.'

This wasn't at all about her looks. It was about trying to protect her virtue, and she didn't seem to realise the risk she was taking.

'I don't hate you,' he said quietly. But the expression on her face said that she didn't believe him at all.

Killian reached out for her hands, warming her palms with his. *Lugh*, she was such an innocent. 'You shouldn't be kind to a man like me,' he said roughly. Already she was a strong temptation, and she represented everything he wanted but couldn't have.

Taryn stared at him, her face confused. 'Why? Is there something wrong with being kind?'

'Aye.' He reached out a hand to trace her scars, caressing the marred skin. Though he had no right to touch her, he wanted to push her away, to make her fear him. It was the only way he could fight against the attraction towards this woman. He cupped her chin and stared into those eyes. 'When I try to keep away from you, as a guard should, you pursue me. You sit beside me, and you want to talk.'

Taryn pulled away, her cheeks flushing. Good. He wanted her to recognise the social distance between them.

She swallowed hard and then regarded him. 'Isn't that what travelling companions do? Talk to one another?'

'I am not your companion. I am your servant.' He wanted the division made clear so she would keep away from him. For if he had his way, he would use that mouth for something entirely different than talking.

A startled laugh broke free from her. 'Killian, not once have you behaved like a servant. You're overbearing, dominant, and you enjoy ordering me around.' She drew her knees up beneath her skirts. 'I never would have ridden that horse if you hadn't forced me to.' The soft amusement remained on her face, and she rubbed her hands together for warmth.

'You should not be so familiar,' he warned.

Her mouth twisted. 'And why is that? Should I be afraid you would behave in a dishonourable way?' She pulled back her hair. 'These scars protect me. I know what men see when they look upon my face.' Though she kept her tone forthright, he knew that she was sensitive about the marks.

'What do you think I see?' He moved in closer, his arm behind her spine.

'A woman who is cursed with the Devil's markings. One who makes men draw back with revulsion.'

With his hand, he touched her forehead, commanding her, 'Close your eyes.'

She obeyed, and he drew his fingers over her eyelids. 'You don't know what men see. Not at all.' He traced the slant of her nose, down to her lips. 'I see a mouth that talks entirely too much. Lips that are soft, almost yielding.' He rubbed her lower lip with his thumb and was rewarded with her sharp exhale. Her blue eyes opened, and he shook his head. 'No, don't look.'

He tilted her chin up, moving his hand down her throat. 'I see a woman with silken skin and

curves that entice a man. And she has no idea
of how tempting she is.'

Her sapphire eyes opened then, and she covered his hand with her own. Beneath his fingers,
he felt her rapid pulse and her uneven breathing.

She should have been afraid of him. But in
those deep blue eyes, he saw no fear—only
wonder. Her hand reached up to his face, mir-
roring the caress he'd given her. As her fingertips edged his rough-shaven cheeks, he went
motionless, like a block of stone.

The moment she touched him, he was lost. He
knew it was dishonourable to take advantage of
her innocence. A good man would release her,
letting her alone.

You're not a good man, he reminded himself.
You're a bastard.

And he knew how true that was, when he
seized her mouth for a kiss.

Taryn couldn't grasp any thoughts at all when
Killian's mouth came on top of hers. She had
never been kissed before, and the sensation was
like fire rippling over ice, melting her resistance.
His warm mouth coaxed her to open, and she
surrendered to him, curious about what it was
like to kiss a man.

The kiss soothed her, his mouth taking possession of hers. A warmth poured over her, through her sensitive skin and down to her toes. Her body sought to get even closer to him, and she was well aware of his arousal pressed between them.

He was forbidden, a temptation she couldn't have. And though she suspected that he truly didn't want to kiss a woman as ugly as she was, she wasn't going to push him away. This might be her only kiss, and she wanted to know what kissing felt like.

He licked at the seam of her lips, and she opened slightly, before his tongue probed her mouth. The sensation was erotic, and she murmured, 'What are you doing?'

He didn't answer, but entered her mouth with his tongue, stroking her. From deep within, she grew wet, restless in a yearning she didn't understand.

The kiss was growing hotter, and she took his face between her hands, kissing him harder. He was stealing not only her breath, but her common sense as well. Never in her life had she ever imagined a kiss would be like this.

He nipped at her lower lip. Then he pulled her hair over the sides of her face, shielding the scars, before he stepped away. Almost as if he didn't want to look upon her again.

She didn't know why he'd done it, but it upset her in a way she'd never expected. During the kiss, it was as if he didn't care at all what she looked like. And now...now she worried that he'd suddenly realised just how terrible it was to kiss such a disfigured woman.

She forced herself to walk away from him, blinking back the hurt feelings. It was what she deserved, letting herself get caught up in imaginings that weren't real. He was a *fuidir*, while she was a king's daughter.

'We should go,' he told her.

And with those words, she understood that the kiss was a lesson to be learned. He didn't want to be her friend or her ally. If she tried to bring down the walls between them, he would only freeze her out.

Chapter Six

They reached the MacEgan holdings at Laochre a few hours past nightfall. Killian led the horse for the last mile, because after riding so close to Taryn, his body ached for her.

He pushed away the needs he didn't want to acknowledge. The kiss had been intended to silence her, to warn her not to befriend him. Instead, it had shaken his senses, making him want to lay her down and touch her for hours. Never in his life had any woman responded to him like that, and it had affected him deeply.

It had stirred her senses as well, and he recognised, too well, the danger. If he didn't shut down the unexpected desire, it would only heighten during the days spent alone with her. He knew better than to court disaster.

And so he'd drawn her hair over her scars,

utterly slicing apart her feelings. He knew the scars bothered her, though he thought nothing of them. But it was a means of protecting her. Better that she should hate him than desire him.

The open land stretched out before them, illuminated by silvery moonlight. Torches lined the stone walls in the distance, flares that reminded outsiders of the numerous soldiers who guarded Laochre Castle. It was one of the greatest strongholds near the southern coast, and *Lochlannach* settlers had their own presence within a few miles. To MacEgan allies, Laochre represented a sanctuary amid the upheaval of the past few years. To enemies, it was a fortress that could never be captured.

When they were within half a mile of the gates, an adolescent boy ran forward to welcome them. He was dressed little better than a slave, but Killian recognised Ewan MacEgan immediately. He was the youngest brother of the King, and he rarely followed any rules, save those that suited him. The moment Ewan neared them, Taryn pulled her hair forward, lowering her face from view.

'Killian MacDubh,' Ewan greeted him, a smile breaking over his face. 'I haven't seen you since last summer. Can you still swing two swords at the same time? I've been wanting to learn that.'

He gave a nod to the young man. 'I can. And one day you will do the same.' He was about to explain why they had come, but Ewan was already chattering.

'You've brought a lady with you. Is she your wife, then?' His voice cracked slightly, but he didn't seem at all embarrassed by it.

'No,' Taryn interrupted. 'He is my escort, nothing more.'

Indeed. It seemed that she had recognised his silent warning and now understood it. Killian hadn't wanted to upset her, but better that than to kindle unwanted feelings.

Before Taryn could say another word, the boy bowed. 'Welcome to Laochre, my lady.' The young man's face lit up with interest, and he added, 'I am King Patrick's brother. Ewan MacEgan is my name.'

Taryn's face softened into a smile. 'I thank you for your hospitality. I am Taryn Connelly of Ossoria.'

'The King's daughter,' Killian clarified. He didn't want Ewan believing that she was an ordinary lady.

'I have come to visit with your kinsmen,'

Taryn explained. 'I am on my way to Tara, and I am seeking warriors to accompany me.'

At that, an eager grin spread over Ewan's face, as if he was more than willing to go with her. 'My brothers and I would be glad to be of service.' His voice cracked again, and he began boasting of how many fighters the MacEgans had and how they were renowned throughout Éireann. Killian risked a glance at Taryn and saw the bewildered look on her face. The boy had barely stopped to breathe as he'd continued talking.

'Has Lady Carice arrived yet?' he interrupted the boy. If she had, Ewan would already be aware of it.

The young man shook his head. 'Trahern went to fetch her earlier today. I don't know when he'll bring her back.'

'When did he leave?' Killian asked.

'A few hours ago. I suppose he'll be back by morning.' He sent another devilish smile towards Taryn, and from the sudden interest in Ewan's face, Killian could tell that the young man was quite taken with her. The Lady nodded to him in acknowledgement, and Ewan proceeded to talk once again without ceasing, as they walked towards the castle gates.

The cat poked his grey head from the basket, and Killian rubbed the animal's ears. Harold looked as if he wanted to jump down from the horse, and he lifted the cat from the basket, tucking him under one arm.

When they reached the castle, he saw soldiers surrounding the battlements of Laochre. It was a heavily defended fortress, particularly since they had been attacked and invaded by Normans in the past. Patrick had married a Norman bride to keep the peace, and there had been few battles since that time.

As Killian led the horse beneath the portcullis, he saw Taryn glance upward at the murder hole that Ewan was gleefully pointing out. She exchanged a silent glance of amusement with him, as if the boy's adolescent behaviour reminded her of a younger brother.

Inside the gates, another wall surrounded the inner bailey. The grounds were immaculate, and Killian helped Taryn dismount so one of the stable boys could take the horse.

Considering how afraid of horses she'd been, Taryn had voiced no complaint for the remainder of the journey. When it was clear that Francis was not going to throw her again, she had seemed to relax. It had allowed Killian to keep the pace swift, and he was glad they had arrived before it was too dark to travel any further.

But when he'd ridden behind her, it had been impossible for him to find any sort of peace. With her body held close, he was all too aware of her curves and her scent. His imagination had tormented him with stolen visions of touching this woman. He never should have kissed her. It had been meant as a warning, as a means of frightening her into keeping her distance. But instead, the physical frustration had become his own.

It was only during the last mile that Killian had dismounted, leaving her to ride alone. She had tensed, but when she saw how close they were, she'd put aside her fears.

They walked inside another gate leading towards the main castle. He shadowed Taryn as Ewan escorted her inside. Though he had spent a summer training among the MacEgan warriors and he knew the men well, Killian felt apprehensive about standing in their Great Chamber as a visitor.

At the far end of the room, he saw Queen Isabel speaking with her husband, Patrick. The King was leaning towards his wife, and their shared look held an intimacy as if they were alone with no one looking on.

Oblivious to their moment, Ewan hurried towards them and began introducing Taryn. 'This is Lady Taryn of Ossoria, and she's come to stay with us.'

Taryn lowered her head, still keeping her face as hidden as she could. 'I am pleased to meet you both. And I would be grateful for your hospitality for a night or two, if I may.'

Killian bowed to the King and dropped to one knee. 'The Lady intends to journey to Tara and is seeking men to accompany her. I was also hoping you might have word about my sister, Carice.'

The King beckoned for him to rise. 'Your sister has not arrived yet.' His gaze shifted over to Taryn and he greeted her, saying, 'Both of you may remain at Laochre as long as you have the need.' He gave orders to a servant to bring them both food and drink.

Queen Isabel approached Taryn with a soft smile. 'I am glad to meet you, Taryn.' She introduced herself and took Taryn's hand, linking it in her arm. 'Come, and we will talk awhile.'

She nodded, keeping her face hidden and drawing up the hood of her cloak as if she were chilled. It was the only way she could hide her scars from the view of everyone else.

Patrick stood until the women had left, and his expression held wariness. When he turned back to Killian, he asked, 'Is she aware that her father is being held for treason?'

'Aye. She means to plead for his life.' He said nothing about Taryn's hope to free the man from imprisonment, sensing that the King would disagree with her decision. But the dark expression upon Patrick's face suggested he knew more about Devlin's capture—and that it involved treachery.

The King of Laochre paused a moment, then added, 'He allied with the Normans in an attempt to overthrow the High King. They will execute him at Imbolc.'

'Lady Taryn wants me to save him,' he admitted to the King. Undoubtedly, her loyalty was a daughter's unconditional love—but given the stories, it was probable that Devlin had indeed attempted an uprising. If Killian became involved in a rescue attempt, his own life would be at risk.

'No one can save Devlin now,' Patrick countered. He sat down upon a carved wooden throne once more, gesturing for Killian to join him. 'Her only hope is to plead for a swift, merciful death.'

'And what will happen to Ossoria?'

The King shook his head. 'Likely Rory Ó Connor will seize command of the territory and give it to one of his allies to govern.'

'Would you be one of them?' he asked, uncertain of where Patrick's sympathies lay.

In answer, the King lifted his silver cup, a smile playing upon his lips. 'I am loyal to my tribe and to my people. I have no wish to take another kingdom for my own. But one of my brothers might agree to rule over the province on Rory's behalf.'

Killian didn't miss the subtle hint that, aye, Patrick might indeed be willing to use his brothers to gain command of Ossoria. Though it shouldn't bother him at all, he wondered if that meant one of them would want to wed Taryn. A sudden tightness took hold of his mood at the thought. He had no right to be jealous—none at all. Taryn was meant to marry a nobleman, and she had no choice in that arrangement. And the sooner he separated himself from her, the better.

'Would you be willing to send men to escort the Lady to Tara?' It would be far safer for Taryn to travel with their warriors, instead of just the two of them alone. Regardless of the King's intentions, Killian wanted additional soldiers to protect her on this journey.

'I could,' King Patrick answered. 'The High King demanded fighters from all across Éireann to help protect us from the foreigners. I have not yet sent my own soldiers to Tara, and my men could guard the Lady.' He stood again and motioned for Killian to follow him. They walked along the trestle tables, towards the back of the Great Chamber. 'But how is it you came to escort the Lady Taryn here alone? You have no ties to Ossoria.'

'It was a bargain made between us,' he answered. 'She agreed to help my sister, and in return, I was to escort her to Tara. But our plans were interrupted.' He explained to the King what had happened with Maeve's soldiers and their subsequent change of destination.

'So you brought her to seek help from us.' King Patrick led him outside. Though it was not customary for a king to walk alongside a man of his low status, Killian knew that the man was seeking his own answers.

'I cannot promise help for King Devlin,' Patrick admitted. 'But if Taryn wishes to see her father before his death, I could arrange that.'

It was likely the best she could hope for. But
a blade of guilt slid within Killian, that he could
not help her. Even if she did plead for his life,
there was little chance that Devlin would be
spared.

Torches flickered in the inner bailey, illumi-
nating the stone wall surrounding the fortress.
The King led him towards one of the outbuildings and offered, 'You may sleep among my
men. I will alert you when your sister arrives.'

With that, the King left him alone. Killian
stood before the door leading to a small tower.
Several men stood at the top, watching over
the wall. He knew from his previous visit that
the men took turns guarding the castle through
the night. If there was more information about
the High King or King Devlin, then these men
might have the answers he needed.

As he climbed up the stairs leading to the
tower, he knew that it wasn't wise to escort
Taryn to the High King, despite his earlier
agreement. This wasn't his concern any more,
especially since she had been unable to uphold
her end of the bargain. But he didn't like the
thought of letting her go alone with MacEgan
soldiers. The men wouldn't harm her—but he
couldn't let go of the worry that she would en-

danger herself with King Rory. The High King would not care that she was innocent—instead, he might use her to torment her father further.

She shouldn't go at all. And perhaps it was best if Maeve's men prevented her from reaching Tara. All he had to do was let them take her.

And yet, she was clearly afraid of her mother. Somehow Maeve was involved with the scars, and if he let her go back to the Queen, Taryn might suffer even more.

It's not your battle to fight, he reminded himself. His concern lay with Carice, not a woman he had known only a little while. He could not leave Laochre until he had seen his sister with his own eyes. He needed to know that she was safe, above all else.

And then what? He had no silver or coins at all. The MacEgans might give him a place here, but he would still be a *fuidir*, albeit a free man.

It wasn't the life he'd dreamed of. He wanted his own land, a place where he was servant to no man. Taryn had offered him silver and vast wealth, in return for his assistance. She had sworn to grant him anything he wanted—all he had to do was save the life of a traitor.

Or he could walk away and remain a *fuidir*.

Common sense told him that this was a grave

risk. His own life might be forfeit, if he made the attempt. But if he did not intervene, King Devlin would die within the sennight. No man was foolish enough to defy Rory Ó Connor.

That is, no one except his bastard son.

His mind began turning over the situation. He did believe he could help Devlin escape, if that was what Taryn wanted. But he would have to remain invisible to the High King so no one would know how it had happened.

If he was caught in the attempt, there was a chance that he would die. But would the High King execute his own bastard son? Killian didn't know. Rory had rejected him once before, so it was a great risk.

But with that risk came opportunity.

For once in his life, the power was in his hands. He could choose whether or not to help Taryn. If he did agree to this dangerous quest, he would demand what he wanted—land to call his own. And even more than land, he wanted his freedom to rule over it.

The thought was outrageous, for he possessed no legal rights. His mother had not been a part of the Faoilin tribe and neither had he. She had never spoken of her own parents or the tribe she was born to, refusing to tell him anything about her family. Even the name MacDubh was an invented one.

He was a man without freedom, without any rights, without even a name to call his own.

Killian walked across the length of the wall, staring out into the darkness. Needles of ice stung his skin, and he rested his hands against the stone. Even in a place like Laochre, he felt the sense of isolation, of not belonging. All the silver in the world could not fill up the emptiness.

Taryn Connelly would do anything to save her father. But could she give him what he truly wanted—a place of his own? The Queen would certainly refuse to grant anything, since she wanted her husband to die. The only person who truly held the right to give him land was the man whose life he had to save: King Devlin himself.

However, it didn't seem that anyone trusted Devlin. The man might make idle promises and keep none of them. Until he met the prisoner for himself, Killian could not judge whether or not Devlin could keep his word. Taryn seemed to think he was innocent of his crimes, but then, she was his daughter.

She was a pawn in this game, a woman who

loved her father and would do anything to save him. The question was, how far would she go?

'His name is Liam,' the Queen said, passing over her son. 'He's just over a year old.' Taryn bent her head towards the baby, and the rush of longing filled her deeply. The child waved his fist, his tiny hands touching her face, as if he could see nothing wrong with the scars. She pressed a kiss to the child's forehead, marvelling at how perfect he was.

'He's beautiful,' she told the Queen. 'And look at his smile.' She cooed over the baby, who squirmed in her arms, trying to get back to his mother.

Queen Isabel lifted her son to her shoulder, patting him. 'He's a sweet babe.' She smiled serenely, then asked, 'Has your father arranged a betrothal for you?'

Taryn's smile faded, and she hesitated in her answer. 'I was almost betrothed once,' she admitted, thinking of Lucas Ó Rourke.

'Almost?' Isabel prompted.

Her cheeks flushed at the memory, and Taryn played with the strands of her hair, wondering if she ought to reveal everything to the Queen.

In the end, she decided Isabel would learn the truth anyway.

'He refused when he saw me.' Taryn pulled back her hair, revealing the scars upon both cheeks. She expected the Queen to flinch at the sight of her marred skin, but Isabel only met her gaze evenly—unlike Lucas.

'He told my father he could never wed a de-formed woman like me,' she continued.

A flare of anger darkened Isabel's face. 'And what did your father say?'

She only shrugged. 'What *could* he say? I cannot change my face.' And although Devlin had ended the betrothal on her behalf, he had taken her out for a walk later that night, offer-ing consolation.

It had been twilight, and the snow had begun to descend, coating the black branches with a layer of frosted white. Their footsteps had crunched upon the layer of ice and leaves, and the stillness had brought a sense of peace, soothing away her anger and sadness. The light was fading, the sun piercing through the trees like an ethereal halo.

'It's so peaceful,' she said to her father. Somehow he had sensed that she needed a mo-ment like this, after Lucas had spurned her.

He took her gloved hand, and they walked for a time without speaking. Then at last he stopped at the edge of the woods. 'You need not let this trouble you. I have had many offers for your hand in marriage. Some men already know of your scars and are willing to overlook them.'

Taryn turned to face him. 'I don't want a husband who merely tolerates me.' The truth was, she wanted a marriage far stronger than the one shared by her parents. It was clear that Maeve loathed Devlin, but the Queen had nowhere else to go. And for some reason, Devlin had not set her aside as his wife. She could never understand why they continued to live as husband and wife.

'I will not force you to wed one of them,' Devlin acknowledged, 'but you must wed another king. Or at the very least, a chieftain. If I have no son to claim Ossoria, then your sons will fight for that honour.'

She didn't ask what would happen if she did not bear a son. Instead, she tried to dream of a future where a man would not judge her by what he saw.

'I suppose my bride price wasn't low enough for Lucas to overlook my scars,' Taryn said quietly.

'I believe I might have hit him for that,' Isabel
offered. 'Certainly a man who would say such
a thing would deserve it.'

Taryn brightened a little. It felt good to have
a woman sympathise with her. 'He did deserve
to be struck down, aye. But I told him I would
not marry him.' Since then, she'd hidden herself
away, refusing to consider other suitors, despite
her mother's attempts to arrange a marriage.
She didn't want to admit to anyone how much
Lucas had hurt her feelings. It was easier to
pretend to be a strong woman, to behave as if
she didn't care.

But she did. And she'd spent the past year
learning how to become a good queen. It was
easier to involve herself in the lives of others
than to face her own bleak prospects.

'It sounds as if you are well rid of him.'
Though her face held curiosity, Isabel did not
ask how Taryn had been scarred. 'My husband
may be able to help, after you return from Tara,'
she offered. 'Several of his brothers are unwed.
Although they do not have lands of their own,
if it is your wish to wed one of them and stay
in Ossoria, it is a possibility.'

Taryn suspected the Queen's offer was born
out of courtesy, nothing more. She knew, too

well, that men judged what they saw, not the person she was. But she gave the expected response, 'Perhaps.'

She did want a husband and children of her own, one day. But it was hard to let go of the hurt feelings from Lucas's rejection. She had never forgotten the distaste in his expression when he'd viewed her scars.

'You don't want to wed one of the MacEgan men, do you?' the Queen predicted. 'I can see it in your face.'

Taryn shook her head. 'Oh, it isn't that. If they look anything like your husband, they will be handsome men.'

'Of course they are,' Isabel agreed. 'And men like Trahern or Connor are beloved by all the women.'

'Which is why they would never even look at a woman like me,' Taryn reminded her. Though she supposed it sounded like self-pity, in her mind, it was the truth. She knew she could find a husband who wanted to rule at her side. But she wanted more than that, and pride kept her from lowering her standards.

Isabel tucked her son into his pallet upon the floor, then turned to face her. 'The MacEgan men see beyond a woman's appearance, Taryn.

Despite my Norman ancestry, my husband grew to love me for the woman I am. A man who sees your true self is one worth keeping.' She offered her a warm smile. 'Why don't you stay with us a little longer and meet them?'

'I cannot stay for long,' she said, though the offer lifted her spirits. 'I want to make sure Killian's sister arrives safely. Then I must go on to Tara.'

The Queen's smile widened. 'Killian *is* a handsome warrior, isn't he? My ladies all have their eyes upon him.' She tilted her head and asked, 'But why is it that you travelled with *him* towards Tara and not your father's men? Were you running away?'

The woman's intuition was sharper than Taryn had guessed. 'My mother did not want me to plead for the King's life,' she admitted. 'In truth, she forbade me to go. I came to seek your help, and Killian agreed to escort me here.'

The Queen walked towards the window, as if she was deep in thought. Taryn waited for the woman to speak, but when Isabel remained silent, she voiced another question. 'How do you know Killian?' He had told her he was little more than a slave among the Faoilin tribe.

Why, then, would he be so familiar with the MacEgans?

'He spent several summers training with our men.' The Queen added, 'The women were heartbroken to see him go.'

Strangely, there was a twinge of discontent at the thought of women offering themselves to Killian. He must have enjoyed their attentions, and truly, why should she care? Yet Taryn remembered, too well, what it was like to kiss him. It had startled her, stealing the very breath from her lungs.

'I imagine he left because of his sister, Carice,' Taryn guessed. 'She's been very ill.'

Isabel turned grave. 'Then I do hope Trahern will be able to bring her here, even if it is only for a short while. We have good healers whose knowledge of herbs and medicines is unsurpassed.' The Queen hesitated a moment. 'She will be safe, so long as the High King does not know that we helped her to flee.'

Taryn nodded, but her mind was more preoccupied with thoughts of Killian. She didn't know if he would agree to help her any more, after she had failed to keep her bargain about Carice. Her mother's pursuit had made it far more difficult, and she did not doubt that

Maeve would try to stop her from reaching the High King.

A few minutes later, a servant arrived with a small repast of wine, bread, roasted boar, and cheese. Taryn sat with the Queen and ate while Isabel told her stories of her husband's encounters with the Norman invaders. She learned that Isabel's marriage to Patrick had been arranged to keep the peace between the Normans and the Irish. They had begun as enemies, but had ended up falling in love.

'An arranged betrothal *can* make a good marriage,' Isabel said. 'If it is with the right man.'

Taryn knew what the Queen was implying, but right now, her greater concern was saving her father. 'I do hope to marry one day,' she said. 'But not yet.' There was too much at stake right now. Until the pieces of her life were put back together, she could not imagine another betrothal.

'I understand.' Isabel grew serious for a moment. 'But if your father cannot be saved, your family will need alliances to help keep the peace in your own kingdom.'

Taryn didn't want to even consider that possibility. She had to believe that Devlin could come home again. 'Perhaps,' she hedged. Then she said, 'I would like to speak with Killian again before I retire for the night.' She wanted to know if it was his intention to leave her behind, once Carice was safe. Though it was likely, she rather hoped he would change his mind.

'I will send for him, if you wish,' the Queen offered. 'He is staying among our soldiers.'

'I would be grateful,' Taryn said. Even so, she was wary of treating Killian like a servant, to come at her beck and call. Already he was tense, since Carice had not arrived. He was a man on edge, ready to do whatever was necessary to defend his sister. She prayed that the young woman would arrive here safely.

Isabel spoke to one of the servants and then turned to Taryn. 'I will leave you alone to speak with him, but if you have need of me, I won't be far away.' Her gaze was searching, as if she sensed that there was more between them.

After the Queen left, Taryn paced across the solar. The fire burned brightly on the hearth, and she could hear the low murmur of conversation from the people around them. Laochre Castle was a bustling settlement, filled with Irish and Normans blended together.

The stone rooms were not as cold as she'd expected, for tapestries lined the walls and the hearth brought a sense of comfort to the solar. But there was no peace within her now. She could not set aside her worries about Tara. It would take only two or three more days to reach the High King's fortress, and she had no idea what she could say that would convince the *Ard-Righ* not to execute her father. A woman's pleas meant nothing to the King of all Éireann.

The door to the solar opened, and Killian stepped inside. From the moment he entered the room, he took command of the space. There was no deference in him, and the look in his eyes held an intensity that made her uneasy.

'I was wanting to speak with you again,' he said without any greeting at all. In one hand, he held out a woollen cloak with a hood. 'Put this on and walk with me.'

'We can speak here,' she said. 'There is no one to overhear our conversation.'

'There are always eavesdroppers within a castle. Ewan MacEgan, for one,' he said. Then he crossed towards her and placed the cloak over her shoulders, drawing the hood over her face.

It felt as if he were trying to hide her appearance, and she felt a pang of frustration. *You're being overly sensitive,* she told herself. It was midwinter and freezing outside.

Killian led her down a narrow hallway and into a room that opened on to the battlements. Outside, the wind roared against the stones, the air filled with cold sleet. She shivered within her cloak, pulling it tightly over her body.

'Is there any sign of Carice?' she asked, when they were alone.

He shook his head. 'Not yet. But it's too soon for her to be here. I trust in Trahern MacEgan—the man will bring her to Laochre as soon as he can.' His grey eyes narrowed upon her, and she had a sinking feeling deep inside.

'Our agreement has changed,' he began. With the words, a chill whispered over her skin, and she knew, without him saying a word, that he was going to leave her here.

'I thought you might say that.' She had hoped he would continue escorting her to Tara, but the look in his eyes suggested that he did not want to any more. 'I am sorry I could not help your sister. But I could do naught to stop my mother's men from pursuing me.' She was only one woman, and Maeve had no intention of letting her go.

'No,' he agreed. 'And they will try to stop you from reaching Tara. It is likely that they will succeed.'

She faced him, staring into his grey eyes. 'You've given up, haven't you? Once Carice is here, you would rather walk away from what I have to offer.'

'Not necessarily,' he countered. The coldness in his voice held a ruthless air, and she suddenly suspected that she would not like what he was about to say.

He crossed his arms and studied her. Freezing droplets of ice caught in his dark hair, and she was held spellbound by his iron eyes. This man, though little more than a slave, was accustomed to getting what he wanted. He was breathtakingly handsome, and she had now experienced what it was to be kissed by this man. It had shaken the foundation of her good sense.

'I could take you to Tara,' he said slowly. 'And I might be able to save your father's life. But it isn't silver that I'm wanting as my reward.'

Her nerves tightened at that. 'What is it you want?'

'I want land,' he said quietly. 'I want a place of my own in Ossoria.'

For a moment, his words hung within the space. She wanted to tell him yes, of course, she could grant him a place. But she hesitated, needing to be truthful with him. 'Land may not be within my power to give. Especially if my father is exiled from Ossoria. I do not know who will become the new king.' Taryn took a step closer and pleaded, 'Let me give you silver or wealth. Or you could become one of our tenants with all the rights of a tribesman.'

'No.' He studied her a moment and said, 'My land will not be part of Ossoria, for I will have no man as my king.' Within his eyes, she saw the frustration of a man who had been powerless all his life. But he was asking for too much.

All she could say was the truth. 'Then I will have to get help from someone else.'

In his bearing, she saw years of resentment and frustration. For a moment, she wondered how she would feel if she were a serving girl, forced to obey the commands of others. She understood why he wanted another life…but she held so little power in Ossoria. Her father and mother commanded the people—not her.

Killian crossed his arms, and she caught a glimpse of the stone-hearted man he was. All his life he had lived with invisible chains—she understood that. But she could not divide her kingdom for his sake.

'My father is the only one who can grant that wish,' she admitted. 'If he is pardoned, then I have no doubt he will give you the reward you deserve.'

The expression on Killian's face suggested that he didn't believe that at all. 'He can never return. You know that as well as I. Rory will not forgive a man who tried to seize his throne.'

She suspected as much, but she didn't know what to say any more. It felt as if all the pieces of her life were shattering around her. 'You are Rory's son. Do you not think you could intervene on my father's behalf?'

'I do not know,' he said. Turning back, he added, 'I may be able to free your father in secret. But I doubt if the *Ard-Righ* even cares if I breathe.'

She stared at him, the wind icing through her cheeks and hair. Killian went to stand at the edge of the battlements while the rain battered his face. As she watched him, she saw a man who had been isolated all his life—a man who had never relied upon anyone but himself.

I care if you breathe, she wanted to say but didn't. The thought frightened her, for she was indeed getting too close to this man. She took a step towards him but forced herself to stop.

'I am sorry to hear it.'

He stared out into the darkness, seemingly

unaware of the harsh weather. Taryn held her
hood over her face to shield her from the freezing rain, choosing her words carefully. 'Would
you rather not go?' she asked. 'I could still speak
to the High King myself and plead for mercy.'

At that, Killian faced her. There was a dark
expression on his face, as if he didn't at all like
that idea. 'He will not listen to a woman's desires.'

He drew closer, and she grew nervous beneath his gaze. The water and ice clung to his
face, but the cold did not appear to bother him.
'And he might threaten you in other ways.'

It was disconcerting to be the focus of this
man's attention. He was so handsome, almost
as if he were not real. She found herself watching his mouth, remembering the aching pleasure of his kiss.

'No man would threaten me at Tara,' she said.
'I know what I look like and how I seem to outsiders.'

But he caught her chin and tilted it up, forcing
her to face him. With his hands, he framed her
scarred face, staring into her eyes. She watched
as a droplet of water rolled down his cheek, and
the instinct to touch it came over her.

'Believe me when I say that men do not care

about a woman's face. Some will take what they desire, whether a woman wills it or not. You would not be safe from the High King's men.'

She supposed that could be true of some soldiers. Thankfully she had never been in such danger. But even so, most men shunned her presence.

'They say I am cursed,' she said softly.

His fingers passed over her marred skin, and the touch was so light, she felt it spiral down her body. For a moment, she wondered what it would be like to have smooth skin. Or to have a man like Killian look upon her with interest. The sudden flare in his eyes made her go motionless. He did not take his hand from her face, and his thumb edged her lips.

'Perhaps you are,' he answered. But in his eyes, she saw an intensity that frightened her. He was watching her in a different way, one that made her cheeks grow warm.

He does not want a woman like you, she reminded herself. *All he wants is land of his own.*

And there was no means of granting that to him.

'You won't go to Tara alone,' he swore. Her skin rose up with gooseflesh beneath his stare. For a moment, she imagined what it would be like if this man were her protector. The thought only heightened an unspoken yearning.

'I know the MacEgan soldiers have agreed to be my escorts,' she said. 'But will you come with me as well?'

He didn't answer at first. Then he slid one hand against her waist. For a moment, he kept it there, watching to see what she would do. His touch burned through her gown, making her wonder why she was so fascinated by this man. Was it because he saw past her scars? Or was there something more?

He is using you, her mind warned. And that could indeed be true. But at this moment, she hardly cared. This handsome warrior was watching her with the eyes of a man who was interested in her. And her wayward heart wanted so badly to believe it.

'I suppose I should confront the man who sired me,' he said at last. His thumb edged a circle over the base of her spine, and the gesture melted away her reservations. Killian added, 'If he allows it, I will ask for mercy on your father's behalf. If not, then I will attempt to free Devlin in secret.'

'If you succeed, I will find a way to get you

the land you want,' she promised. 'I will do anything necessary.'

His hands moved to her shoulders, then down her arms. The warmth of his palms sent a rush of longing through her. 'Anything, *a mhuirnín*?'

Though she knew he was only teasing, the words were a secret caress upon her. Her breath caught as he leaned down, resting his nose against hers.

'There is a way for both of us to get what we want,' he said quietly. His voice was deep, and she leaned back to look into his grey eyes. 'If you are willing.'

A sense of warning heightened inside her. 'What is it?'

'You could wed me.'

She blinked a moment, trying to grasp what he was saying. Wed him? For what purpose? At her startled silence, he continued, 'If I am your husband, no one can deny me a place at your side—not even the new king. You would have your freedom and my protection.'

The brittle disappointment fractured inside her, for her instincts had been correct. He *did* want to use her for his own gain. It wasn't about wanting her or protecting her from her enemies—it was about a slave wanting to become a king. She should have known that his interest in her wasn't real.

He drew her against him, his arms around her waist while she faced the darkened landscape. 'Let me go,' she said suddenly. She couldn't think clearly within his embrace. 'I know what you want, Killian. But your price is too great.'

Her feelings tightened inside her, but she forced herself to speak the truth. 'I want to save my father's life…but not at the cost of my kingdom.'

Killian wasn't surprised at her refusal. And yet, he'd meant his offer in good faith, as one where she could have her freedom to do as she chose, and he would have the lands he lacked.

'Would a marriage to me be such a sacrifice?' he asked quietly, drawing nearer. She tried to move away, but he backed her against the stone wall. 'You did not push me away when I kissed you.'

'It was my first kiss,' she admitted. 'I wanted to know what it would be like.'

He moved in, but she turned her face aside, revealing the puckered skin of her cheek. She'd done it on purpose, to show him that side of her.

'You kissed me back.' He wanted her to realise that a marriage between them did not have to be merely an arrangement. She intrigued him, and he wanted to know her better.

'I did. But that doesn't mean it will happen again.' She pressed her hands upon his chest, trying to hold him at a distance. 'Once was enough.'

He studied her, searching those blue eyes to see the truth. She averted her gaze, but he sensed that she had lost herself in the kiss, just as he had. This woman was a tangle of contradictions—brave and frightened…scarred and beautiful…vulnerable and strong-willed.

'I don't think it was,' he argued. He held her hands, warming them in his palms. Though she could have pulled away from him, she didn't. And he knew that she was as interested in him as he was in her. 'Kiss me again, Taryn. Remember what it was like between us.'

The wind and ice battered both of them, tearing at her long black hair. 'I don't want to.'

He tilted her chin up to face him. 'You don't want to admit that you are drawn to a man like me. One so low-born, like the dirt beneath your feet.'

'I have never treated you like that,' she protested. 'And I know well enough that you are only drawn to my kingdom, not me.' Her blue eyes burned into his, flashing fire.

He touched the scarred cheek, feeling the rough skin beneath his fingertips. She flinched the moment he touched her. 'I was born into a life that I didn't want. Is it so wrong to want more?' He slid his palm down the reddened skin, then turned her to face him.

She tried again to push him away. 'You know nothing of my people or our ways, Killian.'

'Then teach me.' He murmured the words against her lips, tasting the doubt. 'And in return, there are many things I will teach you.'

She turned her face away once more. 'I want nothing from you, Killian MacDubh.' Though her words were quiet, he didn't believe that she was entirely immune to him. To prove his point, he ignored her words and trapped her against the stone, seizing her mouth. He didn't care that he was being cruel. Right now he was too interested in the soft sweetness before him, of the way she had opened to him, her breath catching in her throat.

Shocked by his gesture, she yielded beneath his kiss, letting him take what he wanted. Her gasp caught in her throat, transforming into a moan when he invaded her mouth. He kissed her hard, shaping her mouth to his, tempting her.

Whether she knew it or not, there was an undeniable attraction between them. He threaded his hands in her hair, tipping her head back. Her hand came up to his chest, and the longer he kissed her, the more he wanted this woman. Like Carice, she had never once treated him as a slave. And he wanted to give back to her a taste of what she'd given him.

If he wedded Taryn, it would not be a cold arrangement. Aye, he'd been ruthless in his proposition. But if he got what he wanted from her, he would give her an equal place at his side. She'd said she wanted a husband and children. A woman like her deserved many children, and he could easily see her holding a young child's hand, with another babe cradled at her breast.

He framed her face, his fingers resting against her throat. Her pulse thrummed rapidly, and at last, she shoved him back. Her lips were swollen, her eyes dazed as if she couldn't quite calm her beating heart. 'Listen to me, Killian.' Her eyes flared with anger, and she said, 'I am not a woman who will surrender her kingdom, simply because you kissed me.' She squared her shoulders, looking ruffled and upset.

'I never asked for your kingdom.' He knew better than to demand something like that. 'I offered you the chance to determine your own fate, before Rory demands that you wed a man of his choosing.'

Her face turned vulnerable as if she hadn't thought of that. 'There are times when I feel as if I have less freedom than you do.'

He leaned in and stole another kiss. 'Think upon it, *a chara*. And if you're wanting that freedom, the way lies before you. Wed me in secret, and no one can command you.'

'No one, except you,' Taryn corrected. She stared at him as though he'd lost his mind. And perhaps he had, to think up such an arrangement. 'You might be very good at kissing, but you have a great deal to learn about women, Killian MacDubh.'

Chapter Seven

Some time in the middle of the night, it had begun snowing. By the next morning, the ground was coated in a sheet of white, and there was no sign of it ending. Worse, Carice still had not arrived.

Taryn had no desire to see Killian after their last conversation. Instead, she walked towards the Queen's solar, intending to spend the morning with the other ladies. She wore the same emerald silk gown and had left her hair loose around her shoulders. When she opened the door, she found the solar empty, and she went to stand by the fire. The cat, Harold, was curled up nearby. He yawned and stretched, arching his back.

She didn't move, but the animal padded over to her, seeking affection. Though she was uncertain, she bent down and scratched the cat's ears as Killian had done. The animal purred, rubbing his head against her. She let out a slow breath, marvelling that the creature seemed to be enjoying her touch. Then he flopped down before the hearth once more.

There was a moment of peace, and Taryn warmed herself, still troubled by her conversation with Killian. His demands were unreasonable, far too ambitious for the man he was. Never had he seemed to be a man governed by greed. Why, then, had he asked her to surrender everything, including herself?

The door to the solar opened, and Taryn turned. The moment she did, the young maid screamed, turning her head away. A flush of embarrassment came over her, and the maid muttered an apology.

'I am sorry, my lady. I did not know anyone was here.' But Taryn didn't miss the way the young woman crossed herself, as if to ward off a demon.

Queen Isabel entered the solar and saw the young maid's gesture. Her face darkened, and she ordered the girl to spend the morning helping in the kitchen. When the maid was gone,

Isabel apologised again, 'I am sorry. Renna is a silly girl, and her behaviour was thoughtless.'

'I am used to it,' Taryn said, pulling her hair forward. But it *had* stung, realising that nothing had changed. She had let her guard down, only to be reminded of who she was—an ugly woman whose face frightened others. 'There was a great deal of snow last night,' she said, by way of changing the subject.

'A snowstorm will not stop Trahern from bringing Lady Carice here,' Isabel reassured her, misreading her frustration.

Taryn went to stand beside the Queen. 'I believe he will, aye.'

'That isn't why you're upset, is it?'

She shrugged. 'I have only until Imbolc to save my father, and I have no idea what I can do. Killian offered to help me, but now—' She began pacing across the floor. 'Now he doesn't want silver in return.'

'What does he want?'

'He wants me to wed him in secret.' Taryn picked up a wooden cup of mead, wishing she could hurl it into the fire.

'That *is* rather bold,' Isabel mused. 'Why would he dare to ask for such a thing? Especially when you could wed one of my husband's handsome brothers instead.' There was teasing in her voice, but Taryn suspected that the Queen was indeed trying to find a match for the young men.

'He said Rory will appoint a new king who might force me to wed. Killian offered his protection, in return for part of Ossoria. I do not even think it's possible or even legal.' She drained the mead, feeling foolish for it.

'Well, I think you should get to know my husband's brothers. Connor is visiting, and Trahern should return tonight with Lady Carice. We can hold feasting and dancing to entertain everyone. My husband's brothers are quite charming.'

'Ewan is, indeed,' she agreed. But despite Isabel's claims that Trahern and Connor would not care about her scars, she had no desire to be the centre of attention—especially after the maid's reaction.

The Queen's smile was bright, though in her eyes, there was a shadow of exhaustion. 'I am certain they will be glad to help you when you speak with the High King. You can meet with them, and ask.'

'I don't know if the MacEgan men would be interested,' she admitted, standing by the fire to warm herself. 'And while I appreciate your offer, I would not want everyone to be staring at me. I wouldn't want to embarrass the men in that way.'

'Believe me when I say they would not care,' Isabel insisted. 'But if it makes you uncomfortable, we could hide your scars. If you wore a veil or arranged your hair differently, we could keep most of them covered.'

'It's a deception,' she argued. 'It would be wrong to make them think that I am the same as other women.'

Isabel frowned and crossed the room to stand before her. '*Are* you so very different, on the inside? Will you let your fear and embarrassment reign over your confidence?'

In other words, she was behaving like a coward. Taryn met the Queen's gaze. 'Many of my scars are not on my face.' They were deep inside her, for she was too accustomed to seeing the horror on strangers' expressions.

Isabel reached out and squeezed her hand. 'It does not make you less of a woman. But if you would rather remain here instead of joining in our celebration, it is your choice.'

'I don't want to hide myself away,' she said. 'But neither do I wish to be stared at.' Isabel said nothing, but merely waited for her to make a decision. With a reluctant sigh, Taryn said, 'Help me to hide the scars, and I will meet them.' Though she doubted if any arrangement would be made, she supposed there was no harm in it.

Isabel brightened. 'Good. I will give you one of my gowns to wear, and we will arrange your hair.' She sent Taryn a sly smile. 'None of the men will be able to take his eyes from you. Don't trouble yourself about your father—you need not marry a common soldier to save Devlin *or* your kingdom.'

But there was nothing common about Killian. He was a natural leader, a determined man who intended to claim the birthright he'd never had. His kiss had stirred her senses, making her feel desire for the first time. If he had...cared for her, even a little, she might have considered his suggestion.

And yet, she knew he was using her to get the land he wanted.

Queen Isabel summoned her ladies and spoke to them quietly beforehand. Taryn suspected she was warning them not to speak a word about her scars.

'Come and sit down while we arrange your

hair, my lady,' one of the women said to her, smiling. But Taryn didn't miss the sympathy in her eyes.

She obeyed, surrendering to their ministrations, while she let her mind drift. They combed her hair and arranged it with a veil. But instead of feeling excitement at a MacEgan gathering, anxiety formed within her stomach.

'I want you to enjoy yourself tonight, Taryn,' the Queen insisted. 'No one will dare to insult one of my guests.'

She knew the Queen was attempting to play matchmaker, but it was difficult to imagine that Isabel could keep others from talking about her. 'I will try.'

Killian's anxiety heightened over the next few hours as the snow continued to fall and Carice still had not arrived. All around him, the MacEgan tribe members were enjoying a celebration, though it was not yet Imbolc. The children had spent hours braiding straw into St Brighid's crosses. Others worked on a larger doll in Brighid's form that would be paraded from house to house during the feast of Imbolc. Later, the MacEgans would leave items of clothing outside their homes for the saint to bless, while others would leave food and drink for her spirit. The Faoilin tribe had done the same, all the years of Killian's life, though he'd had to create his own cross out of stable straw and twigs.

It should have been an atmosphere of celebration and anticipation—but he could not help but worry over his sister.

Where was Carice? If she didn't arrive by nightfall, he would have to abandon Taryn here and try to find Brian's travelling party. He continued pacing, gulping down a cup of mead while he waited for Trahern to arrive. Outside, the snow continued to fall, and some of the children brought snowballs into the Great Chamber, hurling them with enthusiasm before the adults ushered them outside.

There was no sign of Taryn or the Queen, as of yet. Killian went to stand inside, and a serving maid refilled his cup.

In the corner, he saw crowds gathered around a wise woman, who was divining the fortunes of others. She sat before a silver basin, staring into the reflection of the still water. Young women were lined up behind her, hoping she would tell them whom they would marry.

The men, in contrast, stood far away from the

women, not wanting to be involved. He could understand that sentiment. For although he had made the marriage offer to Taryn, a part of him had known that she would never agree to it. She did not need him to save her father, for she could easily hire any man to do her bidding. Many men would risk their lives for any amount of silver. She owed him nothing.

But he realised that he *wanted* to help her. He knew how fearful she was of horses, and he wanted to ensure that she reached Tara safely. And once she was there, he didn't want to leave her side. She didn't seem to recognise the dangers that lay ahead.

He drained his mug and continued towards the back of the Great Chamber, weaving in and out of the crowd. It was then that he glimpsed Taryn descending the stairs.

The Queen had given her a gown of cream, trimmed with silver threads. When she moved with the firelight behind her, the gown gleamed like sunlight upon the river. Her hair was pinned up in an elaborate formation, and golden balls were hung all around it. Two of the balls hung against each cheek, with her dark locks of hair shielding the scars.

From a distance, no one would know of her

disfigurement. But in spite of it, Taryn appeared uneasy about being the subject of so many stares. She was twisting her hands together, as if she was nervous. She need not be afraid, for she was easily one of the most beautiful women here.

Killian moved in closer, still keeping his back to the wall. Although he was permitted to move about the Great Chamber among the guests, he knew it would not be fitting for him to approach her. When she caught him watching her, she straightened, lifting her chin coolly.

Ewan came to stand beside him and nodded towards Taryn. 'Do you suppose I could ever find a woman like her to wed?'

'Your family will arrange it.' Killian accepted another cup of mead, hardly tasting it.

'Aye. When I'm older,' Ewan agreed. The young man's gaze followed Taryn, and Killian's mood darkened at the sight of all the men staring.

Several of the musicians began to play, and the sound of pipes and the harp filled up the space. He recognised Lady Genevieve, Bevan MacEgan's wife, at the harp. Taryn chose a seat to listen, and in time, Killian saw a dark-blond-haired man approach and sit beside her. He was speaking in a low voice, leaning close.

It was Connor MacEgan. The man was slightly younger than himself, but he'd always had a smile for the ladies. He took Taryn's hand and held it while the music continued.

There was a low buzz in Killian's ears, his blood heating as he watched them. Would she let Connor take her into a darkened corner, telling him of her worries and fears? Would he soothe her, stealing a kiss?

Killian's knuckles tightened over the cup. He knew what she was doing—looking for someone else to fight her battles. And from the looks of it, Connor was more than willing. Damn them both for it.

He took a step forward, only to have Ewan block his path. 'You look as if you're about to murder my brother. Do you have a claim upon the Lady Taryn?'

Killian steadied himself. No, he didn't. And no matter that he'd tasted her lips, feeling the pleasant touch of her body against his, this was *her* choice.

He shook his head at Ewan but began walking towards the benches, not caring that others were beginning to stare at him. He was well aware that he was interrupting the musicians, but before he could wrench her away from Connor, a hand seized his shoulder.

Reacting on instinct, he swung his fist and found himself staring at King Patrick. He caught himself before throwing the punch and dropped his hand to his side. 'You startled me, Your Grace.' He raised a knee in deference and lowered his head.

'My men will accompany the Lady to Tara as her escorts,' the King said. It seemed to be a subtle way of telling him that his task was ended, and he should go back home.

Killian inclined his head. 'I understand.'

The King held his gaze for a long moment before nodding and walking away. Killian remained where he was, still staring at Connor and Taryn. A slow burn of anger flowed through his veins as he watched the man tease her.

His anger heightened with every minute that passed. *It's what you deserve,* his common sense reminded him. *She was never going to wed a man like you.*

But she'd kissed him back. And more than that, when she'd looked upon him, she had looked upon him as if she felt something for him. As if she cared.

No one had ever cared about a man like him. They used him for their own selfish needs and walked away. He supposed that was why he wanted to be selfish for one moment in his life. He wanted to know what it was like to have a home of his own…a woman of his own. *He* knew, even if no one else did, that Taryn was a courageous, beautiful woman. He wanted to guard her, to keep her safe. For she belonged in his arms.

At the moment, Connor MacEgan was looking into her eyes with fascination.

Touch her, and you die.

His fists clenched, and he saw her blushing beneath the man's look. Not only was Connor MacEgan the brother of a king, but he had enough charm to win the heart of any woman he wanted.

And when the man dared to lean in and steal a kiss, his rage shattered. Killian crossed through the crowd, heedless of the guests and musicians. He grabbed Connor by the tunic and hauled the man backwards.

A fist slammed into his ear, and the world tipped sideways. Killian staggered, swinging until his fist connected with Connor's jaw.

'Killian, wait,' Taryn protested. 'What are you—'

'She's mine,' he gritted out to Connor. 'Do not touch her.'

A strong arm seized him, and the King jerked him back. 'I will have no fighting at this gathering.'

But Connor was already on his feet, rubbing his jaw. 'Stay out of this, Patrick. We were just having a bit of fun.' He cracked his knuckles and began circling Killian. 'It's been a long time since we've had a good fight, hasn't it, Killian?'

'A year or two,' he agreed.

'And what of the rest of you?' Connor called out to the onlookers. 'Would you be wanting us to fight for your entertainment?'

There came a raucous cheer, and Killian added, 'I'm going to break every bone in your body, MacEgan.'

Connor's answer was to beckon him forward, and the guests began placing wagers over who would win.

With reluctance, the King stepped back. 'So be it. It ends when blood is drawn.'

Killian gave a slight nod to show that he'd heard, but Taryn's stricken expression made him pause. 'Please, do not fight over me, I beg of you.'

'Now, then, Lady Taryn, that's what men do over a beautiful woman.' Connor swung a blow, and Killian dodged sideways. 'Was he telling the truth? *Are* you his?'

'He's my escort,' Taryn answered. 'And I'm not—' Her words broke off, but Killian heard the unspoken thought. *I'm not beautiful.* In her eyes, he saw the embarrassment and confusion of having two men fight over her. She wasn't at all accustomed to such a thing. And it infuriated him that she couldn't see that there *was* beauty in her.

'I'm not worth fighting over,' she finished, taking a step backwards.

'You are,' Killian disagreed. 'And it means I'll be defending your honour from anyone who dares to steal a kiss.' Especially a MacEgan.

Connor held up his fists, his weight balanced on the balls of his feet. 'Come on, then. Let's see what you remember.' He sent a flirtatious smile towards Lady Taryn. 'This will be a good fight.'

And so it would, as soon as he ground Connor's face into the dirt, Killian thought to himself. He swung a blow towards his opponent's face, but MacEgan ducked, and his fist struck only air.

Connor tried to grab him, but Killian side-stepped the man, ignoring the sudden dip in his balance. He fought to steady himself, circling his opponent in turn.

'Her lips are sweet,' Connor said. 'Worth fighting for.'

At the man's grin, Killian spun and punched the man in the stomach. It felt good to fight, to release the anger and frustration he'd been holding back for so many days. He struck the man a second time in the ribs, staggering when Connor gave an answering blow. They grappled together, and Killian forced the man to the ground. His mind blurred from the drink and from the pent-up aggression.

Jealousy tore through him. Not only because the man had dared to touch Taryn…but because Connor MacEgan had everything Killian wanted. He had a fine home, the respect of his family and friends, and enough charm to win any woman he wanted.

But damned if he'd let the man get closer to Taryn. He shoved Connor against the hard dirt of the Great Chamber. A fist cracked across his face, and the pain of the answering blow was nothing at all. This was about defending her honour.

Yet when he risked a glance at Taryn, he saw only horror on her face. 'Stop this, please,' she pleaded. 'I don't want either of you to be hurt.'

A trickle of blood formed at Connor's lip. 'You could kiss me to make it better.' Then he grinned and reached out a hand to Killian. With great reluctance, he helped the MacEgan up.

'Kiss her again, and I'll make you unconscious,' Killian swore. Dimly, he was aware of his sore jaw and a bleeding nose.

Connor clapped him on the back and said, 'The Lady Taryn can choose which of us she prefers.'

'I don't prefer either of you,' she answered. 'It was foolish for you to fight.' She turned away, walking towards the back of the gathering space. Her cheeks were red, and she lowered her face as she retreated.

Killian felt certain that she wouldn't return if he let her go, so he caught her by the wrist. 'Come with me.'

'I don't want to,' she protested. 'Just leave me be.'

But he ignored her and drew her back towards a corner of the room, pulling out two low chairs for them to sit upon. Aye, she was angry with him right now. But he wasn't about to let her go off alone. Not yet.

'You do look beautiful tonight,' he said in a low voice.

'You humiliated me in front of everyone,' she whispered. 'All of them were staring at me. It wasn't right.'

He reached for her hand, but instead of taking his palm, she reached out to touch his swollen jaw. The gentle path of her fingers sent a roaring heat through his skin.

'He kissed you, Taryn. I couldn't stand there and let him do that.' Though he knew that it was only flirtation on Connor's part, he couldn't understand the dark feelings of possession that had overcome him.

'You have no claim upon me,' she argued, looking down at her lap.

'Don't I?' He reached out, sliding his hand through her hair. 'Is it him that you're wanting?'

She turned to look at him, and her blue eyes held confusion. 'You weren't fighting over me because you found me beautiful. You were fighting because you want part of my kingdom. If I had nothing at all, you would not even look at me.'

It troubled him to know that she believed it. But more than that, she was wrong. 'I would strike down any man who tried to touch you. And land has nothing to do with it.'

Her eyes welled up, but she did not shed the tears. 'I don't believe you.' This time, when she stood up, he let her go.

His mind was muddled from the mead, and he was now beginning to feel the effects of the fight. Taryn walked towards the entrance, but the Queen stopped her from returning upstairs. They spoke together quietly, and Killian didn't miss Isabel's iron stare.

He leaned back against the stone wall, wondering why he'd reacted as violently as he had. Was it because he'd indeed formed a claim upon Taryn? Was it because he wanted her to belong to him, regardless of the land?

Her accusation, that he would not even look at her if she had no wealth, was wrong. It was a startling truth, to realise that he'd have done the same, even if she'd been naught but a serving maid.

Harold came padding towards him, weaving around his legs. Killian reached down to rub the animal's ears. The feline reached his paws up and nudged him.

Given the direction his life was going, he soon would have only animals for his companions. He needed a way of bridging the distance with Taryn, a way of regaining her trust.

He lifted the cat under his arm, intending to travel back to the tower, when he heard a slight commotion at the back of the Chamber.

The crowd shifted, and he spied Trahern MacEgan emerging, his tall form lightly dusted with snow.

And holding his hand was Carice.

Trahern MacEgan was supporting Lady Carice as she walked forward, and his expression was grim. He was a giant of a man with dark hair and a dark beard. Though he smiled warmly at his brothers and at the Queen, Taryn didn't miss the shadow in his eyes.

'Both of us are in need of food,' he called out as he helped Lady Carice walk forward. Though the woman braved a smile, it didn't meet her eyes. Something must have happened on their journey.

Killian hurried forward and embraced Lady Carice. The young woman appeared better, but she was still pale and shivering. They spoke quietly for a moment, and Carice ruffled Killian's hair the way a sister would.

When her gaze passed towards Taryn, there was an unreadable expression upon her face. Carice leaned upon Killian now as she walked, while Trahern went to speak with the King. He was leading her towards the dais, but she beckoned for Taryn to join them. It wasn't clear why, but she obeyed the silent request.

'I am glad you arrived safely,' she told Carice, while Killian helped the young woman sit down.

'So am I.' She tried to smile again, clenching her fingers to keep them from trembling. 'It was not easy to escape my father.' Carice did not elaborate further, but added, 'Has your mother pursued you here?'

Taryn shook her head. 'Not yet.' She didn't doubt that Maeve lay in waiting on the road to Tara. There was no reason for the Queen to move in pursuit, when her desire was merely to keep her daughter from pleading with the High King.

'Do you still intend to speak to King Rory?'

'Yes. The MacEgan soldiers have agreed to escort me, as well as your brother.' A flush rose over her cheeks at the thought of Killian. To disguise it, she gave Carice a trencher of roasted meats and cheeses.

'I am glad you are going,' Carice said to him. 'Your father will want to see you.'

'I've my doubts on that point,' Killian said. 'But aye, I think it's time he knew of my existence.'

The young woman toyed with the cheese and studied him. 'Be careful, Killian. Don't do anything dangerous.'

'As you say.' His gaze suddenly locked with Taryn's. This man knew how to melt her defences, how to make her feel desire. He was the last man on earth she should ever be with, and well he knew it. She decided that now was a good time to slip away. But before she could excuse herself, Carice reached out to take her hand.

'Don't go yet,' the young woman begged. 'I would like to stay and talk with you awhile.' She turned to Killian. 'Give us a few moments alone, won't you?'

He inclined his head, but before he left, he caught Taryn's gaze. The look in his eyes was enigmatic, as if he wanted to say something to her but couldn't find the words. 'As you will.'

Carice waited until he'd gone, and motioned

for Taryn to sit beside her. 'Something has happened, hasn't it?'

'I don't know what you mean.' Her words were calm, but Carice could see right through her.

'He hasn't taken his eyes off you. I've never seen my brother give such attention to a woman before.'

Because I am a means to an end, Taryn thought.

When she only shrugged, Carice probed further. 'Does it bother you, that a low-born man would desire a king's daughter?'

Taryn sent the woman a sidelong glance. 'Has Killian *ever* behaved like a low-born man?'

Carice laughed suddenly, nearly choking on her food. She took a sip of mead to clear her throat and beamed at her. 'No, never. He might be a *fuidir*, but there is no doubting he is the High King's son. And that is what I wanted to speak to you about.'

Taryn leaned in, and the woman continued. 'Knowing Killian, he will attract attention. There are tales about the High King's cruelty, of how he is a man who punishes his enemies. It is why—' Carice paused for a moment to choose her words. 'It is one reason why I did not wish to wed Rory Ó Connor.

'But…if Killian goes with you to Tara,' Carice continued, 'there is an opportunity for him to leave behind his old life. If he swears fealty to King Rory, it might be that he would have a place of his own. I do want that for him. Even if it means humbling himself before a man like the High King. Would you take him with you?'

Though she knew Carice was only trying to help the man she thought of as a brother, Taryn wanted her to know the truth. She traced the edge of a silver goblet, wondering how to put this without offending Carice. 'I agreed to give Killian a place in Ossoria, if he can save my father's life.' She deliberately said nothing about his offer of marriage.

The young women sobered. 'And if he cannot save him?'

Taryn didn't know how to answer that, but she admitted, 'He may still dwell among us. But if Rory takes command of our lands, I can do nothing.'

Carice stopped eating, and she thought for a long moment. 'Killian will have to gain the favour of the High King. And that may not be possible if they believe he was responsible for my escape.' She rested her chin on her hands, mulling it over. 'Perhaps I am wrong, and it *is* too dangerous.'

'I am going, regardless. My father will die if I don't plead for his life.' Taryn glanced over at Killian and realised that he had not taken his eyes off her. 'Besides, I have the MacEgan men to accompany me on the journey.'

Carice frowned. 'The men can protect you from any outside threats, yes. But they cannot protect you from the High King himself.'

'My face is my protection,' Taryn reminded her. 'The High King will have no interest in me.'

The young woman took a breath and shook her head. 'You misunderstand me. I mean that the High King might try to use you to punish Devlin even more. He could try to hurt you, in order to bring greater consequences to your father.'

A chill rose over her skin at the thought of being tortured at the hands of the High King. 'But I've done nothing wrong.'

'Your father has. And Rory will not hesitate to use you for his own purposes.' Carice sent her a look of sympathy. 'You should keep

Killian near you always. Trust that he will keep you safe.'

Behind her, Taryn saw Killian leaning against the wall. He was still watching, but there was a sense of isolation around him, as if he was an outsider. One of the maids sent him a warm smile, but he ignored her invitation.

Instead, all of his attention was focused upon Taryn. And she was beginning to realise that travelling with Killian MacDubh would be dangerous indeed—a temptation she'd never expected.

Chapter Eight

Killian stood by the stone hearth in the solar, warming himself while he waited on Taryn. The Queen had promised to send her there so he could have a moment to speak with her alone. And though she might not want to see him, he intended to apologise for the earlier fight.

The door to the solar opened, and Taryn stepped inside. She had removed the golden balls from her hair, and long black locks hung over her shoulders. Her face was pale, and she wore a grey *léine*. It made her appear as if she were about to go to bed, and he found himself transfixed by the simple garment. 'Isabel said you wanted to see me.'

'Aye.' Though the effects of the mead lingered, he wasn't drunk—he could feel the bruises and swollen joints from the earlier fight. 'I know you're angry with me.'

Her lips tightened. 'Now, why on earth would I be angry? Could it be because you embarrassed me in front of the MacEgan tribe by fighting with Connor?' She drew closer, her hands clenched at her sides. 'Or perhaps it's because you think I should run away and marry you.'

She was upset, he knew, but he was more interested in the way her blue eyes were shining with frustration. That sweet mouth was moving, talking about the High King and her father, but he wasn't paying any attention at all. He was more interested in the softness of that skin and what he could do to those lips.

'Connor wasn't lying, you know,' he interrupted.

'Connor? What does he have to do with this?' She crossed her arms and glared at him.

'Men *do* fight over a beautiful woman.' He caught her by the waist, keeping her there. Her face was flushed, and she appeared indignant.

'Let go of me, Killian. And I'm not a beautiful woman.'

'If I let go of you, that vicious animal might eat you,' he teased. Harold was lying on his back beside the hearth, his long body stretched out with his paws tucked up. 'I'm guarding you, don't you see?'

She elbowed him in the ribs, and struck the spot Connor had beaten earlier. Killian cursed and rubbed his side. 'Son of Lugh, woman. Was that necessary?'

'Was it necessary for you to fight over me?'

He rose to his feet gingerly, trying to breathe with the bruised ribs. 'Did you think I enjoyed watching him kiss you?'

'It meant nothing,' she protested. 'I only just met Connor MacEgan.' She blinked a moment and added, 'But I don't need to explain myself to you.'

When he approached, she backed away, until her shoulders were pressed against the wall. Killian rested his hands on either side of her. 'I didn't like seeing him kiss you.'

'Because you're afraid a man like Connor would want to wed me instead? Because you'd lose your chance to steal Ossoria from me?'

Was that what she thought? That he wanted only her kingdom?

Killian leaned in so that his face was a breath from hers. 'Do you think that's all I'm wanting from you, Taryn?'

Her blue eyes stared back at him with fury. 'Of course that's all you want. If I had no kingdom at all, you would never want anything to do with me.'

'You're wrong,' he countered. 'I'm not expecting you to believe me, but you are.' He nuzzled her earlobe, leaning in to take it in his mouth. She exhaled sharply, her hands resting on his shoulders as if to push him away.

'You do feel something for me,' he said. 'I can see the shivers rising upon your skin.' He grazed his fingers over the gooseflesh there, and she closed her eyes in response. 'I'm no good for you. And yet, you want what I offer you.'

'You have nothing to give.' She turned her face away, but though his hands remained upon the wall, she did not flee.

He stole a kiss, nipping at her soft lips. Her mouth drifted open, and he kissed her lazily, stroking her mouth with his tongue. Her fingers dug into his shoulders, but again, she did not pull away.

This time, he grew bolder, moving his hands to her waist. Lightly, he rubbed the base of her spine while he continued to kiss her. She was falling beneath his spell, her eyes closed while he seduced her with his mouth.

He moved his hands higher, and against the linen underdress, he could feel the outline of her curves. When his hands moved beneath her breasts, he deepened the kiss, asking a silent question.

'You are a wicked man,' she breathed against his mouth. 'I know what you're trying to do.'

'I cannot give you a bride price of silver or gold,' he said in a low voice. 'No riches or land. I have nothing at all.'

Her blue eyes opened, and in them, he saw a hunger that mirrored his own. He had awakened her, opening her consciousness to another kind of temptation.

'All I can give you is this.' He cupped her breasts, gently caressing the erect nipples. She jolted as if he'd set her on fire, but she only bumped against the wall. Killian paused, keeping his hands in place while he leaned in to kiss her again.

This time, he invaded her mouth with his tongue, all the while stroking her erect breasts. His own body was hard with need, and God, what he wouldn't give to take her. But this wasn't about satisfying his own lust. It was about pleasuring this woman, and showing her what there could be between them.

'Y-you should stop,' she murmured, gasping when he kissed her throat, still touching her breasts. 'I can't breathe.'

'I don't want you to breathe,' he answered, loosening her laces. 'I want you to feel the madness that's burning inside me. I want you to lose yourself to my touch.'

She was arching against him, fighting to catch her breath. And when he pushed back the shoulders of her underdress, he revealed her creamy breasts, tipped with darker nipples. Son of Lugh, she captivated him.

'I want to taste you,' he said, kissing the delicate skin of her shoulder as he moved lower. 'I want to kiss you here.' When she didn't deny him, he gave in to the impulse, trailing a path down to the rosy nipple.

She cried out when his mouth covered one breast, suckling her hard. Her hands locked in his hair, and she shuddered. Her knees buckled, and he caught her, clasping her hips and letting her feel the rigid erection. She was panting now, mindless to everything but him.

'Wed me, Taryn, and I'll touch you like this, night after night.' He took the opposite breast into his mouth while he fingered the first. She was ragged, utterly aroused. 'You can be free to do whatever you wish,' he murmured against her skin. 'No man will force you to do his bidding.'

He knew she was wet, and the image of sliding into her depths was tormenting him.

'Or if you don't want me as your husband, I'll leave you alone.' He broke away, leaving her there. Her hair was tangled around her face, her lips swollen. Her underdress hung open, exposing her large breasts with glistening nipples from his mouth. She flushed beneath his stare and tried to cover herself.

'I never meant to embarrass you in front of the castle, *a stór*,' he said. 'But I will kill any man who touches you in this way.'

Her face was crimson as she clutched her gown. 'No man has ever touched me the way you did just now.'

'And no man ever will,' he swore, stealing another kiss before he left her alone in the solar.

The next morning, Killian prepared a mount for Taryn while the MacEgan soldiers gathered supplies and their own horses. He hadn't spoken to her since last eventide when he'd touched her so intimately. All night he had ached for her, haunted by her innocent reactions. He'd wanted to watch her come apart in his arms, but instead, he'd left them both wanting. If he hadn't stopped then, he would have taken her innocence.

Carice had sworn that she would stay behind, but he'd caught a glimpse of an unknown emotion in her eyes. She was too weak to travel, he knew, and Laochre was the safest place for her. But he sensed that his sister had plans of her own that she would not say. It did seem that her health was improving, and he was glad of it.

When he saw Taryn approaching, he saw the wariness in her eyes. Her face blushed, and she admitted, 'I still don't like horses.'

Killian lifted her on to the calm mare he'd chosen. 'This one's a gentle *cailín*. She won't be harming you.'

Taryn gripped the reins so tight, her knuckles were white. 'Ride beside me, won't you, please?'

Her fear of horses hadn't diminished at all, though at least this time, she hadn't outright refused. She knew, as he did, that her father's time was running out. It would still take a few days to reach Tara, and walking was not an option.

'Are you wanting me to catch you if you fall?' he said, recognising her fear.

She sent him an embarrassed look, and he supposed that was exactly it. 'I can endure this if

I know you might be there to prevent me breaking my neck. Animals like you. They despise me.'

'Now, that's not true. Harold is quite fond of you.' To prove his point, he scooped up the cat and settled the smoke-grey feline in the basket beside her.

'Killian...' she warned, but he swung up on his own mount, bringing it beside her.

'It's only a few days. You can survive this journey,' he assured her. He was about to turn his horse around, to join the guards and servants at the end of the procession, but he saw the discomfort in her posture.

Her hood was pulled up to hide her scars, and she was staring straight ahead, her back stiff. The mare was fidgeting, conscious of her anxiety. If she didn't relax, the horse would grow skittish.

'You need to calm yourself. The mare can feel your tension.'

She gave a slight nod to show that she'd heard him, but it did nothing to diminish her rigid posture. Killian reached out and took her gloved hand. She gripped his palm tightly, and he said, 'You've done this once before. You can do it again.'

She didn't look as if she believed that at all.
To lighten the tension, he added, 'You're going
to be breaking my fingers, if you don't stop
squeezing that hard.' But still she didn't look at
him, nor did she relinquish her grip.

Killian pulled his hand back and removed
Taryn's glove, placing it in the basket beside
the cat before taking her palm in his. Her skin
was cold, and he warmed it with his own hand.
Somehow the contact did help her to settle her
nerves, and she loosened her hold.

'Steady yourself, Taryn.' He stroked her hand
with his thumb, and she let out a slow breath.
Her shoulders lowered, and he continued to
soothe her nerves.

'I know I should not be afraid.' Her voice was
wooden, holding no faith in herself.

'It takes time to let go of fear,' he said. 'And
I will be here.' He laced his fingers with hers,
and she did seem more at ease. For a while, he
rode alongside her. They remained in the midst
of the MacEgan soldiers, with men leading the
way and others behind them.

Though she didn't speak to him, he suspected
she was embarrassed by what had happened between them. All night, he had been haunted by
the visions of her soft skin and the way she'd

sighed when he'd touched her. He wanted her in a way he'd never expected. And the more he kissed Taryn, the more he craved her.

Killian fixed his gaze ahead, shifting uncomfortably in the saddle. They would ride until nightfall for the next few days. And after that, he could not say what would happen. The High King might deny that he'd ever fathered a son. Or if Killian dared to try a rescue, he might lose his life in the attempt.

There were so many paths leading towards disaster, and it all depended on the High King's decisions. Lugh, but he wished he held power of his own, a means of controlling the outcome of this.

The cat peered out from his basket and began sniffing at Taryn's other hand. She yelped when the animal placed his paw upon her hand. The mare whinnied, tossing her head at Taryn's cry.

'Easy,' Killian soothed. 'Harold was only wanting a bit of your affection.'

'He startled me.' She lowered her shoulders, visibly trying to relax. 'I cannot believe I am travelling with a cat. You should have kept him beside you.'

He took her hand once more and brought it to the animal's head. She appeared wary, but allowed him to guide her fingers. 'He likes it when you stroke his ears. A curious beastie, is young Harold.'

For a time, he guided her hand over the animal's soft fur. The cat purred contentedly, and Taryn did seem to relax. 'There, now. He does like you, do you see?'

She gave a nod. 'I suppose so. But his claws make me nervous.'

'He won't harm you,' Killian promised. He kept a gentle pressure upon her palm and met her gaze openly. Her blue eyes held wariness, and he said quietly, 'He wants to have your touch upon him.'

She looked down, biting at her lower lip, as if she'd guessed what he meant to say.

They rode away from Laochre along the main road. The horses maintained a good pace, their hooves crunching over the ice and snow upon the ground. Taryn kept her heavy cloak over her shoulders, the folds shielding her face. Though he knew what lay beyond the folds of that hood, she was one of the most striking women he'd ever seen. She wore her emotions on her face, and there was a blend of gratefulness and worry over the coming days. The instinct came over him once more, to protect this woman.

'Will you stay at my side, throughout this journey?' she asked.

'If that's what you're wanting,' he answered. 'Or if you need me to guard you from this ferocious beast.' He released her hand and reached over to scratch the cat's head. Harold leaned into his palm, purring and bumping his hand with his paw.

He smiled at Taryn, and she softened to it. A faint smile edged her mouth, and the sight of it caught him low in the gut.

'Take off the hood,' he commanded.

She grew serious. 'No. I don't want to frighten the men around me.'

'You've no reason to hide your face. Not from me or anyone else.' He suspected she'd grown accustomed to veiling her features, keeping herself apart from the world. 'Their attention is on the road ahead and the land around them. Not you.'

She hesitated, flinching when the cat pushed his head against her hand. 'I don't know if that's wise.'

'Then be unwise.' He reached out and pulled the hood off. She had not worn a veil, but her hair hung down around her shoulders. The black strands held a slight curl, and they framed her pale skin, making her features stand out even more.

She could not see past the scars to find the beauty that was there. He could see it, in the soft curve of her nose, the full lips that he'd tasted. And those eyes that looked upon him as if she saw a man, not a slave.

He'd never before met a woman like her. And when she reached for his hand once again, the gesture shot a bolt of heat through him. He imagined those hands moving over his shoulders and down lower. Her fingers had dug into his skin when he'd pleasured her, and he wanted to feel her fingertips upon him once more. Killian let her hold his hand, not even caring how it must seem to others.

'My father has only a few days left to live,' she said suddenly. 'Unless we can save him.'

He gripped her palm. 'We will try. But when we arrive at Tara, you must not let anyone know who you are. Keep yourself hidden among the other ladies at first until we know more. The High King will be angry enough that Carice is gone. Do not let anyone know that you are Devlin's daughter.'

She appeared uneasy about his orders. 'I have

to let them know. My reason for going to Tara is to beg an audience from the High King.'

Killian didn't like that idea at all. 'He may cast blame upon you for Carice's disappearance. You cannot take the risk.'

'I must,' she argued. 'Surely, he is not a heartless man.'

Aye, but he was. Rory Ó Connor was merciless to his enemies and had gained his position as High King because of his ruthless nature. Killian didn't want Taryn endangering herself by the misguided belief that he would listen to a woman's pleas.

'You cannot let him see you,' he commanded. 'It is far too dangerous.'

'I've come this far. I don't want to turn away because of cowardice.' She faced him, and her demeanour held a stubbornness that he hadn't expected.

'You don't know the King and what he will do.' How could she believe she could reason with a man who had ordered her father's execution?

'Neither do you,' she pointed out. 'And that is why we will keep on with this journey and meet our enemy face-to-face.'

Killian let go of her hand, keeping his horse

alongside hers. 'This is a mistake, Taryn. He will not heed your wishes.'

'We won't know that, unless we ask.'

Somehow, Taryn endured the journey northeast. The hours on horseback had been exhausting, and after she dismounted, it was as if the ground were still moving beneath her feet. Killian had set up a tent for her, and there were several fires outside. Though he was keeping his distance, she noticed that he had brought hot stones inside the tent to warm the space. There was also a pile of furs for sleeping, as well as a flask of wine and food he'd set aside.

Though she supposed he'd carried out the duties of a servant, it felt more personal than that. And that was her own fault.

Never should she have allowed him to kiss her or touch her so intimately. Last night, her defences had crumbled like sand against the onslaught of the feelings he'd conjured. She supposed it was her own vanity. The physical touches had made her ache inside, awakening dormant feelings of longing. And though it was likely that Killian wanted only her kingdom, for a moment, she'd wished that he wanted *her*. The rest of the world had slipped away, and she'd surrendered to the mindless feelings of desire.

As she ate, she wondered if he was dining among the other men. Would he share a tent with the other guards, or was he expected to sleep outside? The night air was bitterly cold, and she was grateful for the heat within the tent.

Inside, she felt restless, not knowing what the next few days would bring. All day, Killian had remained at her side in silent support. Although she was still frightened of horses, she was thankful that she'd managed to get through the day without being thrown off.

He didn't want her to face the High King, and likely would be even more insistent as they neared Tara. But somehow, she wanted to believe that Rory could be merciful.

There was a faint rustling outside her tent, and she saw Killian sitting in front of the opening. She went to pull back the flap and asked, 'Was there something you needed?'

He glanced at her and shook his head. 'I'll stay outside your tent to keep watch over you.' Without waiting for her to agree, he pulled a hood over him and turned his back.

Was he intending to sleep outside, in the cold? She didn't like that at all.

'I'll be fine,' she assured him. 'You may sleep with the other men and there is no need to worry about me.'

'There is always reason to worry about the safety of a woman in a camp of soldiers,' he said. 'And while most of the MacEgan men are honourable, I cannot speak for all of them.'

She didn't want to think of him sleeping outside with no shelter. But it didn't seem that he would listen to reason. He was a proud, stubborn man who would suffer outside in a winter storm before he would leave her unguarded.

'Come inside for a moment,' she told him.

He obeyed and entered the tent, closing the flap behind him to keep the heat inside. 'What is it?'

'Sit down,' she told him. Killian's gaze moved around the small space, but he obeyed. When he was seated near to the hot stones, she sat across from him. 'That's better.'

'Well?' he prompted.

'I didn't want you to be outside,' she admitted. 'You went to the trouble to get hot stones for me, so I thought you should warm yourself.'

He didn't look at all pleased by her invitation. Instead, he tried to stand up again. The space within the tent was too small and his head brushed the ceiling. 'It will only make it that much colder when I leave, Taryn.'

Her heart began to pound, but she blurted out, 'You don't have to sleep outside.' Her words came out as a whisper, and she didn't know where she'd found the courage to voice them. Colour rose to her cheeks, and she clenched her hands together. It was meant as a kindness, though she knew how it must sound.

His expression narrowed, and he moved down on one knee until he was facing her. 'What are you asking, Lady Taryn?'

She took a deep breath. 'I am asking you not to remain in the ice and cold. I would not rest well, knowing that you faced such discomfort.'

'I am a soldier and little more than a slave,' he answered quietly. 'I am used to sleeping outside.'

'I don't want you to.' Her voice came out hushed, more worried than she'd intended to sound. 'It isn't right, nor is it necessary.'

'I am your guard,' he reminded her.

And he was, but it was more than that. She squared her shoulders. 'If you want to sleep here, in a warmer space, you may.' When he didn't answer, her nerves tightened. 'Or…or if you'd rather not, you can go back to the other tents with the rest of the MacEgan soldiers. Just…not outside.' She drew her knees up, pulling the hood of her cloak over her hair to shield herself from the embarrassment.

'What would the others say about you?' he asked quietly. 'You know what they will think.'

The frustration gathered up inside, and she shrugged. 'Does it matter any more?' She had reached the end of her hopes, and now she simply didn't care. This was about giving him shelter for the night, nothing more.

He sat facing her, and beneath his gaze, she was even more wary. 'You would not invite any of these other men into your tent, would you?'

She shook her head. And though she wanted to deny that there was anything between them, she knew it was not true. 'I trust you,' was all she said. 'You would never hurt me.'

She lowered her hood once again, facing him openly. Though it was difficult to see in the darkness, she was aware of his shadowed form and the way the atmosphere between them had shifted.

'No. I would not.'

The interior of the tent seemed to close in on her, and her heart faltered at the way he was looking at her. She yearned for things she shouldn't have, and beneath her skin, she warmed to his presence. He didn't speak, and she felt the need to fill the silence. 'I also know you won't listen to me. You'll sleep outside my tent, whether I want you to or not.'

With that, he admitted, 'I would, aye.'

The amusement in his voice broke apart even more of her defences, and she recognised the danger to her heart. She was falling beneath his spell, wanting so desperately for this man to care about her. It was a foolish hope, and she steeled herself, trying to raise up her defences again.

'Are we not friends?' she asked. 'Can you not simply sleep over there and accept the comfort I offer you of a warm place to sleep?'

He moved in closer. 'You don't understand, do you?'

She had no idea what he meant. 'Understand what?'

'A beautiful woman invites a man into her tent…and you believe nothing will happen?'

Her face was on fire, but she distracted herself by rearranging the pile of furs. Was he suggesting that he was unable to resist her? She thought it very unlikely. 'Of course nothing will happen. It's a place to sleep, and I will remain on the opposite side.'

'No,' he said quietly. 'You're wrong.'

She didn't understand what he meant. Before she could ask, he continued, 'Kiss me the way you did last night. And then tell me if you think it's wise for me to share your tent.'

The blood rushed through her veins, and it suddenly felt warmer within the space. 'There's no need for that.'

'I think there is,' he countered. 'You have no grasp of what could happen.'

Her cheeks flushed, and she lowered her gaze. 'You're wrong.' But the truth was, she didn't know what was between them. He had behaved in a jealous manner when Connor had flirted with her. And he had a possessive nature, wanting to claim her and the land in Ossoria. Yet she couldn't tell what he truly desired.

He moved in closer and brought his hands to rest upon her shoulders. 'I'm not wrong, *a mhuírnín.*'

She was stunned when his mouth descended on hers. Against his mouth, she was aware of his hot breath and the way it felt to be taken like this. She could only hold on to him as he threaded his hands through her hair, capturing her lips and beckoning her towards sin. The kiss went on and on, pressing tendrils of desire through her body. She was aching to be touched, and a moan escaped her when his tongue tangled with hers.

He took her past the edge of madness, her body softening against him. Between her legs, she grew restless, wanting to know more of this carnal pleasure.

It *was* dangerous, to be taken like this. Perhaps he was trying to frighten her into pushing him away.

Instead, he was tempting her closer. She wanted to know more of this blazing desire, to be touched by a man who stole her inhibitions and made her want so much more than the life she had.

His lips travelled down her throat, and shivers rocked through her. She gripped his head, and a moment later, he laid her down against the furs. It had grown darker, and she could hardly see his face.

But she could feel his touch. His hands moved down her back, drawing him closer. He palmed her bottom, pressing her against him. Between her legs, she could feel the blunt erection press-

ing, and instead of terrifying her, it made her
want to open to him.

No husband would ever touch her like this. If
she went to her wedding night a virgin, it was
likely that he would shove her legs apart and
drive between them. He would take her only
a few times, perhaps once to consummate the
marriage, and again to conceive a child.

Or perhaps he'd never touch her again after
the first time, taking other women to satisfy
his urges.

He certainly would never kiss her senseless,
his body rocking against hers. She was ach-
ingly wet, and if Killian asked it of her, she
might have surrendered to the needs overflow-
ing inside her.

Instead, he shoved her back, cursing beneath
his breath.

'Wh-what is it?' she stammered. She hadn't
wanted him to stop, but he was behaving as if
he despised her. It took a moment for her brain
to realise that he wasn't going to continue touching her.

'Don't ask this of me, Taryn.' He was behaving as if this was her idea. She had kissed him
back, aye, but that was because she'd wanted to.

She realised suddenly that he'd kissed her in

an attempt to frighten her, so she would force him out. Her response wasn't at all what he'd expected.

Likely, he hadn't wanted her to kiss him back. A pang of hurt formed inside her, but she sat up and faced him. 'I offered you a place to sleep, so you wouldn't be out in the cold,' she pointed out. 'I never invited you to share anything more. And if it bothers you to be so close to me, perhaps you *should* go back to the soldiers and stay with them. It matters not to me.'

Killian stood without speaking a word. Then he left, as if nothing at all had happened.

Taryn closed off the entrance, tying it shut. Her heart was still beating rapidly, and her feelings were bruised from this. She should have known that this was a mistake.

He's not your friend, her common sense reminded her. *This is about his own personal gains. Not you.*

She huddled in the furs, even knowing that sleep would not comfort her this night.

Chapter Nine

They rode out the next morning, through the forest and past the brooks and waterfalls. After travelling most of the day, they reached the region of Glendalough. The ancient round tower stood high, clustered by stone outbuildings used by the monks. Then they continued riding further north, until they reached an older road at the top of the hillside. From here, the green hills embraced the land, while a silver lake gleamed against the morning sun. It was a serene landscape, and few of the men spoke.

Killian's mind took no peace from their surroundings. He'd distanced himself from Taryn, not understanding what had happened last night. She had granted him a place within her tent, and he'd behaved cruelly in return.

The truth was, she saw past the walls of stone

and ice surrounding his heart. She had offered a friendly warmth that he wasn't used to. Women wanted him for only one thing—to warm their beds. And though he'd taken his pleasure from it, it had never been anything but emptiness.

Last night, when he'd kissed her, her response had taken him apart. Her eager willingness to meet his kiss and the sweet taste of her tongue had made him want to lay her down and slide into her wet folds. He was angry with himself for trying to push her away, only to find out that she was a woman of passion.

He knew that no man had ever given her such attention. She was isolated from common men and didn't understand the consequences of her actions. Another man could take advantage of her innocence, and Killian might not be able to stop him.

Rage tightened inside at the thought of anyone touching her. Taryn deserved a man who could protect her, honouring her. And though he knew he was unworthy of wedding a woman of her stature, he craved the scent of her hair, the softness of her curves.

He urged his horse faster, the frustration beating stronger within him. In the distance, he saw the road curving through the hills, down into a valley. A flash of silver caught his eye, along with motion.

He rode faster, trying to grasp what it was he was seeing. And the moment it became clear, he turned the horse around and went to speak with Taryn. She hardly met his gaze, her eyes locked upon the green hills. There was an icy chill in her demeanour, as if she didn't want to speak with him at all.

'We have a problem,' he told her. 'Your mother's men are waiting for us in the valley. They are camped along the side of the road.'

She grimaced but nodded. 'I was expecting that. She knows I am travelling to Tara, and there is only one road leading in that direction.'

'We don't have to stay on the roads,' he pointed out. 'If you're wanting to avoid them.'

'No,' she said quietly. 'I suppose I must face her and make it clear that I will not abandon my father.'

He agreed with that. Queen Maeve would not stop hunting for Taryn, and they needed to come to an agreement now, before they reached Tara. 'Do you want to ride ahead of the others and meet with her?'

She thought a moment and agreed. 'I suppose there's no need to bring the rest of them into our disagreement. They can maintain their pace, and we'll ride ahead.'

'Can you manage on the horse?'

There was a glimpse of fear on her face, but she shrugged. 'I don't like the idea of going faster, but I suppose I have no choice.'

'Lean in and let your mare follow my horse,' Killian said. 'And don't try to pull her too hard.' He didn't miss the fear she was trying to hide. But she had managed to stay on the horse thus far.

He led them towards the front of their travelling party and told the MacEgan men to keep their distance until they had come to an understanding. There was no need to provoke a fight between the soldiers. To Taryn, he said, 'Stay close, and don't fall behind.'

She inclined her head and nudged the mare faster. Her fingers gripped the reins, and Killian urged his horse into a hard canter. Glancing behind, he saw her following, though her eyes were tightly closed.

The road shifted downward, and though she leaned forward as he'd instructed, he didn't know if she knew how to command the horse to stop. He kept the horses together, bringing them down into the valley. Mile after mile they travelled, until he saw that Maeve had gathered her soldiers together on the road to block their path.

So be it.

When they were within a few hundred paces, he moved his mount beside Taryn's and seized the reins of her horse. Slowly, he guided the horses into a trot and finally into a walk. Only then did she open her eyes.

Her face was flushed, her mouth tight, but she gathered her composure. As she drew closer to her mother, she straightened in the saddle.

Maeve walked forward, her expression holding back a mixture of worry and anger. Killian pulled his horse to a stop, letting Taryn go to meet her mother alone. For a moment, the Queen studied her daughter, as if determining whether she was unharmed. Taryn dismounted and then beckoned for Killian to come closer.

He swung his leg off the horse and led it by the reins, seizing her mount as well. He decided to play the role of servant in this, for it was less threatening.

'You can go no further,' Maeve was telling Taryn. 'We must return to Ossoria.'

'You've been waiting on me all this time?' she guessed. 'You must know that I have no intention of abandoning my father.'

Her mother's gaze turned discerning. 'I know that you are as stubborn as always, and you do not believe what I have said. But Devlin is not worth saving. Come, and we will speak.'

Taryn turned and gestured for Killian to come with them. He held himself motionless, knowing it was not his place to accompany her.

'I will speak with you,' she told her mother, 'but only if Killian is present.'

The Queen cast him a look, and her face paled. She looked as if she were about to say something but held her tongue. 'We will walk through the hills for a moment. He may protect you, but he does not need to hear what I have to say.'

'He will hear everything,' Taryn argued. 'Else, I will not go.'

The Queen shook her head. Killian could tell that the nature of the conversation was nothing she wanted an escort to overhear. But he merely walked the horses over to a tree and tethered them, letting them graze. And when Taryn summoned him to join her, he obeyed.

Maeve sent him a dark look and said, 'I would prefer it if your servant left us. This is not for his ears.'

'He is not my servant.' Taryn straightened

and added, 'Furthermore, I trust Killian more than I would ever trust you. He has kept me safe, and he has sworn to help Devlin.'

Maeve's expression twisted, but she relented. When he reached Taryn's side, the Queen frowned. 'I know who you are. Rory's blood runs in your veins.'

He didn't respond, but sent her a slight nod to show that he'd heard her.

'I will not let you go any further on this journey,' Maeve told her daughter. 'You cannot risk your life for Devlin. I won't allow it.'

'I know you do not care for him,' Taryn began. 'But he does not deserve to die in that way. Surely you must recognise all that he has done for our people.'

'I despise him,' Maeve snapped. 'Believe me when I say that we are all better off without him. The High King is delivering justice that was owed to us years ago.'

Killian saw the dismay on Taryn's face, and he took a step closer to her. Though he didn't know why the Queen loathed her husband, he didn't miss the protective way she watched her daughter.

'What is this justice you speak of?' Taryn asked softly. 'All you've ever done is speak ill of him. What did he do except keep the peace in Ossoria? And all you did was issue orders of how everything was to be done, how quickly, and in what manner. You treated everyone like a slave. Whereas he—'

'You know not of what you speak,' Maeve said. 'I did keep a tight rein over our servants and tribe members, yes. To protect them from his anger.'

Taryn sent a look back towards Killian, and her face revealed her disbelief. 'My father was never angry with anyone.'

'Because I placated him. I obeyed his orders and ensured that everyone did his bidding without question.'

Killian studied the Queen and saw traces of fear, not a woman who was desperate for power. He was beginning to wonder if Taryn's father had revealed only what he'd wanted her to see.

'If you believe that he was a kind man, you are wrong,' Maeve said. 'You know nothing of the sort of person he was.'

'That's not true.'

Killian moved forward and rested his hands upon Taryn's shoulders, heedless of the Queen's glare. He wanted her to know that she need not listen to any of this. In silent answer, she reached up and clasped his hand.

'It is true,' the Queen insisted. 'Those scars happened because of *him*.' Her face was bone white, and when she met Killian's stare, there was anguish within it.

'What do you mean?' Taryn's voice held the coolness of a woman who didn't believe the Queen's words.

'After your brother died, Devlin went into a fury. You know how he doted upon Christopher. He blamed you for the accident. When you ran towards your brother, the horse reared up.'

Taryn's hand tightened upon his, but she said nothing.

'He was furious,' she said quietly. 'I had never seen him so angry. He held on to Christopher's body, grieving…and then a…a sort of madness came over Devlin. He set his dogs upon you,' Maeve continued. 'They ripped your face apart and would have killed you, had I not stopped them.'

A violent anger roared through him when Killian heard this. If it were true, then the Queen was right. Devlin deserved to die.

Tears were streaming down the Queen's face. 'Every day that I see you, I blame Devlin. I was devastated when Christopher died, but I would never have punished you. You were only four years old.'

Taryn's voice was cool. 'If that was true, then why did you stay with him? Why didn't you tell me what happened?' The tone of her voice suggested that she didn't believe Maeve.

The woman's shoulders were trembling, and she added, 'I had nowhere else to go. And I was afraid of what else he might do to both of us if I tried to take you away.' Her face whitened. 'He spent a great deal of time with you. At first I thought it was his remorse for what he did. But I never stopped worrying that he might lose his temper again. I promised myself I would help you find a husband quickly to get away from Devlin.' The Queen pressed her fist to her mouth, as if trying to keep herself from saying too much.

A hardness formed in Killian's gut at Devlin's actions. But Taryn was shaking her head in disbelief. 'No. I cannot believe my father caused these scars. He would never hurt me.'

Killian kept an arm around her, intending to guide her back. He couldn't be certain what was true, but there was no questioning Maeve's desire to protect Taryn.

The Queen straightened her shoulders. 'I swore that I would never let anything happen to you again. And I will keep that promise.'

Taryn didn't reply, and Killian saw the doubts upon her face. She had gone motionless, and without a word, she began walking back towards the horses. His instinct was to follow, but instead, he faced Maeve. He wanted to judge whether or not she was telling lies.

'I won't let my daughter go to Tara,' the Queen said. 'She can't endanger herself like that. But more than that, Devlin should not be freed.'

If her words were true, then he agreed with Maeve. But the Queen had not yet finished. 'Know this. I will take my daughter back to Ossoria by force if I must. I care not if she hates her imprisonment. Her well-being means more to me than her feelings.'

'If you take her by force, she will despise you,' Killian countered. 'She will blame you for his death.'

'Devlin deserves to die,' she shot back.

'Maybe. But let her learn that for herself. Or she'll be hating you forever.' He crossed his arms and stared at the Queen. This was not her decision to make.

'Better for her to hate me than to die at the High King's hands.' In her eyes, he saw the cold resolution. Maeve was never going to let Taryn go. 'He will use her. And I cannot allow Rory to hurt my daughter.'

'I will not let any harm come to her,' he countered. 'I am the High King's son. And that gives me a means of protecting her.'

'*I* will protect my daughter. And you will not interfere with that.'

He faced her and saw the underlying fear in her eyes. She might be insistent upon keeping Taryn away from the High King, but there was more to this. He sensed that she was hiding more secrets, and there were strong reasons why she had kept all of this from her daughter.

Or if she was indeed lying—to rid herself of an unwanted husband and claim the kingdom for herself—then he would only learn the truth by confronting Devlin.

'The choice is Taryn's,' he said. 'If your daughter wants to continue her journey, you will not stop us.' He sent her a hard stare, letting her know that he would not yield in this. Then he turned and strode back towards Taryn.

She was standing alone, staring off at the silvery lake. Her face had gone pale, and the dark strands of her hair hung against her cheeks, barely disguising the scars. Her hands were gripped together, and he came to stand beside her.

'You believe her, don't you?' Her words were tinged with ice. 'You're not going to let me save him.'

'*Is* she telling the truth? Do you remember what happened to you?'

Taryn shook her head slowly. 'I don't, no. I remember falling hard and—' she closed her eyes against the memory '—the terrible pain of my face being torn. Someone pulled me away from the dogs, but I never saw who it was.'

She reached up to touch the scars, turning her blue eyes towards him. 'I always believed it was my father who got me out. I never thought he could ever hurt me.' She shook her head. 'I still can't believe it. But I don't know why Maeve would try to turn me against him. Is it because she wants to rule Ossoria alone?' Frustrated tears welled up in her eyes, but she would not let them fall.

Damn it all, but he was weak when it came to vulnerable women. Without asking, he pulled her into an embrace. She stiffened the moment he touched her, but he didn't let go yet. Instead, he rubbed her spine lightly. 'She's going to try to force you to go back with her.' There was so much tension radiating from her, and he didn't know if it was anger or something more. He stroked the back of her head, letting the silky strands fall through his fingertips. 'What do you want to do?'

She glared at him. 'I want you to take me to the High King. I want to move forward and forget about her lies.'

He didn't ask what she would do if the Queen wasn't lying. Taryn would have to make that decision for herself when she saw her father. And if it turned out that King Devlin was not to be trusted, Killian fully intended to leave him where he was.

'Release me, Killian,' she demanded.

'Not yet. Your mother is watching us.' He moved his palm up her spine. 'And I know how to free you from her commands. She will have no choice but to let you go.'

Her blue eyes narrowed with confusion. 'No matter what you say to her, Maeve will never give up.'

In that, Taryn was wrong. There was a way to force the Queen's hand. 'If you want to see your father again, follow my lead,' he said. 'I swear to you, I can get you out of here without violence. She will have no choice.'

Taryn would be indignant and furious, but the deception would work. He grazed her cheek with his thumb. There was worry in her eyes, but he took her face between his hands. He was well aware that Maeve was watching them, and this would work to their advantage.

Lightly, he leaned in and kissed Taryn. 'Trust in me.'

What was he doing? Taryn wanted to fight against his kiss, to push him away and demand an explanation. But he was doing this for a reason. She knew, after last night, that he wanted to show Maeve that there was more between them than a lady and her guard. But why?

The softness of his mouth poured over her like a river of suppressed needs. She couldn't deny that she craved his mouth upon hers, or that she enjoyed his touch. But her cheeks were burning at the knowledge that they were being watched.

And soon enough, as she'd expected, Maeve hurried forward. 'Take your hands from my daughter, *fuidir*.'

Killian kissed her harder, as if to taunt the

Queen. Then he pulled back, his silver eyes demanding that she do everything he asked.

She didn't want to. He was domineering, demanding that she bend to his will. For a servant, he had more arrogance than any man she'd ever met. And she suspected that his actions had something to do with getting the land he wanted.

'We are returning to the rest of our men,' he told Maeve. His arm slid around Taryn's waist in a blatant show of possession.

'She will go nowhere with you.' The Queen gestured for her men to step forward, and Killian placed his hand upon the blade at his waist.

'In that, you are wrong, Queen Maeve. No longer do you have the right to say where Taryn goes.'

What was he doing? Taryn couldn't quite grasp it, but she held her tongue, waiting for the answers.

'I am her mother,' Maeve insisted, striding forward until she stood before them. 'I have every right.'

'And I am her husband,' Killian answered. 'That gives me command over her. Not you.'

Taryn blinked at the lie, her heart pounding.

She buried her face in his shoulder, knowing that her expression would give everything away if she dared to look at her mother.

Her husband. Someone she had sworn he would never be—and yet, she saw the wisdom of the deception. A husband *did* have the right to command his wife, over her parents' wishes. She became his property, to do with as he wished.

Her mother's face went white with rage. 'I don't believe you. You could not do such a thing.'

'We took sanctuary at the round tower,' he informed her. 'And we said our vows before we left, in the presence of the priest there.'

Her mother was arguing that it was impossible, that such a marriage could never be real. But when she lifted her head, Killian was facing down the Queen, his gaze like ice. 'I am taking my wife back to our travelling companions. You will allow us to continue our journey without interference.'

'My daughter would *never* wed a slave,' the Queen insisted. But Taryn saw the flicker of doubt in her mother's eyes.

'I am not a slave.' Killian released her and took a step forward, using his height to intimidate her mother. 'I am the High King's son. And it is my right to bring her home to Tara.'

That put an end to her mother's protests. Taryn could see the shock giving way to fear. No, Killian had not admitted that he was a bastard. But it seemed that he bore a strong enough resemblance to the High King that her mother could not deny it.

Taryn felt the need to say something, instead of remaining silent. She moved forward and took Killian's hand. 'What he says is true, Mother. And we are going to leave now.'

'I don't believe you,' Maeve snapped. 'Why would the High King's son choose a bride with a scarred face…when he could have anyone else? And why would he wed a traitor's daughter?' She shook her head, refusing to acknowledge the possibility.

Black rage covered Killian's face. 'Do not speak ill of your own daughter.' His hand remained upon the hilt of his dagger. 'I would suggest that you leave us. Now.'

'The marriage can be annulled,' the Queen started to argue, but Taryn held up a hand.

'No. It will not be.' Daring a look at Killian, she realised he was right. This truly was the best way of overcoming her mother's control. 'The marriage has already been consummated.'

Maeve paled, but sent Taryn a look. 'This isn't finished. I will never let you endanger yourself at Tara.'

'She is under my protection,' Killian answered. 'And you can do nothing to change it.'

Her mother's mouth set in a hard line. 'We will accompany you to Tara,' she stated. 'My men will join with yours.'

And I will learn if you are lying, her tone seemed to say.

Taryn stared back at her. 'I care not what you do. But I intend to find out the truth about my father.' She put her arm around Killian's waist to underscore her words. There was a hint of approval in his eyes, and he led her back towards their horses.

In a whisper, she leaned in. 'I cannot believe what you just said to my mother. But it worked.'

'Of course it did.' He appeared entirely confident in the ruse. And although she could not know what would happen once they reached Tara, for now, she was grateful to him. She could travel freely, with no worry about an army pursuing them.

Relief filled her up, and he lifted her on to

her horse. His hands lingered upon her waist for a moment, and his expression turned enigmatic. After he swung up to his own mount, he sent her a sidelong look.

'Is something the matter?' she asked, as they began their journey back to the MacEgan men.

His eyes held a glint of wickedness. 'Well, now, that all depends, *a mhuirnín.*'

'On what?' She urged her horse forward alongside his.

'If we are now "married", then it seems that we'll now be sharing a tent,' he said. There was an unspoken question, one that warmed her skin with promise.

She understood what he was asking, and she straightened in the saddle. 'Don't fear, Killian. Your virtue is safe with me.'

And with a smile, she rode back to the men.

Chapter Ten

The Queen was as good as her word. The moment Killian returned with the MacEgan soldiers, she joined them. Though Maeve did not dare to issue commands, she kept a close eye upon Taryn.

He was well aware that she didn't believe their story at all. Her insistence upon controlling her daughter, though out of a mother's love, had made him realise that only a husband had the right to supersede Maeve's authority.

Taryn, thankfully, had recognised the deception as a best means of reaching Tara with no further interference. He had no doubt that her mother would have prevented a marriage at all costs. It was only his resemblance to the High King that made her falter. She would learn, soon enough, that he was a bastard. But for now, he had the right to travel with the Lady Taryn.

They would reach Tara within another day or two. Night was falling, and he finally chose a place to make camp. Taryn was looking weary, but he knew she was grateful that she still had her freedom, such as it was.

He set up their tent away from the others, knowing that they would have to share a space tonight. The thought of being so near to her was a raw temptation, and he worried that he would be unable to keep his distance. Each night, he thought more about touching this woman, about lying beside her.

The truth was, he wanted her with a fierce need he didn't understand. He was like a flask of oil, ready to ignite with a single flame. Every time he kissed her, he thought of what it would be like to pleasure this woman, to teach her what it was to surrender to his touch.

They ate among the other men, and he didn't miss the Queen's resentful look when he escorted Taryn back to their tent. But his so-called bride took his hand and went with him obediently.

Instead of walking inside the tent, she stopped him for a moment. 'She is watching us.'

He knew that and didn't care. 'She doesn't believe what we told her.'

Taryn nodded. 'Will the men tell her the truth?'

Killian shook his head. He'd given orders to one of the MacEgan captains to spread the word among the soldiers. The guard had understood the need immediately, and he was confident that the men would maintain the illusion to prevent bloodshed.

He took Taryn's hands, and she lifted her face to his. In the shadowed moonlight, her eyes glowed. 'I suppose, in this instance, I am using you to avoid a conflict with my mother. But you needn't worry that it will come to anything more than this.'

He lifted her hands to his chest. God help him, but he had never desired anyone more than this woman. He traced her scarred cheeks with his thumbs, not caring that most of the camp was finding a reason to watch their shadowed silhouettes. 'I think we are using each other, *a stór*. And this night, I find that I don't care.'

He claimed her mouth in a fierce kiss, needing to taste the lips that had haunted him. She yielded to him, kissing him back and opening to him. Against his mouth, she whispered, 'Are they still watching us?'

'Aye, they are.' He drew her hips to his, knowing that she could feel the length of his arousal.

'Good. Perhaps my mother will believe this.' She deepened the kiss, opening her mouth and touching her tongue to his. Her boldness sent a white-hot bolt of desire rocking through him. He met her kiss with his own, ravaging her mouth until he could hardly remember anything at all. She tempted him beyond measure, and he hissed when she slid her hands down to his hips, moving her body against his.

'You're pushing against the boundaries, Lady,' he murmured against her ear. He sucked at the soft lobe, and she released a gasp. 'Do you know what I'm wanting to do to you now?' She shook her head, shuddering when he trailed a path to her throat. Her responses were innocent and so perfect, he could spend all night touching her.

'I'm wanting to run my hands beneath your skirts. I want to caress your ankles, rising up between your thighs.' At her shocked expression, he added, 'Aye, *a mhuírnín*, I'd touch you there, too. And if you were wet, I'd pleasure you until you were desperate to take me inside you.'

Her face was flushed, and he drew his hands over her bottom, moving his thigh between her legs. She clung to him for balance, and he said, 'I could lift your skirts and put myself inside you. You'd feel me moving within your body.'

Her fingers dug into his shoulder, and he could see her eyes staring into his with her own arousal. When he moved his leg, she let out a faint moan.

'Your legs would be wrapped around my waist while I thrust inside you,' he said. And she closed her eyes as if to imagine it.

Without asking, he led her inside the tent and drew the flap shut. In the darkness, he could no longer see her face. But he sensed that he'd brought her to a desire she'd never felt before.

'Killian,' she whispered. 'What you said outside…it made me feel so…' Her words drifted off, as if she was too embarrassed to speak.

'I don't think anyone would doubt now that our *marriage* is consummated. They saw enough.'

He was giving her the chance to pull back from him, to sleep on her side of the tent and maintain her virtue. But inside, he was aching for her. He wanted to do exactly as he'd said, sliding into her body and thrusting until she cried out from the pleasure of it.

'They did, yes,' she whispered.

He heard a slight rustling as if she were lying down upon the furs. 'And I am grateful for what you said to my mother today. It might have been a lie, but you convinced her it was truth.'

Killian doubted if the Queen believed them, but she had not tried to stop them. It made him wonder whether Maeve was telling lies of her own.

Silence fell between them, and he stretched out on the cold ground. Despite the leather ground covering, he could feel the frost beneath his cheek. His shaft was aching, and he gritted his teeth against the discomfort. He'd brought this on himself by touching her.

It was only to prove to others that she is yours. Not because you care about her.

Not because he had grown to admire her over the past sennight, in the way she fought for someone she loved. In the way she continued to believe in him, despite what others had said. Taryn was a woman of fierce loyalty, and he envied Devlin for that.

'Killian,' she whispered. 'Why did you touch

me like that, in front of everyone? It wasn't necessary to go that far.' Her voice held no chas-
tisement; instead, he detected an emotion he
couldn't read.

'You know why.'

'But…what you said to me outside this tent.
There was no reason to say those words, for no
one could hear you.'

That was it. He heard the shyness of disbelief
in her words. He moved in closer until he was
lying beside Taryn, his knees touching hers. 'Do
you not believe that you are a desirable woman?'

'I don't know what to believe.' She rested
her folded hands against his chest. 'Most men
don't look at me in that way. I've grown accustomed to it.'

'Most men are fools.' He reached out to cup
her cheek, running his hands through her hair.
Though he kept the touch light, his imagination roared with forbidden visions. He wanted
to touch her bare skin, to make her feel things
she had never felt before.

Taryn said nothing, but her fingers moved
against his chest in a silent caress. 'Last night—
when I invited you in, it was only meant to be
an offer of shelter.'

He didn't take his hand from her hair. 'Being

with you at night is dangerous to both of us, *a mhuírnín.*' And though he knew he could not leave her now, he sensed that the boundaries between them were shifting.

'I am not afraid of you.' She reached for his palm and covered it with hers. 'I am more afraid of what will happen at Tara.'

He could give her no answer, for they both knew the danger that lay ahead. 'What are you most afraid of?'

She moved in closer, turning to rest her cheek against his heart. He wrapped his arms around her, breathing in the scent that haunted him at night. 'I'm afraid that I'll be powerless to help my father. That I'll be forced to watch him die, and there will be nothing I can do to save him.'

There was a soft tremor in her body, and he held her close. Her pain reminded him of what he'd felt for Carice—of all the years of helplessness, wondering when she would die. And though his sister was now safe, he knew the illness could take her at any moment.

'Do you think Devlin was to blame for your scars?' he asked.

'No.' Her answer held the quiet weight of a daughter's love. 'I don't know why she said what she did. Maybe it was greed. Or maybe it was her own hatred. But I can never believe that my father would do anything to harm me.'

The whisper of her voice held years of pain and regret. He stroked back her hair, not knowing what to say. But the sudden intimacy between them was like nothing he'd known before. Here, in the dark, it seemed as if she was laying herself bare before him.

'I used to go out walking with him. He talked to me, and no matter what Mother said, he did care about me.' She paused a moment and added, 'I know he had a terrible temper. My parents fought often, and I tried never to make him angry. He liked it when I obeyed him and remained quiet while he talked.'

Killian said nothing, but her remark sent a warning through him. 'And what did your mother think about the time you spent with him?'

Taryn pulled back. 'She hated it. I never could tell whether it was jealousy that he spent time talking with me or whether she was afraid of him. Maybe she thought he would set their marriage aside and send her away.'

Killian said nothing, but inwardly, he sensed that there *was* a threat towards Taryn. And whether it came from her father or her mother, he couldn't be certain. But he remained guarded, not trusting either of her parents.

'I don't know what will happen any more,' she continued. 'I don't know if my father will live or die.' She paused for a long moment and touched her fingertips to his face. 'And I don't know if you'll help me or leave. For you only want my kingdom…and that is not in my power to give.'

He wasn't going to leave her. Though he cared nothing about King Devlin, he wasn't going to walk away from Taryn Connelly. Although she now had the MacEgan soldiers, she needed someone who could intercede with the High King on her behalf.

'It is not only your kingdom that I want,' he said, moving his hand down her spine. The curves of her body pressed close to his, and the ties of her gown rested beneath his palm.

A tremor passed over her at his words. 'I don't need your pity, Killian.'

Deliberately, Killian caressed the puckered skin upon her cheek. 'These do not define who you are.'

'Yes. They do.' She covered his hands with hers and pulled them back from the scars. 'And I am well aware of it.'

His skin tightened with the knowledge that she had been hurt for so long. Selfishly, he wanted to push back all the years of pain, teaching her what it was to be admired.

'Don't say it,' he commanded. He didn't want her to be anything other than what she was. 'You are beautiful, Taryn. Anyone who cannot see that is unworthy of you.'

He kissed her lips lightly, even knowing that it would not convince her. It was a kiss of invitation, a silent thanks. But this time, she did not kiss him back.

'I think you are only saying what I want to hear,' she said against his mouth. 'This isn't real.'

He understood that she was trying to distance herself, to prevent him from touching her. She was vulnerable this night, wanting him to stay away. Words would not convince her. But perhaps actions would.

'Then believe this is real.' He took her mouth again, not letting her catch her breath. He kissed her hard, tasting her and enjoying the rush of sensation that roared through him. It was reckless and unrelenting, in an attempt to show her how desirable she was. He slid his tongue inside her mouth, coaxing her response, before he pulled back.

'Did you think I liked watching Connor MacEgan kiss you the other night?' He captured her face between his hands, forcing her to look at him. 'Does he make you feel this way?'

She rested her forehead against his. 'No one makes me feel the way you do.' This time when he kissed her, she responded with her own kiss. Her tongue met his tentatively, and he never ceased his assault upon her senses. He wanted her to stop thinking about the past, to live only in this moment.

Her hands moved around his neck, drawing him closer. Her legs were twisted in her skirts, and she adjusted her position until she raised one knee, bringing him closer on top of her.

God above. No longer was he the conqueror, but instead, he was trying to learn what she wanted. Her hands moved beneath his tunic and the hauberk of chain mail, her fingers caressing his back. A surge of heat flooded through him. And if nothing else happened this night, he wanted her to know that she had a profound effect upon him.

'Whatever you want this night, Taryn, I will give.' He wanted to spend the hours pleasuring her, until there were no doubts that he desired her. He was so aroused, craving this woman in a way that went deeper than the need to breathe. 'I will be a slave to what you need, if that is your wish.'

Taryn broke away, tracing the lines of his face. 'You are not a slave and never will be, Killian MacDubh.'

Her words were an invisible touch upon him. Never had she treated him as a *fuidir*. When he was with her, she seemed to see the man he was instead of the servant. He could not deny that he wanted her in a way he could never understand. She was his, and he would kill any man who dared to touch her.

'I am yours to command, Lady. So long as I have permission to touch you the way I'm needing to.' He loosened her laces, wanting her. Were it possible, he would rend the gown in half to bare what he desired.

She was quiet, giving no answer yet. 'And what if my kingdom is taken from me? What if my father is killed and there is nothing left?'

'Your kingdom be damned,' he answered. The only thing he cared about was protecting Taryn.

He lowered her gown, baring one shoulder.

His baser instincts were raging within him, and he wanted to take her over the edge of release.

She kissed him again, and he spoke against her mouth, 'If we continue this, Lady Taryn, I won't be able to stop touching you. Your innocence will belong to me.'

God help her, but she wanted that. She wanted this man to touch her, to satisfy the longings that burned within her. And though a maiden was meant to save her virtue for a husband, she rather doubted if she would ever marry. This might be her one chance to discover what a bride felt upon her wedding night.

'What is your command, my lady?' Though he spoke as if he were her servant, she knew differently. *He* would reign over her, touching her in the way he wanted to. And she did want to experience the same thrilling touches he'd given her before.

'Remove your clothes,' she said softly.

'Only if you do the same.'

She pulled back from him and got to her knees. Though her hands were shaking, she removed her overdress and set it aside. Her *léine* beneath it was made of linen, and in the cold night air, her breasts puckered against the fabric.

Beside her, she heard Killian removing his own garments, setting aside the armour.

Don't be afraid, she tried to tell herself. *He will not hurt you.*

Of that, she had no doubt. And for once in her life, she wanted to know what it was like to feel cherished…beloved even. She had no doubt at all that Killian's touch would feel wonderful.

'Let me help you,' he offered. But instead of removing the *léine*, he pressed her body beneath his. The heat of his skin was welcome, but she could not stop herself from shaking. She could feel the outline of every hardened muscle, the planes of his body shielding hers.

He balanced his weight on both arms, and he lightly kissed her. 'Are you certain this is what you're wanting, *a mhuírnín*?'

'Yes.' She didn't doubt her decision—it was only her fears of the unknown that held her back. 'I want you to touch me the way you did before.'

'Don't be afraid.' He shifted his weight so he was lying on his side, but he lifted her leg over his hip. She was aware of his hardened shaft nestled against the fabric of her *léine*, and the knowledge that it would soon be inside her made her grow wet between her legs.

His hand passed over her shoulder to her breast. She bit back a moan when his fingers found the tight nub and stroked the nipple. The urge came, to press herself against his arousal, and he let out a hiss of air when she did.

'Not yet, *a ghrá*. We've all night for this.'

Although the linen *léine* was normally soft against her skin, tonight it felt almost abrasive. It was an unnecessary barrier, and she wanted his hands against her bare skin. 'Help me take this off,' she urged.

But there came only a low laugh. 'Later.'

He pressed her back, stroking both breasts with his fingers. The tremulous sensations echoed between her thighs, and she squirmed against him.

'I love the way these fill my hands,' he murmured, cupping both breasts. 'I want to suckle them and make you moan.' He fingered the nipples, and they hardened, sending a flood of heat between her legs. 'I dreamed of you last night.'

His words wove a spell over her, and she reached out to his chest, feeling the ridges of muscle beneath her palms. 'Tell me.' She stroked him, learning the shape of his torso and the way his body felt beneath her hands.

'I dreamed of tasting you like this.' He bent

his mouth to her nipple and sucked her through the fabric. Tempestuous needs stormed through her, and she dug her fingers into his dark hair, her legs tangled against his. He sucked and nibbled, and she was arching against him, wanting so badly to be joined with this man.

The feelings gathered up into a tight ball of desire, and it was as if he were unlocking a secret part of her. This time, he moved lower, grasping the hem of the *léine* and drawing it up to her waist. His fingers skimmed her thighs, opening them gently as he moved higher.

She realised what he wanted, and though she was embarrassed, she parted her legs. His fingers moved to her intimate place, and he let out a low growl when he touched the wetness there.

'You're ready for me, aren't you, *a ghrá*? This is where you want me to be.' He slid a single finger inside her, and she couldn't stop the cry that broke forth. Slowly, he moved the finger in and out, coating it with her essence. His thumb moved against the delicate skin above her entrance, and she felt a blossoming sensation.

'Don't stop,' she commanded.

And he obeyed. He was opening her, preparing her for the invasion of his flesh. In return, she reached out to him, feeling the large erection. He was so thick, she could hardly curl her palm around him, and he stilled when she began to stroke his velvety shaft.

'What else do you want of me?' he asked. 'Shall I kiss you here?' He passed his fingers along the wet seam of her entrance, and the shocking idea made her shudder.

'Later,' she said.

She continued caressing his length as he guided her to sit up. It was a revelation to touch his bare shaft, to feel the bead of moisture at the thick head, her palm surrounding him. The slightest motion made him react, and she gave in to her curiosity, enjoying the way he gasped at her attention.

'This is about you,' he said, removing her *léine* at last. 'I want to pleasure you until you can't hold back your scream.'

But she was finding her own pleasure in touching him. In the darkness, she could almost pretend that she was a woman of beauty, that he truly didn't see the scars. When she transformed her rhythm, moving her hand up and down, he suddenly forced her back, pinning her wrists to the ground.

'Enough,' he said. 'I won't last if you keep doing that.' He kissed her again, and she pulled his hips on top of her. The feeling of his hard length nestled against her curls was so tempting. His tongue entered and withdrew, just as he reached down to slide his finger inside her. The sensation drove her wild, and she arched against him.

She was desperate for more, and he guided the tip of himself into her wet entrance. Taryn braced herself for the joining that would come, knowing there would be pain when she surrendered her virginity.

Instead, Killian didn't move. He remained barely inside her, and with one hand, he began stroking the hooded flesh above her opening. Every part of her was sensitive to him, craving his body inside hers.

'I won't join with you until you've been well pleasured,' he swore. Though she didn't understand what he meant by that, she gasped when he began suckling her breast. It felt as if her body were turning itself inside out, fighting against the onslaught of arousing feelings. She was unable to stop herself from moving her hips, and he kept up the rhythm, stroking her into a frenzy. Her body was trembling hard, and a white-hot core of need began to shimmer within her. He had found a hidden place, and as he stroked it, she heard herself begging him for more.

She was pressing against his hand, feeling the blunt head of him teasing her. And the shimmer transformed into an ache. He sensed her need and began rubbing harder, driving her towards the brink of surrender. He sucked hard against her nipple, and she couldn't stop herself from arching her back while a thousand pieces inside her shattered into a molten blast of desire. She let out a gasp as a release slammed into her, and her fingers dug into his shoulders.

My God, she'd never felt anything like this in her life.

He surged forward, and she felt a slight pain as he breached her. The pain was quickly forgotten as their bodies joined together. She raised up her knees, and he filled her completely, taking a moment to catch his breath.

It was right having him buried deep inside her. The weight of his body upon hers was welcome, but the yearning had not diminished. He kissed her gently. 'We haven't finished yet, *a mhuírnín*.' With that, he withdrew lightly and filled her again. Her breath hitched as he began thrusting in a slow rhythm. It was like being caressed on the inside, and she welcomed the intrusion.

Instinctively, she tightened herself against his erection, and he groaned at the sensation. 'Do that again.'

'Does it feel good to you?' she asked.

'Aye, Taryn. It does.'

She obeyed, and he kept up the slow penetrations until her body began quaking with the tremors. 'More, Killian.'

'I'm trying to be gentle with you.'

She realised that he was holding back for her sake. When he was deeply embedded within her, she framed his face with her hands. 'I don't need you to be gentle right now. I want you to feel the way I did.'

He rewarded her by increasing the pace. 'Am I hurting you?'

The sensation was so overwhelming, she was hardly aware of anything else. 'Only if you stop.'

She knew the moment he surrendered to his own desires. He began plunging hard, lifting her leg against his waist, and she could hardly breathe from the pleasure of being filled. She gave everything of herself to him, meeting him thrust for thrust.

Then he gripped her hips and let out a groan, shuddering hard as he emptied himself within her. They were one flesh, joined together as only a man and a woman could be.

For a moment, she lay beneath him, savouring his touch. She would not think of the weeks ahead, when he would leave her. Nor would she let herself dwell on the reality that it was unlikely any man would touch her like this again.

For now, she would be with this man and pretend that the lies were real. That he was her husband and not her guard.

And she held no regrets at all.

Chapter Eleven

They reached the High King's fortress by the second night. Killian led their travelling party with Taryn following behind him. He was conscious of her every move, and he could not stop watching over her. During the past two nights in their shared tent, he'd spent most of the hours in her arms, finding all the ways to pleasure her.

And yet, it still wasn't enough. She had indulged in their night trysts, but she had grown quieter within the past day, hiding her thoughts from him. He knew not what would happen when they met with King Rory. But he would guard Taryn with his life.

'Will we seek an audience with the High King this night?' she asked, after she led her horse beside his. The cat was curled up in the basket upon her saddle, and he saw her quietly stroking Harold's ears.

'Not yet.' He wanted to slip inside the fortress and disappear among the folk while he learned what he could about Rory. 'Stay here and make camp,' he told her. 'I will go alone and find out what I can about your father's fate.'

'When will you come back? By midnight, do you think?' There was a tendril of worry within her voice.

He leaned across to take her hand, kissing the knuckles. 'If I don't, I've no doubt you will come riding in after me.'

She didn't smile, as he'd expected her to. Instead, she squeezed his hand. 'I know I shouldn't be afraid. I've done nothing wrong, and the only reason I came here was to plead for my father's life. Yet I cannot help but feel the coldness in this place.'

'And that is why I need to know what lies behind those walls,' he told her. 'You said before that the men you sent on Devlin's behalf were killed. We need to know why.' She nodded and pulled him close for a kiss. He tasted her fear and tried to soothe it. 'If I have not returned by dawn, do not come after me.'

She was already shaking her head. 'His men

will know that ours are here. We cannot hide fifty men for more than a few hours.'

'The MacEgan guards have come to join with the High King's men. They might believe that Maeve has come for the same reason, to bring soldiers and atone for her husband's mistakes.'

Killian could see the unrest in her eyes, the unwillingness to obey him. He rested his palm against her cheek. 'If it's safe, I will come back for you, Taryn. This, I promise.'

'And if it isn't safe? What if you don't come back?'

'Then you must return with your mother. Turn away from all of this.' Her safety mattered more than all else. Though he doubted if the High King would pursue them, he didn't want Taryn to face any danger.

'Walk with me a moment,' she said quietly, swinging down from the horse.

He dismounted and she led him away from the others. Her hand was cold, and when they were alone, out of view of the others, she said, 'I don't want anything to happen to you.'

There was far more longing in her voice than there should have been. He knew what was happening between them, and he regretted his earlier coercion regarding her kingdom. No matter what happened, he had to keep her safe, at all costs.

'I know how to defend myself, *a stór.*'

She stared at him, and then drew her arms around his waist, resting her cheek against his heart. 'I need you to stay alive, Killian. Don't do anything dangerous.'

'I know how to blend in with my surroundings, Taryn.'

She squeezed him tightly and then drew back, lifting her face to his. 'Be safe.'

Her words slid into him like an invisible embrace, and he kissed her hard. This woman had somehow reached inside him, giving herself to the man he was instead of the man he wanted to be.

'What will you do if they recognise you?' she ventured.

'The only soldiers who have seen me before are those searching for Carice.' He slid back a lock of her hair. 'If they have not returned, I will be fine. If they have told the High King about my sister's disappearance, then we are both in danger. Brian may blame me for her disappearance, to save himself.'

She paled at that. 'I don't like this, Killian.'

Neither did he. There was a greater risk now,

with more to lose. He was venturing into a place where he knew no one, where he would be seen as an enemy. And though he could remain unseen, if he made the wrong move, it might cost him his life.

'I have this feeling I won't see you again,' Taryn whispered. 'And it frightens me.'

He gripped her hard, kissing her temple. 'You will see me again.' As a teasing note, he added, 'I need my land, don't I?'

She didn't smile. For they both knew that the chances of him sharing a true marriage with her were nearly impossible. More likely the High King would execute Devlin and seize control of his lands. Rory might force both Maeve and Taryn to wed men who were loyal to him. Even if Killian did wed Taryn in secret, the King could easily dissolve the marriage by having him killed.

He kissed her softly. 'Remain with the soldiers until dawn. Do not let anyone see you.' He needed her to remain safe while he explored the outbuildings at Tara.

'I will.'

For a moment, he palmed her cheek, taking a moment to memorise her features. Deep blue eyes studied his with worry, and she covered his hand. Her long black hair framed a face that haunted him now. He would never forget those features or the way her expression transformed while he was moving inside her.

And though he feared he had to give her up after this, he wanted to savour these last moments.

'Be careful,' Taryn urged.

He gave a hard nod and disappeared into the night.

Hours passed, and still, Killian hadn't returned. It was dawn now, and Taryn slipped outside the tent, hoping to catch a glimpse of him. All night, she had worried that he'd been caught by the High King's men. She couldn't bear it if anything happened to him. Aye, it had been unwise to join with him and spend the night in his arms during these past few nights. Yet she was not sorry for the choices she'd made.

It no longer mattered that she was the daughter of a king and he was the bastard son of Rory Ó Connor. He was the man she cared deeply about, and he had never once turned away from her scars. But the danger in this place had slid within her bones, making her fear that they would threaten Killian.

She crossed through the rows of tents, walking up the hillside to get a better view of Tara. The sun had barely risen above the horizon, but she hoped she could see the High King's territory. Sheep grazed upon the long grasses, and morning dew coated her skirts. She had bound a veil over her head, trying to keep her scars out of view.

Just a glimpse—that was all she wanted. She moved closer, towards the fortress enclosed by a large wooden fence. For a moment, she studied the High King's vast holdings, wondering whether there was any mercy within him at all. Was it even possible that he would let her father live?

She shielded her eyes against the morning sun and then a small group of men began to approach. It was soon clear that they had been watching her.

Taryn hesitated, wondering whether to retreat. If she ran, they would undoubtedly pursue her. She remained in place while she tried to decide what to do. As the men came closer, she saw a familiar face. The leader of the soldiers had been among the High King's men who had come to fetch Carice.

A faint smile edged his mouth the moment he recognised her.

No. Her pulse beat faster, even knowing she had done nothing wrong. But the moment he called out, Taryn spun around, hurrying towards the hill. She lost her footing and sprawled hard on the ground. Though she tried to call out to the MacEgan men, the High King's soldiers surrounded her within seconds.

'We've been looking for you, my lady,' the captain said. Two of the men seized her arms and dragged her to her feet. 'King Rory wants to have words with you. He wants to know where his bride is. And I think you know the answer to that.'

'I have not seen her since you left me at the round tower,' she countered. 'I had nothing to do with Carice's disappearance.'

'Then why did you run?' The knowing look on his face made her cheeks flush.

She tried to gather her composure. 'You frightened me when you approached with your soldiers. I came to seek an audience with the High King, for my father's sake.'

'Oh, he will be wanting to see you,' the man replied with a thin smile. 'My orders are to bring you for questioning.'

Her heart quaked at that, even while her logical mind argued, *This was what you wanted*. It wasn't as if she had a choice, either. Steeling herself, she met the captain's gaze. 'You need not treat me as a prisoner. I will speak with the *Ard-Righ*.'

But the captain ignored her. To the men holding her, he ordered, 'If she resists, drag her upon the ground.'

The men obeyed, and Taryn had to struggle to keep up. Her skirts tangled against her legs, and more than once, she stumbled. Her pulse quickened as she searched for a sign of Killian. But he was nowhere to be seen.

Rory Ó Connor's holdings consisted of a large fortification built of wood, known as the *Rath-na-Rígh*. Two walls surrounded the structure with a deep ditch between them. The men led her over the trench and inside the gates. Hearth fires were set up outside, and dozens of men and women moved throughout the space. Some were cooking food in iron pots, while others were treating animal hides stretched over heavy frames. A few boys wrestled in the open spaces, laughing as they tried to pin each other to the ground.

Taryn drew nearer and spied a smaller hillside within the walls. *Duma nan Giall*, it was named. She had never before seen the mound of hostages, but she had heard of it. An iron gate closed off the small house made of timber, and she wondered if her father was held within it.

As she passed through the grounds, she was struck by how vast the King's holdings were— and there were soldiers everywhere.

The men forced her towards the banqueting hall, a tall building made of timber that was heavily carved and painted in bright colours. It stood between two parallel mounds of earth, and Taryn counted six doors on each side.

'Bind her,' the captain said, 'until the High King is ready to see her.'

Taryn lowered her head, her mind spinning. She would have to plead with the King for mercy and pray that he did not hold her responsible for Carice's disappearance. Her heart was pounding when they led her inside the main door.

Inside, she smelled roasted mutton and vegetables. Her stomach roared with hunger, for she had not broken her fast this morn. But all hunger vanished when she heard the heavy footsteps approaching. She did not dare to look up, but she knew the High King was drawing nearer. She bit her lip so hard, she tasted blood.

'Your Grace, this is the traitor's daughter,' the captain said. 'We believe she was the reason why Lady Carice disappeared.'

'Was she?' came a deep baritone voice. 'Let go of her.'

The soldiers released their grip, and Taryn sank to her knees. She knew better than to attempt anything less than deference.

For a moment, the *Ard-Righ* stood in front of her. Taryn stared at his leather boots, her heart pounding.

'You do resemble Carice Faoilin,' he admitted. 'I can understand why my men made a mistake at first. But they did not see you clearly.' He reached out a hand and touched her chin. Taryn kept her gaze averted, knowing that this man held her life in his hands. 'Rise.'

She got up from her knees, and the moment she stood, he tore the veil from her hair. The linen slipped to the floor, and she felt the fear gripping her once more. Rory jerked her back by the hair, forcing her to look at him. His grey eyes were the same as Killian's, and it was like seeing an older, crueller version of the man she cared about. His dark beard covered his face, and his mouth was a thin slash.

Dear God. Her mother had been right. The moment anyone saw Killian, they would recognise him as Rory's son.

The High King pulled back her hair and revealed her scarred face to the men. 'Think you that I would wed a woman so cursed?'

Taryn didn't move, nor did she dare to speak. The wrong words could end her life or her father's.

'I want to know where Carice Faoilin is,' the High King said. His voice held such caged fury, she didn't know how to answer that. 'You will tell me this, if you value your life.'

She was not about to betray Killian's sister—especially not to this man.

'I d-don't know.' Fear gripped her roughly, and she admitted, 'My mother's men came for me, and I left Carice behind. I was travelling with her to the wedding, but then I had to leave her.'

But the captain was already shaking his head. 'On the first day we saw her, this woman claimed that *she* was your bride, my liege. She intended to deceive us during our journey towards Tara, and Lady Carice disappeared soon after she stayed behind. It could not have been a coincidence, for we have not seen your bride since.'

She knew these men were trying to save their own necks by blaming her. Best to tread carefully. 'I lied to them on the first night out of fear,' Taryn said. 'I was seeking sanctuary with the chieftain and was afraid I would not be allowed inside. It was a mistake from the first.'

'Why did Lady Carice run away? Was she trying to break our betrothal?' Rory demanded. His hand gripped the back of her neck, and Taryn froze. If this man intended to kill her, he would do so. She could do nothing at all to stop him.

'Lady Carice was dying,' she told the King. 'She was hardly able to leave her bed.'

His gaze darkened, and for a moment he passed judgement over her. 'But she was strong enough to flee this marriage.'

Taryn straightened, reaching for a courage she didn't feel. 'I do not think you would want a bride who is so ill, Your Grace. There are other women who would suit your needs better.'

'Not you,' he said coldly.

Though she had expected such a reaction,

she could not stop the colour from rising to her cheeks. 'No, Your Grace. Not me.'

The High King drew back his hand and said, 'I presume you came here to plead for your father's life.'

She gave a faint nod. 'Yes, Your Grace. If you would but grant him mercy, surely he—'

'I will not grant mercy to a traitor. He will die for his attempt to seize the kingship for himself.'

Taryn clenched her hands together, feeling as if all the blood had drained away from her body. Killian had been right. The High King had no intention of listening to any of her words.

But she would humble herself before him, begging for mercy. 'He is my father, Your Grace. And whatever he has done, I would ask that you consider another punishment. Perhaps exile…or—'

'The only mercy I would consider is granting him a swift death,' Rory finished. His iron tone made it clear that he would not be swayed in this.

The ice rose up from Taryn's heart, descending into her limbs. But she lowered herself to her knees, asking, 'May I see him?'

'Not unless you wish to join him.' To the guards, he ordered, 'Take her to the mound of hostages. She may be more willing to talk in the morning, once she has spent time with the other prisoners.'

Killian let out a curse when he saw the soldiers seize Taryn and take her away. He had hidden himself among the King's subjects, never letting any man see his face. And though he could not know how they'd taken Taryn without alerting the other soldiers, he had to get her out.

There was only one way to do so. He had to confront the High King and reveal his identity.

Although he knew his features were similar to Rory's, it was a rare moment when Killian ever saw his reflection. He hardly cared what he looked like, and he knew not what others would say when he claimed to be Rory's son.

But he had to act swiftly before Taryn was harmed.

Slowly, he rose from his place where he'd been washing a wooden table. He dried his hands upon the rough wool that he wore. Then he walked to the place where Taryn had been standing. He held back his shoulders, still keeping himself hooded. It took a moment for the men to notice him, and the captain approached. 'Go back to your place, *fuidir*.'

Killian ignored him, striding towards the High King. 'I would like an audience with you, Your Grace.'

The captain reached out to seize his arm, but Killian twisted it and sent the man sprawling to the floor. His strength seemed to startle the others, and he saw men reaching for their blades.

But he had their attention now.

Rory Ó Connor turned and stared at him. It was clear that the High King was lacking in patience, and the moment would soon be lost.

Killian reached up to his hood and pulled it back, revealing his face. He waited, before he spoke, to see if anyone saw the resemblance. By the gods, he hoped so. This was his best hope of keeping Taryn safe.

For a moment, the High King froze. He stared hard at Killian, and the expression on his face was not at all the rage or disinterest he'd anticipated. Instead, there was a look of stunned silence. There was no doubting that Rory recognised him as another bastard son. But instead of dismissing him, the High King moved closer. 'Who was your mother?'

Killian straightened. 'Her name was Iona.'

A strange smile spread over the High King's

face, and he shook his head. 'No. Her name was not Iona. It was Liona MacPherson.'

Killian didn't move. There was a low buzzing sound in his ears, and he didn't know what to believe. He'd expected the High King to dismiss him, to brush him aside. But instead, Rory's face had turned hard.

'She disappeared, a very long time ago. I suppose she altered her name to remain in hiding.'

It was indeed possible, for his mother had never once travelled to visit her family. She had named him MacDubh, refusing to even grant him the knowledge of her tribe's name. The MacPhersons lived far to the northeast, and he had never been there before.

'Describe what she looked like,' Killian demanded. He wanted to know if Rory was telling the truth.

'She had dark hair, like yours, but her eyes were green. She stood as tall as my shoulder, and she had a small freckle near the corner of her mouth. I was the King of Connacht when I first saw her.'

So it was true. The details were precise, and he was certain the High King was telling the truth. But there came an icy chill over Killian's spine. 'If you remember her so well, then why did she change her name and flee?'

The High King shrugged. 'Because I forced her to wed me.'

Married. His mother had married Rory Ó Connor. The blood seemed to rush from Killian's body, and he stared into Rory's eyes. There was no denying that he was this man's son. Their hair, their height—every feature was the same, save the beard and the slight tinge of grey at the man's temples. His emotions tangled up in a turmoil of fury and shock.

'What is your name?' the High King asked. 'What did she call you?'

'Killian MacDubh,' he answered. For a long moment, he couldn't speak, could hardly grasp what had happened. He wanted to demand answers, to know why Rory had refused to foster him—why he had never searched for them. In the end, he twisted off the silver ring his mother had given him long ago.

Rory accepted the ring and let out a slow breath. 'I gave her this ring when I wed her. Which means you are my son and heir.'

'Get up,' a guard commanded. Taryn's back was aching, but she moved to her knees. Her hands were bound in front of her, and she struggled to rise. She had not been taken to the mound of hostages, as the High King had commanded. There were only men there, and instead, the captain had confined her below the ground, in a chamber used for slaughtering sheep and cattle. There was still blood in the trench before her, and the frigid stone wall at her back.

'Where are we going?' she asked the guard. Her hands were freezing, and she stumbled as he pushed her forward.

'You will be imprisoned elsewhere,' was all he said.

Elsewhere? She was terrified to think of why. Did it have something to do with her father, or was this still about Carice?

Taryn trudged along the dirt pathway, lowering her head again. She was beginning to realise why her mother had wanted to keep her from Tara. A fresh wave of fear passed over her at the realisation that Maeve had likely entered the gates with her soldiers, once she learned that Taryn wasn't there. And though she was not on good terms with her mother, she could not fault Maeve for trying to protect her.

The guard led her back towards another out-

building that stood high above the others. From
its placement near the banqueting hall, it was
well guarded. She searched again for a glimpse
of Killian or her father but saw neither one. She
trudged up a narrow staircase, before the guard
opened the door to a tiny chamber and shoved
her inside. Taryn struck the wall, barely catching her balance. 'You'll wait here until he comes
for you.'

He? Was he referring to Rory Ó Connor?
Dear God, she hoped not. But there was one de-
fence she had remaining. With her bound hands,
she pulled her hair over one shoulder, revealing the hideous scars on her cheeks. Then she
straightened, well aware of the guard's sudden
wince. Good. Perhaps that would be her protection against rape.

He slammed the door shut behind him, leaving her alone. Inside the narrow room, a thin
slit served as a window. She moved towards it,
trying to see her surroundings. There were soldiers everywhere, leaving nothing unguarded.

Where was Killian? She had not seen a trace
of him, and she worried that he was being held
prisoner somewhere. Or worse, tortured. Her
spirits sank, as she was beginning to grasp the
hopelessness of her situation. The High King

was furious with her for Carice's disappearance, and he would surely punish her if he believed she was responsible for helping the young
woman flee.

Taryn closed her eyes, the unknown fears
washing over her. Why had she dared to come
here? It had indeed been her own *naïveté*, believing that she could somehow change the High
King's mind.

The door opened, and she spun, her heart
beating wildly when she saw Killian standing
there. He lowered the latch, and she ran forward, letting him crush her in his arms. He used
a blade to slice through her ropes, and she was
free to hold him close.

'What has happened to you?' she demanded.
'Have you seen my father? Does the High King
know you are here?'

Killian ignored her queries and leaned in to
kiss her. 'So many questions.' He kept his nose
touched to hers. 'And you didn't listen to me, did
you, *a mhuírnín*? Else, you'd not be confined.'

'I only thought to have a look at the ring fort,'
she admitted. 'I never imagined there would be
so many soldiers here.'

'Rory is raising an army, gathered from all

the tribes. He wants them to fight against the Norman invaders.'

She noticed then that his clothing was different. Instead of the rough, dark wool and chain mail, he wore a tunic of fine woven silk and trews befitting a king's son. Taryn stepped back, noting that he had shaved, and his black hair was combed back.

He had received a welcome from Rory Ó Connor, whereas she had been taken prisoner. She didn't know what to think of that.

'Tell me what has happened to you,' she urged. 'I suppose the King was glad to see you, if your new clothes are a means of judgement.'

There was a trace of unrest upon Killian's face, but he nodded. 'Rory did not know what had become of me. My mother fled when she was with child and remained in hiding for the rest of her life.'

Taryn sensed that there was more he wasn't telling her. His expression was unsettled, and he was clearly keeping information from her. Though the King might be glad to see his bastard son again, she rather doubted that he would treat Killian so well. Certainly, he would not clothe him in finery or treat him as a lost son. Unless…

Understanding dawned within her, and Taryn straightened. 'You are his legitimate son, aren't you?'

He made no denial. 'It seems my mother wed Rory when he was King of Connacht. It was an arrangement to ally their lands, but she did not want the marriage. Instead, she turned her back on her family and sought help from Brian Faoilin.'

It should have been welcome news to learn that Killian had a true birthright now. But instead of being happy for him, she felt a sense of loss. The High King's son would not be allowed to choose a bride for himself. He would have to make a political marriage, one that furthered the alliances.

He certainly could never wed a traitor's daughter.

She tried to push back the hurt, but it rose up inside her. Somehow, within the past few days, she had seriously begun to consider marrying Killian. Though she'd known their lives were not meant to be joined together, she had been happy with him. He had made her feel beautiful, and her heart had fallen hard.

Now it seemed he had been raised up to an

unreachable place—whereas she had fallen low, because of her father's misdeeds.

'As the High King's son, you now have what you always wanted. The land and the chance to be a leader of men. I am happy for you.' She tried to brave a smile, but he seemed to guess her uncertainty.

'Not everything I want,' he admitted. His hands moved into her hair, and she felt a pang of longing. When he kissed her, she opened to him, feeling as if their last moments were slipping away.

'Rory blames me for Carice's disappearance,' she confessed, breaking the kiss. 'I am being kept prisoner because I would not reveal where she was.'

'So I heard. I was there when you were brought to him.' Killian drew her close for a moment. It reminded her of the nights they'd spent together and the way he had brought her to pleasure, again and again, and she wound her arms around his neck.

'I will intervene on your behalf,' he promised. She knew not if he was speaking of her fate or her father's, but she was grateful for it. And yet, the moment he walked away, he would become more deeply entwined in the High King's affairs.

'Thank you,' she murmured.

His eyes were silver, and though there was very little light within the chamber, she saw the look of longing on his face. She wanted so badly to have a last stolen moment with him.

'You will stay here until I have arranged for your release,' he told her. 'It will be safer.' He stepped back, but before he could walk towards the door, she moved before him.

'Don't go yet,' she whispered. She took his hands in hers and brought them to her waist. 'Please.'

His eyes darkened, and he leaned against her lips. 'What are you wanting, *a mhuírnín*?'

She didn't know what to say without sounding desperate. 'I don't wish to be a prisoner here. And I know that once you leave me, everything will be different between us.'

And it already is, she thought to herself. Here, he belonged. He had a father who was grateful to find him alive and a place of his own. Whereas she was seen as only a traitor's daughter.

'You won't be a prisoner,' he promised. 'But it's not safe for you outside this chamber.'

She knew that. And yet, it troubled her to be left behind. 'After this day, I don't suppose we can be together any more,' she admitted.

His hands moved up her back, and he rested his forehead upon hers. 'Is that what you've decided?'

'You won't want someone like me any more. Not if you are the High King's son.'

'As the High King's son, I can have any woman I desire. And you are the only one I want.'

'Why?' she whispered.

'Because you never saw a *fuidir*. Only a man.'

I love you. She held the thought inside herself as she threaded her hands through his hair and kissed him with the force of her emotion. Though she wanted to believe that he wanted her as well, she knew too well how complicated political alliances could be. It was rare that a man could wed the woman he wanted.

'I will ask Rory to let me take Ossoria in your father's place,' he said. He did not mention the execution, but she prayed that there was still hope to save Devlin's life.

'Imbolc is tomorrow,' she whispered. 'There's hardly any time left.' Not only for her father, but also for them. She rested her cheek against his chest, holding him tight. 'I don't know what else we can do.'

'Trust in me,' he said, framing her face. 'I will need to spend time with the High King. If I get closer to my father, I may learn what can be done to save Devlin.'

She understood the unspoken words. He could not be seen with her for a time. He would have to distance himself to uncover the truth. 'Do what you must, then.'

He didn't let go of her. 'There's something you should know, Taryn.' He kissed her mouth again. 'If it comes down to choosing your life or Devlin's... I won't be choosing his.'

She gave a nod, but inside, her feelings were breaking apart. 'No matter what happens, I need to see him.' Surely then, she would see the truth in Devlin's face. Surely her mother had lied about what had happened. Maeve's claim, that he had been responsible for her scarring, seemed impossibly untrue.

'I will do what I can,' Killian promised. 'But I need time to get close to Rory. He'll be watching both of us. He may be glad that I am here, but he does not trust me. He'll be wanting me to prove my loyalty to him.'

Killian touched her scarred cheek and helped

her straighten her gown. 'I must go now. There are guards posted outside this door. They will tell Rory every time I come to see you.'

Though it pained her, she whispered, 'Then you should stay away.'

He brushed a kiss upon her cheek. 'I'm not wanting to leave you at all, *a mhuírnín*.'

Neither did she, but she understood the game they were playing. One wrong move, and lives could be lost.

'Be safe,' she whispered, 'and come to me when you can.' She suppressed the desire to tell him of her feelings for him. If anything happened to Killian, she didn't know if she could bear it.

'I won't fail you in this,' he swore. He kissed her one last time, and despite his reassurance, she couldn't help but worry.

And when he left her at last, she felt the walls closing in, her time slipping away.

Chapter Twelve

'Where is she?' Maeve demanded, when Killian approached their camp. 'Is my daughter alive?'

While he understood the woman's terror at her daughter's fate, it irked him that she would question his ability to protect Taryn.

'She is,' he said, 'and I have arranged a place for her. But I will not risk her safety by bringing in more soldiers. The MacEgans may enter the grounds, for King Patrick sent these men who were willing to join the High King. But were I in your place, I would stay behind.'

Maeve quieted at that. Then her gaze passed over his new clothing, and she saw the gold ring Rory had given him. 'I see you were telling the truth about being his son. I hope it means you are able to protect your *wife* from Rory's cruelty.'

He didn't bother to explain himself, for there was no reason to do so. Instead, he ordered Maeve, 'You should return to Ossoria. I will keep Taryn safe.'

'No,' the older woman argued. 'She will be in danger, with every moment she is here.' Her gaze fixed upon the banqueting hall, and she looked as if she wanted to speak against Rory. Then she risked a glance back towards the hillside. 'No matter what my daughter has told you, I beg of you, do not free Devlin,' she begged. 'Nothing good can come of it.'

'That is for Taryn to decide. Not you.' He started to turn back, but Maeve hurried forward.

'My daughter is blind to the truth. If Devlin is freed, he will only hurt her again. I will not let that happen.'

Killian resented her insinuation that he was powerless to help her. 'Your daughter is under my protection now. And no man will ever hurt her, so long as I have breath in my lungs.'

It was clear that Maeve did not trust him to take care of Taryn. But more than that, she was desperate to be rid of her husband. He studied her face, wondering if Devlin had harmed her in any way. It did not seem so. But there were other ways to gain a woman's fear and loathing.

The only way to learn those answers was to confront the man himself. Killian turned his back on the Queen, returning inside the gates. He had only recently learned that Rory was keeping Devlin chained in a small underground enclosure.

Killian crossed through the gathering space, well aware of all the eyes watching him. Although Rory had not formally acknowledged him as his son, the gift of new clothing and his own features had gathered enough attention. Even the women were casting him looks of interest. But their coy smiles revealed that their true interest was in gaining the attention of the High King's son. They were nothing at all like Taryn of Ossoria.

He knew Rory's reasons for keeping Taryn confined. So long as she wasn't in chains, Killian wasn't going to argue the point. It was safer to hold her away from the others.

He reached the space where her father was being held and ordered the guard to unlock the iron gate that kept the man imprisoned.

'My orders are not to let the prisoner visit with anyone,' the man protested.

'He will go nowhere,' Killian promised. 'I mean only to speak with him. And if he tries to escape, you have permission to kill him.'

At that, the man acceded. He opened the gate and allowed Killian inside. 'For a few moments, then.'

Inside the underground space, there was hardly any light at all. King Devlin was confined to the opposite wall. That was a torture in and of itself, being kept in constant darkness.

'Who are you?' the man croaked, clearing his throat.

'I am Killian—' He started to say MacDubh, but altered it, finishing with, 'Ó Connor. The High King's son.' The words felt strange upon his tongue, but more than that, the name was so very different.

'What do you want from me?' There was no fear in the man's voice, only resignation.

'Your daughter, Taryn, is here.'

He waited for the man's reaction, but there came only silence. It was as if Killian hadn't spoken at all.

At last, the old man said, 'She should not have come.'

'She pleaded with Rory for your life. She claims you are innocent of treason.'

Again, the King said nothing, and Killian's senses went on alert. Most fathers would react in some way if his daughter had come on such a journey. Instead, this man offered nothing at all. He was beginning to wonder if Maeve was right about Devlin. Was he truly the sort of man who could harm his own daughter?

Instinct told him to walk away and leave the man alone. But then, Devlin had been confined in this place for weeks. It might be that his lack of interest was weakness from imprisonment. 'Your wife is here as well.'

The man's silence suggested that he didn't care that anyone had come for him. Or perhaps he believed that Killian was here to torture him or draw out information that could be used against his family.

Taryn had pleaded with him to save this man, while Maeve wanted him to die. Imbolc would begin on the morrow, and this was Devlin's last day to live.

'Do you want to see them?' Killian asked. He waited for an answer, but Devlin only lowered his head.

'Nay, I've no wish for them to see me like this.'

He could understand that—especially if he

believed their lives would be in danger. 'Your daughter asked me to intervene on your behalf,' he told the King. 'She begged me to set you free.' Killian hardened his tone and continued, 'Why are you worth saving? Or shall I just let you die?'

'I have no intention of dying.' There was enough arrogance in the man's voice to make him wonder what the King's intentions were. 'The High King is trying to use me as an example to other kings. If he executes me, he risks losing the support of his allies. And the Normans will not look upon him with favour.'

The man's treason was clear enough. He had betrayed his kinsmen, and there was no remorse in his actions.

'Why did you ally with our enemies?' Killian asked.

'Rory will not keep his throne unless he forms an agreement with the Normans. His plan to raise an army against them will cause hundreds of men to die. If we negotiate with them, it will save many lives.'

'I suppose you already have an "agreement" with them.' Now he was starting to gain a stronger understanding. If Devlin intended to overthrow the High King, it would give him a position of power among their enemies.

'The Irish will never come together as one kingdom,' Devlin said. 'They raid against the other tribes, and there are so many kings, they squabble among themselves.' His voice grew quieter, and he added, 'Rory is a weak High King. He will never hold his throne against the Normans. Strongbow knows it, and so do I.'

Richard de Clare, a Norman nicknamed Strongbow, had brought his own invasion only a few years ago. His men had remained within Éireann, and the Norman King Henry had visited Tara to establish his own dominion.

Killian probed further, wanting to know more about Devlin's plans. 'And what about the Queen? Your wife intends to rule Ossoria without you.'

'Maeve knows nothing of how to rule,' Devlin said quietly. 'Men do not listen to her.' He turned to face Killian at last. 'I know you were sent to question me. But ask yourself this. What will happen when the *Ard-Righ* is stripped of his throne, because he did not acknowledge the greater power of our enemies? If you do not carefully consider your loyalties, your head will be beside his. Think upon that. For the Normans *are* intending to seize land, while King Henry intends to claim Éireann. Unless he already has a man loyal to him, who takes command as High King.'

Devlin made it sound as if an attack was imminent. And whether or not it was, there was no doubting that the man held no allegiance towards Rory Ó Connor. He was indeed a traitor.

'And what of your daughter? Were you intending to give her in marriage to one of the Normans?' He couldn't keep the fury from his voice. Taryn did not deserve such a fate.

'I doubt she will ever be able to marry,' Devlin said. 'If you have seen her, you know the reason why.'

Anger darkened within Killian. These were not the words of a proud father who loved his daughter. And yet…though Devlin could be lying, pretending as if he didn't care for her at all, the dull tone in his voice suggested otherwise.

'Was it true what Maeve said, that you were responsible for her scars?'

Devlin remained silent. But his lack of a denial was the answer Killian had anticipated. It seemed that he *had* set his dogs upon his daughter. What kind of a man would make her suffer in such a way?

His mood was dark when he stepped back towards the gate. Though Taryn would be devastated by Devlin's death, he could see no reason why the man deserved to live.

'You are commanded to come with me, Lady Taryn,' a young woman bade her. 'King Rory wishes to speak with you.'

It was barely past dawn on the morning of Imbolc. Taryn rose from her place on the floor, feeling numb with terror. Killian had not returned last night, and she knew not what decision the High King would make.

The maid led her outside the room, where two guards shadowed them. Although they did not seize her, Taryn was well aware of their weapons. They continued down the stairs and outside.

Winds tore at Taryn's hair, pulling it back from her face and revealing the scars to anyone who stared at her. Though she wanted to lower her head, it made no difference now. *Let them look,* she thought.

And so she kept her shoulders back, following the maid through the fortress towards a large stone chair. Rows of men stood before the High King, and there was an unnatural silence.

'Why have I been brought here?' she asked the maid. But the young woman only shook her head, offering no answer at all. Taryn took slow steps forward, feeling uneasy about what was happening. Only when she reached the chair did she see her father on the ground before the High King. He was dressed in only a ragged *léine* made of wool, and his black hair was matted. His beard had grown out below his chin, and manacles hung from his wrists.

'Father,' she whispered, dropping to her knees. Tears blurred her eyes at the sight of him. When she looked upon his features, she did not see the face of a traitor.

Instead, she saw the man who had grieved for the loss of his son…and the man who had spent years treating her as a beloved daughter. They had taken long walks together, and he'd taught her how to lead their people. He had never raised a hand against her, and she wondered if what her mother said was true. *Had* he set the dogs upon her and caused the attack? Was that why he had spent so much time with her—out of remorse? Or had her mother spoken lies, meant to make her despise her father and leave him to die?

She didn't know. But it hurt to see him like this, facing his own execution.

God help him, she feared that her mother's prediction would come true. Maeve had said that the High King intended to execute Devlin...and if Taryn pleaded for him, Rory would kill him before her eyes.

Killian stood beside the High King, but she saw no mercy in his eyes. His attention was fixed upon Devlin, and though he had to have seen her approaching, he did not meet her gaze. It could only mean the worst.

Look at me, she wanted to plead. She wanted to gain strength from Killian's presence, to know that he would stand by her and help her free Devlin. Instead, she was terrified that he was powerless to do anything.

Her father's *léine* was stained with blood, and she was certain he'd been whipped or tortured. But instead of fear in his eyes, she saw a restlessness. It was as if he were waiting for something to happen.

Taryn turned to look at the crowd of men and women gathered around. She recognised only a few of the High King's soldiers nearby. Shielding her eyes against the sun, she saw Maeve on horseback in the distance, surrounded by her own escorts. It seemed that her mother fully intended to witness her husband's death.

Again, Taryn raised her eyes to Killian, praying that he would do something to stop this. If he was Rory's acknowledged son, then he could ask on her behalf. But there was a stoic expression upon his face, as if he cared not what happened to her father.

She didn't understand at all. This man had fought for her, lain beside her at night, and loved her until she'd cried out from the joy of it. Why would he not look at her?

'I know that you have come to plead for Devlin Connelly's life,' the High King said to her. 'But this man is a traitor and has allied himself with the Normans, intending to overthrow me and seize command of Éireann.' His gaze was iron, his grey eyes staring hard at her. 'He deserves to die.'

She could not bring forth any words. Aye, she wanted to beg for the High King's mercy once again. But the stony expression on Killian's face suggested that there would be none.

Taryn moved forward until she stood directly before the High King. When she reached her father, her eyes filled up with tears. He appeared half-starved and emotionless.

Slowly, she lowered herself to her knees. The cold earth was damp, and the wetness seeped into her skirts. She remained kneeling before the High King and said quietly, 'I give you *my* loyalty, as Lady of Ossoria. And I would ask for your mercy on my father's behalf. Exile him, if you must. But please…let him live.'

Her words did nothing to soften the High King's ire. Taryn barely heard the King's answer, his diatribe about how Devlin had betrayed them, raising an army against them. Instead, she studied Killian's face, searching for answers within those cold grey eyes.

He'd wanted land of his own, a chance to have his freedom and a different life. She had offered that to him in return for saving Devlin. But now, he had no need of it. And that meant he no longer needed her.

'I accept your fealty,' the High King answered. 'And I am inclined to forgive your part in my bride's disappearance, since you brought my son back to me. But as for your father, I will grant only the mercy I spoke of before.'

Her pulse was racing, her knees aching as she prayed that Killian could somehow intervene for them. A swift death was the only offer Rory had made.

'I must know that my son is loyal to me,' the High King continued. A low buzzing rang in Taryn's ears, and she felt sick with fear. 'I need to believe that his obedience is without question.' Rory unsheathed his own sword and passed it to Killian.

Nausea rose up in her throat, her heart pounding. Dear God, she now understood why she had been brought here.

'I will indeed grant your father mercy and accept your loyalty. Instead of a traitor's death, he will be beheaded. Death will come in one swift blow.'

She stared at the gleaming sword in Killian's hand. The High King was testing his son's loyalty and obedience. If Killian refused to kill her father, then *he* would be accused as a traitor.

But if he obeyed, all was lost.

Don't do this, she pleaded silently. The tears fell down, and she rose from her knees, not knowing what to do.

She moved towards Killian, her heart breaking into pieces. She had given this man everything, believing in him. He had sworn that he would do everything to protect her father.

'Please,' she said to Killian, dropping to her knees before him. Though she could not shield Devlin, it was the only thing left she could do. 'Don't, Killian. I beg of you.'

He did look at her then, but his eyes were frosted and cold. Gone was the man who had loved her at night, who had taken away her fears. No longer did she see the man who had ridden by her side, journeying with her to this place.

And she knew. God help her, she knew that he would carry out this death sentence. The tears flowed freely, and she could not bear it when he stepped past her, his sword raised.

Then he lifted his weapon and struck.

She will get you to safety. I will protect you along the way, but we have to go now.'

Her eyes welled up with unshed tears. 'Were you going to kill my father?'

He gripped her hand and met her gaze. 'I would never do anything to hurt you, *a mhuírnín.*'

She gave a slight nod, squeezing his hand in return. Though her fear had not diminished, it did seem that she believed him. 'Promise me you'll be careful,' she murmured. Her long black hair was windblown, her blue eyes sharp with worry. Both of them knew that his chances of survival were slim, for he was well outnumbered.

'I have a reason to live,' he insisted. 'And someone to fight for.'

She nodded and said, 'I love you, Killian.'

The words were an invisible embrace, encircling his spirit. He kissed her roughly, and then Maeve drew her horse to a stop nearby. The fighting had shifted in another direction, and Killian saw an opening to bring Taryn to the Queen.

'Keep close to me,' he commanded, guiding her towards the outskirts. She gripped his hand, and her fingers were icy cold from fear.

But the moment they were nearly there, four men charged forward, their weapons drawn.

'Killian!' Taryn called out in warning, and he released her hand, unsheathing his dagger.

'You have to go. Now!' he ordered, and she obeyed without question. He lost sight of her, forced to concentrate on the men surrounding him. *Let her reach Maeve safely,* he prayed silently.

His heartbeat thundered in his ears, his body responding from years of training. Time slowed down to a fragile breath of air, and he no longer heard the sounds of battle. He had become frozen, his soul lost, as his blade twisted within men's flesh. He moved like a shadow, his sword weaving a path through the enemy.

Some of the MacEgan soldiers came to his aid, and with their help, Killian defeated the Normans. His muscles ached, but he forged on, searching for a glimpse of Taryn. He needed to see that she was safe, but there was no sign of her among the people.

Perhaps that meant she was with the Queen, out of harm's way. And yet, he could not let go of the suspicion that something had happened to her. The thought was a dark torment, eating away at his patience.

You were never meant to be with her, his conscience taunted.

He didn't want to believe that. For whatever had begun between them had evolved into emotions he'd never before encountered. Taryn had treated him as her equal from the moment they had met. And in his eyes, there was no woman more beautiful.

He fought alongside the MacEgan soldiers and Rory's men, hacking a path towards the edge of the soldiers. Somehow, in the midst of the fighting, he saw that Devlin Connelly was gone.

So be it. There was naught he could do, and what mattered now was surviving and protecting Taryn.

He slashed his way through the men, fighting alongside the others, until he reached the outer perimeter. And the sight of the woman before him nearly stopped his breath.

Queen Maeve lay unconscious upon the ground, her red hair tangled over her face. And there was no sign of Taryn.

Killian hurried forward, his pulse racing. When he reached her side, he shook her gently. Maeve moaned, and when her eyes opened, he demanded, 'Where is your daughter?'

The woman was pale, blinking with confusion. 'I don't know. I fell from my horse, and I have not seen her.'

He helped her rise to her feet and brought her to one of her men, directing him to bring her to safety. In the meantime, he searched the grounds for a sign of Taryn. The Norman army had begun a retreat, and dozens of bodies littered the grass.

An uneasy feeling wrenched within his gut, mingling with guilt. He never should have sent her off alone. Killian hurried through the crowds of soldiers, forcing a path through the fighting. The sound of a woman's scream cut through the violence, and he saw Taryn standing with a blade in her hand.

Two men were closing in on her, and one held a spear in his hand. The other was trying to come up behind Taryn, and he seized her hair, jerking it backwards.

Killian lifted his own sword, prepared to strike down the man, when suddenly he spied Devlin. The man was watching his daughter, but he did nothing to help her. Damn him for it.

With his sword raised, Killian hurried forward, intending to disarm her attacker. But instead, Taryn lunged with her blade. The knife slashed against the man's throat, but it wasn't enough to bring him down. Instead, he seized her wrist and squeezed hard enough for her to cry out in pain. The knife fell from her grip, leaving her defenceless.

'Let her go,' Killian said, raising his sword towards the man with the spear.

'Put down your weapon,' the assailant answered. 'Or I will kill her.'

Killian met Taryn's gaze, but did not lower the sword. 'You are outnumbered by our men.'

'And I have something you want.' He gripped Taryn's hair roughly, forcing her to her knees. 'Give yourself over as my hostage, and I might let her go.'

Killian didn't move at first. It was entirely possible that the soldier would kill Taryn the moment he dropped his weapons. He shifted his gaze towards Devlin and asked, 'Are you planning to abandon your daughter, after all she did for you? Or will you fight and help me save her?'

Taryn was struggling against the man's grip, but to no avail. And although Killian knew he could win this battle, the risk was grave. He had to move swiftly and shield her from harm.

But it seemed that Devlin had no intention

of helping him. Likely the man had intended to escape in the midst of the battle, while the Normans tried to overthrow the *Ard-Righ*. Instead, the High King's men had driven them back.

Killian heard the shouts of the King's men, and a split second later, an arrow struck the ground beside him. Son of Lugh, but he hadn't seen the archers. He froze and glanced behind him. Half a dozen of the High King's men had their bows drawn, aimed at the Norman soldiers surrounding Taryn.

If they loosed an arrow, they might strike her instead. But from the grim look upon the soldiers' faces, he realised that it didn't matter to them. They saw Taryn as a traitor and a threat.

'Don't shoot!' Killian ordered.

But it was too late. He ran to Taryn, intending to shield her from the arrows with his own body…but Devlin reached her first. Time stilled when Killian saw the first arrow pierce her skin. Blood flowed from the wound, and she slumped forward to the ground.

Chapter Fourteen

The hoarse battle cry that ripped from his throat was born of grief and fury. Killian gripped his sword, giving himself over to the madness. Inside, he was hollow, unable to believe what he was seeing. The woman who had given herself freely, breathing life into his frozen heart, was lying on the ground. Her black hair shielded her face, and he knew not if her heart was still beating.

A thousand emotions tore through him—fury that she'd been harmed, guilt that he hadn't saved her in time…and heart-stopping fear. She had given herself to him, teaching him what it meant to love. He had never known what it was to need someone, to feel as if she made up the other half of his tortured soul. With Taryn, he was a whole man, someone of worth.

And Fate taunted him with the knowledge that he'd been unable to save her.

Sprawled across her was the body of Devlin, covered in arrows. Her father had given himself over to shield her, but Killian could not tell if the man's sacrifice had held any worth.

He moved Devlin off Taryn and saw that her complexion was snow white. Blood had soaked the bodice of her gown. Killian pulled her into his lap and examined the arrow wound. Thank the gods, the arrow had pierced her shoulder. It did not seem life-threatening in any way, and he was able to breathe again.

A low moan sounded from her, and Killian murmured, 'It's all right, *a chroí*. I have you now. You're safe.'

Darkness enveloped her, and Taryn smelled the metallic tang of blood mingled with Killian's scent. Her shoulder burned with a vicious pain, but she thought she heard her father's voice.

'Taryn, forgive me,' he whispered in a hoarse voice. 'For I cannot forgive myself. I never should have set the dogs on you.'

Anguish welled up inside her, for she hadn't wanted it to be true. She'd wanted to believe that her father was a noble man, incapable of such horror. Instead, he was the man her mother had said he was.

Taryn couldn't speak, and she struggled to open her eyes. Killian held her in his embrace while her father lay on the ground beside her. At least a dozen arrows had pierced him, and she had no doubt that he was going to die. Every breath was a struggle, and she realised that the blood upon her hands was his.

Dear God.

Her father had thrown himself in front of her, taking the arrows that would have killed her. Grief swelled up within her at the knowledge that, in spite of what he had done to her, he had loved her enough to sacrifice himself.

Her mother, Maeve, stood nearby, her hands covering her mouth. At the sight of her, Taryn saw a woman who had let her hatred and bitterness consume her over the years. Devlin's thoughtless act had scarred her mother, just as surely as Taryn bore the physical evidence of her father's rage.

She had every right to turn her back on Devlin, hating him for the way he had caused her disfigurement. But what good would that do? Nothing could change the past.

Weariness slid over her, and she decided that

she would not take the path Maeve had chosen. Instead, she looked over at her father and granted absolution. 'I forgive you,' she murmured.

He was coughing hard, and his gaze drifted to something behind her. Taryn turned and saw her mother approaching. Maeve walked slowly towards them, her hands gripped together.

'I let my ambitions lead me,' her father whispered. 'I wanted a greater position in Éireann. But all of that is lost to me now.' Lifting his gaze to Maeve, he added in the faintest voice, 'I am sorry. Not only for endangering Ossoria, but for what I did to our daughter.'

Her mother didn't speak, but closed the distance and knelt beside her husband. While there might not be forgiveness between them, there was peace. 'You saved her life today, Devlin. It is enough for me.'

Taryn fought to remain conscious, though a rushing noise filled her ears.

'I do love you, Taryn,' Devlin said, his voice growing fainter. 'And you are beautiful to me. Now and always.'

He gave a last shuddering breath, and she saw the moment the life faded from his eyes. She wept for the loss, but in his death, there was redemption. In the end, she chose to remember the man who had tried to make up for his sins—not the one who had made a terrible mistake.

Killian held her close while she grieved, and she took comfort in his embrace. In his arms, she felt safe and beloved. Gently, he lifted her to stand, but she faced her mother. 'I know you were only trying to protect me.'

Maeve nodded, her eyes filled with tears. 'You are, and always have been, my beloved daughter.'

With her uninjured arm, Taryn reached out to her mother and squeezed her hand. Then she walked back with Killian, leaning against him. Her mind was tangled with uncertain emotion, regret and sorrow foremost. But despite what had happened this day, she took strength from Killian. His expression was rigid, though he remained gentle in guiding her towards his chamber.

'Are you all right?' she asked.

'No.' He stopped a moment, reaching out to the blood-soaked wound. 'You were hurt this day, and I blame myself for it.'

Behind his stony expression, she saw overwhelming regret and fear. But she knew her wound was not a mortal one. Instead, she reached up to touch his cheek. His hand covered hers, as if he needed her touch upon him. 'I would give my life for yours, Taryn.'

'I am glad you did not have to,' she whispered, rising up to kiss him. He took her mouth hard, like a man who needed to convince himself that she was alive. 'Take me home,' she pleaded.

'Where?' he prompted, resting his forehead against hers.

She managed a weak smile. 'Home is wherever you are.'

Hours later, Killian stood before the *Ard-Righ*, awaiting an audience with his father. Taryn was resting, after the healer had helped remove the arrow and had tended her wound. Despite knowing that she would fully recover, he had hated seeing her suffer. Right now, all he wanted to do was take her back to Ossoria to heal. Instead, he had to face the High King's displeasure.

'You disobeyed my orders,' Rory said in a stony voice. He reached for a goblet of wine while a servant tended a minor wound upon his arm. 'You were commanded to kill Devlin Connelly.'

'I disobeyed because there was a greater threat,' Killian shot back. 'You would be dead, had I not lifted my blade.' He took a step forward and crossed his arms. 'I should think that would prove my loyalty.'

His words lingered between them like a gauntlet. Rory stared at him for a moment, before a faint smile broke through. 'Indeed. And for that reason, I will forgive your transgression. The traitor is dead now. But we have not discussed what to do about his daughter.'

'Lady Taryn had nothing to do with Devlin's actions,' Killian reassured his father. 'Already she has sworn her loyalty to you.'

Rory's gaze narrowed. 'She has said so, but I cannot let her return to Ossoria without one of my own men in command there.'

'I will govern Ossoria on your behalf,' Killian said quietly. Though he suspected his father had been speaking of another ally, he had the man's attention now.

'Why should you be given a kingdom?' Rory demanded.

'Because my mother stole my birthright before I was born,' he answered. 'I was given the life of a slave, instead of the life I was meant to have.'

'And you think I will simply hand over a kingdom to a son I hardly know?' The older man looked indignant. 'Especially after you were involved in my bride's disappearance?'

At that, Killian stiffened. He sensed that these questions were yet another test, a means of proving his worth. And yet, he no longer cared.

He met his father's gaze and said, 'I think we both know that Carice was not a suitable bride for you. Not only was she young enough to be your daughter, but she was too sick to be the Queen of Éireann. When I last saw her, she was dying.' It was not entirely the truth, for his sister *had* seemed slightly better among the Mac-Egans. But he would not reveal this to Rory.

His father's mouth tightened and he gave a single nod. 'So be it. Brian Faoilin is still searching for her. If she is alive, we will find her.' He paused a moment. 'Is it your wish to return to Carrickmeath? Or would you rather take your rightful place here?'

My place is with Taryn, he wanted to say. Instead, he answered, 'I have no ties to Carrickmeath. But I have claimed the Lady Taryn as my own. I intend to wed her, and I will see to it that Ossoria prospers.'

Rory would have none of it. 'The Queen and

her daughter will remain here as my hostages. I want neither of them to have any claim upon the kingdom.' He refilled his goblet of wine and continued, 'Lady Taryn is unworthy of the High King's son. And although I am not opposed to you governing Ossoria on my behalf, I would prefer that you choose a bride whose allegiance is unquestioned.'

'I do not question her loyalty at all,' Killian said. 'And the people will want their lady to remain.'

'If you wish to claim her for your own *fuidir*, I have no objection,' the High King said. 'But the daughter of a traitor will never be a queen.'

Killian stood his ground. 'Queen or not, she will be my wife.'

'And if I demand that you leave Tara and deny you as my legitimate son?' The High King rose from the table, the anger glittering in his eyes.

'I would give up everything for her,' Killian answered, with no hesitation. The moment he spoke the words, he knew they were true. For this stubborn woman had laid siege to his heart until he could not imagine living without her. He approached his father and asked quietly, 'Was there no woman you ever loved enough that you would do anything to possess her?'

Rory's face transformed into sadness, and he removed the ring that had belonged to Killian's mother. 'There was one. And not a day goes by that I do not regret losing her.'

One month later

'I do not know if this is a wise marriage,' King Rory said as he stood beside Killian. 'But I am willing to let you take command of Ossoria.'

In the past few weeks, Killian had worked alongside his father, learning the politics of Éireann and understanding the different provincial kings. The kingship was like a game of chess, but he was well aware of the threat that lingered.

Even more startling was the revelation that his sister, Carice, had become involved with one of the Normans. She had slowly recovered from her illness, and for that reason, Killian would be ever grateful. King Rory had agreed to release her from the betrothal arrangement, and she was now free to marry whomever she desired.

Everyone had gathered for Killian's wedding, which was to be held at the *Tulach-na-Coibche*, the hill named for the numerous marriages held there and the bride prices paid. The day had been cooler than usual, holding the threat of snow within the skies.

Several of the provincial kings had gathered—including the Norman leader Richard de Clare, known as Strongbow, and his wife, Aoife. They had claimed Leinster as their own, and though there was a fragile peace between the Irish and Normans, it would take more time before the power struggles ceased.

As for himself, Killian was content to reign over Ossoria with Taryn as his bride.

She walked towards the hillside, wearing a gown of deep blue. Her long black hair was pulled back with ropes of pearls, and a single sapphire rested upon her forehead. This time, she had done nothing to hide her scars.

Although there were whispers among the children as she walked, their mothers shushed them. Taryn walked proudly with her shoulders held back, and beside her walked two queens—her mother and Queen Isabel of Laochre. Queen Maeve had been disgruntled to learn that they had lied in their earlier claims of marriage, but she'd been mollified at the prospect of a grand wedding.

Taryn sent Killian a quiet smile, and it was as if her presence brought a warmth within him even greater than the sun. When she reached his side, he noticed that Harold the cat was following in her footsteps, his grey tail twitching as he stalked the train of her gown. Many of the onlookers chuckled at the sight of the animal.

'Harold seems quite taken with you,' Killian remarked, kissing her lips in greeting. 'But I won't be allowing him to marry you.'

'There is only one man I wish to marry,' she said. 'And that is you.'

He took her hand in his, and as the priest began the blessing, he murmured, 'You are the most beautiful woman I've ever seen.'

She squeezed his hand in answer, smiling. 'I love you, Killian.' Her blue eyes met his, and he leaned in to kiss her deeply.

'As I love you, *a chroí.*'

There was amusement in her eyes when she pulled back from the kiss. 'If you don't stop kissing me, we'll never finish our marriage vows. Our guests will grow impatient.'

He sent her a wicked smile. 'Then they'll have to wait, won't they?'

True to his promise, they did not stay long at their wedding celebration. Taryn barely had a few bites of her marriage feast before her husband took her by the hand. His thumb stroked the sensitive skin of her palm, and she recognised the promise in his grey eyes.

There would be time to eat later. The look on his face revealed that he was hungry for *her* instead of food. She sent him a tentative smile, and he led her away from the crowds. Outside, light snowflakes spun upon the wind, coating her eyelashes and nose. By the time they reached Killian's chamber, her hair was damp.

He opened the door, and behind them, Taryn spied Harold, the cat, who had followed them up the stairs. The feline nudged at her legs, seeking affection.

But Killian was adamant. 'You are *not* joining us,' he informed the cat, closing the door in the animal's face. Taryn laughed when a paw crept beneath the doorway, as if Harold were seeking a way inside.

She had grown accustomed to the animals that seemed to follow Killian everywhere. Not only the horses and the cat, but even the dogs adored him.

A sudden scratching sound upon the door revealed that Harold had not given up on his quest to be a part of their wedding night. Taryn started to laugh as Killian undressed her. 'He doesn't give up, does he?'

'He wants only to be with you.' He breathed against her throat as he unlaced her silk gown, lifting it over her head, leaving her clad in a *léine*. The words flowed over her like another caress, and Killian removed his tunic, standing bare-chested before her.

Her body was alive and yearning for him, but the room was cool from the window accidentally left open. Taryn walked over to close it, but Killian stalked her, pressing her against the wall. Snowflakes blew into the room, dusting her bare skin.

He kissed a snowflake above her breasts, and the sudden shock of ice and heat made gooseflesh rise over her skin. Her gasp pleased him, and as several more droplets touched her body, he kissed them away. 'I'm freezing, Killian,' she told him, moving to his warm body. 'Close the windows.'

But instead, he took a small amount of snow from the ledge and drew it into his palm. It reminded her of boys who scooped up balls of snow, only to throw them at bystanders.

'What are you going to do with that?' she demanded. From behind her, she seized her own handful of snow.

He eyed her with interest. 'Trust me, Taryn.'

'Not when you're holding a ball of snow.' Clearly, he intended to place it somewhere upon her skin. But he closed the window and led her back to the bed. He distracted her with his heated kiss, one that relaxed her inhibitions, reminding her of how much she loved his touch. Taryn removed her *léine*, and her body was warmer now, eager for the joining that would come. She could imagine him sliding into her, making their flesh one.

He removed his own clothing and laid her back upon the bed, his hard body nestled alongside her. Then he took a small amount of snow and rolled it across one nipple, making her bite back a scream. He followed the frigid snow with his warm mouth, suckling and tempting her. The sensation was so shocking, her fingers dug into his back, her legs twisting with need.

'What are you doing to me?' she whispered.

'Melting you.' His voice was husky and filled with desire. 'I want you to feel naught but me loving you this night.'

In answer, she reached for his trews, wanting to feel his length upon her bare skin. He covered her then, and the heat of his skin warmed her to her core. His erection was thick upon her stomach, and she shifted her legs apart while he continued to stroke her nipple with his tongue. She reached down to his shaft, and in her palm, she had a little of the snow she'd taken from the ledge.

He let out a hissing curse, and she laughed at him. 'Careful, Killian. Whatever you do to me may come back upon you.'

His answer was to thrust inside her. 'Then I'll have to warm myself.'

She arched against him as he began to penetrate in rhythm, but it was his eyes that held her captive now.

He took her to the edge of eternity, bringing the familiar rush of pleasure as she convulsed around him. Once, she had been a woman who had hidden herself from the world, believing she was less of a person.

But Killian had changed that, making her into one who was beautiful. She held him close until he found his own release, and when she lay with him in her arms, she traced her hands over his skin. As they spent the remaining hours loving one another, Taryn lay in her husband's arms, filled with satisfaction and joy at their future together.

The silent peace was only broken by the plaintive meow of a lonely cat, followed by a thump against the door.

She laughed and held her new husband close. 'Harold doesn't give up, does he?'

Killian slid his hand over her skin, their bodies still joined together. 'He loves you. As do I.'

She breathed in the scent of this man, revelling in their closeness. 'On the morrow, we will return to Ossoria. You'll have everything you ever dreamed of.'

He kissed her hard once more. 'Nay, *a mhuírnín*. Everything I dreamed of is right here.'

* * * * *

Look for
WARRIOR OF FIRE
the second book in this exciting duet.
Coming soon!

**Don't miss Sarah Morgan's
next Puffin Island story**

*Some Kind
of Wonderful*

Brittany Forrest has stayed away from Puffin Island
since her relationship with Zach Flynn went bad.
They were married for ten days and only just
managed not to kill each other by the
end of the honeymoon.

But, when a broken arm means she must return,
Brittany moves back to her Puffin Island home.
Only to discover that Zac is there as well.

Will a summer together help two lovers reunite or
will their stormy relationship crash on to the
rocks of Puffin Island?

Some Kind of Wonderful
COMING JULY 2015
Pre-order your copy today

0315/MB507

MILLS & BOON®

& HISTORICAL

AWAKEN THE ROMANCE OF THE PAST

0715/04